To my sist[...]
an inspira[...]

With love sandia

Sandra Owen

TERROR IN THE ANDES

Sandra Owen

authorHOUSE®

AuthorHouse™
1663 Liberty Drive, Suite 200
Bloomington, IN 47403
www.authorhouse.com
Phone: 1-800-839-8640

First published by AuthorHouse 3/30/2009

ISBN: 978-1-4389-6187-3 (sc)

Library of Congress Control Number: 2009901974

Printed in the United States of America
Bloomington, Indiana

This book is printed on acid-free paper.

TERROR IN THE ANDES is dedicated to my Welsh husband and best friend Tom, for sharing many of life's adventures, and to my family who are always there for me.

IN MEMORY OF:

Geraldine Morris

Who shared this incredible experience of backpacking through the Andes in 2008.

PROLOGUE

The coca leaf dates back to ancient civilizations for at least five thousand years. It was used in religious rituals as an offering to the gods, including Pachamama. (Mother Earth) The traditional chewing of the sacred leaf still carries on today among the indigenous people of the Andes. It is widely used for medicinal purposes and is known to boost energy.

Over the past several years in the hidden corners of the Andes, in the lush jungle areas, Peruvian farmers have switched their former crops of coffee, fruit and vegetables to growing the more lucrative coca plant. As a result, hidden processing plants close to these remote areas have been set up to produce refined cocaine in lieu of transporting the raw product to processing plants in nearby Colombia or Mexico. This makes Peru the second largest producer of cocaine in the world.

Some gorilla groups including the Sendero Luminos {Shining Path} have joined up with drug traffic cartels from Colombia and Mexico to protect and expand their business. The Peruvian government and army have been fighting a losing battle in their attempt to eradicate the unlawful activities connected with the illegal use of the coca plant.

CHAPTER 1

Malcolm Murray, age forty six, had been successfully smuggling cocaine from South America for five years and his luck was running out. Business had always been good when there was a growing market for his product. There was never a shortage of willing and eager buyers. He wasn't a user himself, nor did he ever have the desire to be. He figured that people had choices in life, if they wanted to take drugs, that was *their* choice. There was nothing *he* could do about it. And someone had to supply them. It might as well be *him* rather than someone else making all the profit. That was his logic although not everyone would agree with him.

He was cautious, intelligent, and cunning in this dangerous line of work, and of course, he had to be ruthless. If anybody tried to double-cross him, they would pay a high price if caught. To him, it was a matter of principle and pride rather than taking his loses. He wouldn't let anyone pull the wool over *his* eyes when making a deal. If they wanted to try it with someone else, fine, but just don't try anything funny with him. He made plenty of dough to support his comfortable lifestyle. Sure, just like anyone else, he had debts to pay but they were nothing he couldn't handle. Fortunately for him, he was basically a loner and this enabled him to maintain a low profile. Socially, he didn't need to impress anybody. He didn't care to join the 'in crowd' competing for the best car, the finest wine, the most beautiful women, or any of that nonsense.

He enjoyed individual sports and seldom passed up the opportunity to participate, should the occasion arise. Although he didn't like to lose at any challenge that confronted him, he would secretly admire a winning competitor. He relished playing mind games, especially when the other person was at his most vulnerable.

His hired hand José Peres had been with him for three years but at times he still wondered whether or not to trust him. He not only couldn't keep his mouth shut when he should, but it appeared that he lacked common sense and was prone to occasionally having a soft heart. Malcolm had often warned him not to say anything, or give the merest hint if he was ever asked about his employment. But when José was amongst friends and family, he would make a slip of the tongue and did a poor job of correcting himself. He could afford to be generous, sometimes too generous. This in itself aroused curiosity but so far he obeyed orders and that was important.

Malcolm was a bully both physically and verbally. His short broad physique and piercing black eyes projected an air of brutality with which José was totally familiar. At the age of seven his father had turned to alcohol. That was when his mother had abandoned them for another man. His father refused to talk about it. So he never knew whether his mother left because of alcohol, or whether his father had turned to alcohol because his mother left him. Either way, Malcolm had grown up questioning himself about what role he had played in the breakup.

The huge unsightly scar over the bridge of his nose occasionally reminded him of his wild youth. His losing opponent in a pool game refused to pay up at the end of the night. A brawl ensued whereby he was whacked across the nose with a broken beer bottle. He had since then grown accustomed to the stares, especially from the children.

José was a little wiry guy with a crooked grin exposing tobacco stained teeth. He was a nervous person who learned how to survive at an early age. He grew up surrounded by poverty and was accustomed to fending for himself. He landed his employment with Malcolm accidentally by being at the right place at the right time, at the camouflaged hanger deep in the Amazon jungle. It was a case of mistaken identity. Malcolm's newly assigned aide hadn't shown up when José happened to be wearing the aide's coveralls. José learned quickly to do what he was told. As far as their employer-employee relationship was concerned, they were an unlikely pair.

January was into the beginning of the rainy season in the Central Highlands of Peru. The countries in the highlands of the Andes had only two seasons, the wet and the dry. The coastal region in the west, along the Pacific Ocean was mostly desert and rainfall was a seldom but welcome delight.

Heavy clouds hung low in the early morning as the pilot steered his twin-engine Cessna through the canyons and over the high Andean peaks heading north. Up until now he was in a good mood. Things were going well and he would take a nice long vacation after this run. He was smiling as he daydreamed about sailing in the Caribbean aboard his recently acquired forty- foot sailboat. He would do some deep-sea fishing, one of his life's passions. But the daydreaming didn't last long. The pilot became alert when he thought he detected a slight sputter but he wasn't sure. He scanned the dash.

'No indication there! Maybe it was just my imagination.'

His passenger apparently hadn't noticed or he would have said something. His mind wondered back to his daydream where he was reeling in a big one. Then the Cessna did it again. He was surprised. He never had a problem with his 'Baby' before. That's what he called her, his 'Baby'. It was almost like he was having a love affair with her. He knew her like a book and she had always been reliable. Then suddenly the engine began to sputter and spurt and the plane began losing altitude. Malcolm Murray scanned the dashboard for indications of the malfunction. His face twisted as his eyes widened. It appeared that everything was malfunctioning. He couldn't believe it.

'How could this be?'

For a brief moment he wondered if someone had sabotaged his plane. It had to be that new mechanic.

"What the hell is happening?" he shouted in a panic. He was talking to himself rather than his passenger whom he usually ignored unless he needed him for something.

"I don't know," yelled José above the din of the engine.

3

"Maybe that new mechanico he do something, or maybe he do nothing Señor Murray."

Malcolm was too preoccupied to think about any possible errors made by the new mechanic. He was busy with his attempt to maintain control and gain altitude. He was seething and would deal with that later. Right now, more important things needed tending to. The red engine lights flashed and the warnings beeped. Señor Murray was confused and at his wits end. It was crucial that he keep his cool in a crisis like this. He had to carefully plan his next move if he wanted to save his 'Baby' and stay alive.

'Damn! I can't radio for help!'

He knew he had two options. He could bail out, but then he'd lose his cargo and where would that leave him? No, that wasn't a good idea! He would take his chances and stick with the plane. He knew this route well and was grateful that José remained calm. José sat quietly in the passenger seat. It was one of the few times in his life that he prayed.

CHAPTER 2

Phil MacAllister and John Emerson ages nineteen and twenty-one, two Canadian University students had taken a year off between their studies to do some traveling. John was studying chemical engineering while Phil was studying journalism. They eventually wanted to experience different cultures from around the world. It was one of the reasons they had chosen a career that would enable them to work and travel at the same time.

On this particular trip they had spent time in the Amazon jungle and were now touring the Central Highlands of Peru. They were grateful for the change in climate. The heat and humidity of the jungle had been unbearable, but on hindsight, they agreed it was worth every minute. The mosquitoes and other insects had also driven them crazy. The only relief for them was under a net or beside a smoky fire. But they wouldn't have traded the experience for any other in the world.

Several days ago they had left Huancavelica and were presently camping somewhere between there and Santa Inés. That is not what they had planned but it was as it had turned out. The driver of an old pick-up dropped them off in the middle of no man's land. They really had no choice but to make the most of their situation. That was the day before yesterday. So they carefully selected a secluded area to pitch their small pup tent behind a large hill away from the dirt and gravel road. Their goal was twofold, protection against the elements, and protection from the possibility of an encounter with any local bandits. They had been warned to be cautious having met other backpackers since their arrival in Lima. Although it was highly unlikely in this area, it was a habit they had adopted. Their ultimate goal was to make the grueling four-day journey with a guide up the Inca Trail to the ancient ruins of Machu Pichu, the lost city. The ruins are remnants of the Inca civilization that briefly conquered and ruled over South American warring tribes after the Wari Empire. Machu Pichu was the central resting-place for the royal kings and their families. The Incas were known for their skill in carving stone architecture that was very much intact today and unmatched by modern standards. The two students planned to tour the ancient city of Cuzco and explore the Sacred Valley.

In the meantime, they would do a little exploring on their own and enjoy the chilling fresh air and breathtaking views of the snow-capped peaks surrounding them. Yesterday morning they had slept in, due to the harrowing experience of the day before when they thought they were being kidnapped. They spent the rest of yesterday catching up on long overdue resting of their weary young bones. They had been travelling almost nonstop and it was time to chill out and take it easy.

It was early morning on the second day. Last night's rain had lulled Phil to sleep and he had slept soundly. When he awoke, he unzipped the tent door, flipped it open and peeked outside to investigate the weather. As sunrise was breaking in the east, clouds were beginning to form but he wasn't discouraged. He felt energized. He quietly dressed, careful not to awaken his friend. John didn't flinch one bit. John was in dreamland.

Phil emerged to 'a brand new day' as he stretched his arms inhaling the clean, brisk mountain air. The wind swept across his tanned face as he smiled with delight and marveled at the spectacular scenery surrounding him. It was like being in a post card. He felt like he was standing on top of the world. It was a privilege to be here. It was his turn to light up the small stove and make breakfast. He was grateful to have stocked up on dried food packages, militia rations a friend had given him at the last minute before he left. "Here take these," he said. "They might come in handy. They're light and don't take up much space."

He pulled out a couple of breakfast packages and tore them open. It was advisable to boil water briskly for at least three minutes before drinking it to kill any bacteria. But because the boiling temperature of water is so much lower at this high altitude, they carried bottled water at all times. Phil was frugal with the water supply since this was an unplanned stopover. He also carried a small amount of iodine. The iodine was for water purification. A few drops per liter would do the trick. He lit the stove and began his task. He called out to his friend as he poured water into the billycan.

"Hey John! Wake up! You're missing the best part of the day."

By then John was already awake enjoying the warmth and coziness of his sleeping bag. He could see his breath and was lingering a little while longer until the sun provided some heat of the day. But he was famished. Should he arise now or later?

"I'm up. Why are you up so early?"

"I couldn't sleep. I was hungry but I'm glad I'm up. It's beautiful out here."

"Call me when the food is ready."

As Phil sat on a rock waiting for the water to boil, he couldn't help but recall the day he made his decision and didn't regret it one bit. It wasn't difficult to steal time from his studies and take John up on his offer. He was happy that his friend had invited him to join him on this trip. Besides, John had said, he would prefer not to go alone, that when one traveled to a third world country there was safety in numbers. If Phil didn't join him, then he would find someone else who would.

Phil's parents were dead set against his traveling before he completed his education. They were afraid that he wouldn't go back to university. But Phil had convinced them that yes he would go back and finish his education. Nothing would deter him from pursuing his goal in life. This was an opportunity to broaden his outlook and add to his future career in journalism. When he finished his education, he would end up being a globetrotter anyway.

Yes, he nodded his head, so far he had no regrets whatsoever about this trip. The trip up the Amazon was awesome. Never in his wildest dreams did he imagine himself cruising up the Amazon and trekking through the jungle taking in the unique and diverse flora and fauna reserves and meeting tribe members who hunted with spears and poison darts. Just then, he heard John's familiar voice.

"Hey Phil! Where's the food? I'm starving."

"Come on out. It's waiting for you, you poor hungry soul," Phil chuckled.

"It ain't no gourmet breakfast but it will have to suffice."

They sat there eating their breakfast and gulping it down with their coffee. After breakfast, being conscientious about the environment, they would pick up every trace of themselves having been there.

"What do you say we pack up and head out today?"

Phil assumed that John would agree. They usually planned their agenda a couple of days in advance but at the moment they were in a state of limbo.

"That's not a bad idea. We'll get things rolling right after breakfast and head down to the road. The sooner we get started, the better our chances of hitching a lift. It might take us a while before someone picks us up since there's hardly any traffic."

"You're not kidding. As long as we don't climb in with that crazy guy who dropped us off here." Phil was grinning from ear to ear.

"He'll be after us for his sixty soles."

That was a private joke between them and that was another matter. John burst out laughing as he entered the pup tent and began stuffing his belongings into his knapsack. It was still early and he was in no hurry to leave. He decided to keep his diary out and update the last couple of days of his journey

CHAPTER 3

"I can't get this damned thing under control!" Malcolm yelled and cursed under his breath at the same time. José's eyes bulged with fear as he cried out,

" Arriba! Arriba!"(Up! Up!)

He was going to die. He was petrified. He wasn't ready to meet his maker. Prior to this flight he had mustered up the courage to visit the village shaman, a forbidden deed according to his religion, but everyone else did it. He didn't want to admit that he was superstitious, but he was. He gaped at the pilot as if he were cursed.

"I can't afford to lose this cargo!"

The pilot yelled as he stretched his thick neck looking back to inspect his valuable investment. He was thinking out loud rather than expressing his concern to his passenger. The content of the plane was worth more to him than his employee ever was. *He* was the one who had more to lose if they went down. He owed people money, lots of money and this was a major investment for him. Sure, he always carried plenty of cash on him, but not enough to pay off his debts. He didn't trust banks. Just like any other financial institution they always ripped you off. And besides, it wasn't a place to hide your profits. He took care of his own money laundering. There was a quiver in his passenger's voice.

" You forget about the stupid cargo and worry about our mortality."

José quickly made the sign of the cross as if it would speed up the connection between himself and his potential Savior. He could see the mountain ridge fast approaching before his very own eyes.

"Son of a bitch! We're going down!" shouted the pilot as he quickly scanned the terrain around him. There was a small plateau ahead if he could make it. His hand clutched the control stick pulling with all his might. His knuckles blanched as he attempted a landing slightly uphill in order to avoid the speed and force of a downhill disaster.

" We're not going to make it," thought José as he sat there chewing his nails.

With presence of mind the pilot managed to gain slight altitude at the last minute and pulled the Cessna over the incline, level with the plateau, narrowly missing the ridge by inches. He was a good pilot and if he could land it safely he might be able to fix the problem and be on his way before anyone discovered him. That was his plan. He had no intentions of dying, not yet. He had too much living to do if he could protect his livelihood and hang onto his resources.

'That stupid new mechanic! I shouldn't have been in such a hurry. Why did I trust him? From now on I'll do the repairs myself'.

That was his last thought before he felt the impact.

CHAPTER 4

The backpackers had finished their breakfast and morning coffee. The Primus stove was ideal for this trip because there was very little, if no source of wood to burn for a campfire. The stove was small and not much of a burden to carry. En route, the two had observed the common practice of Peruvians, usually women, roaming the hills with their multicolored woven material tied uniquely to make a pouch behind their back. They used this method to gather small sticks and medicinal plants placing them into the pouch. The mountains had been stripped of trees because of years of deforestation. As a result, the locals were forced to scrounge for firewood. Mothers also carried their babies and toddlers in these pouches. It enabled them to work in the fields while at the same time, care for their children.

Phil MacAllister was of medium height and muscular build. He had deep set brown eyes and kept his dark hair in a brush cut. He inherited the dimple in his smooth young skin from his grandfather. Both he and John had a terrific sense of humor and a special way of cheering one up.

This was Phil's first trip to South America and at first he was nervous. He had read the warnings of the dangers to tourists. It was said that Peru was one of the most dangerous countries in South America. Because of the country's widespread poverty, muggings and theft were not uncommon. But John explained to him,

"Just like in any other country, there were some corrupt police and some criminals. We just have to keep our eyes peeled and exercise caution. I'm not going to let that stop me. Are you?"

John was right and it wouldn't stop *him* either.

Phil was pleased that he had taken a beginner course in Spanish. It was optional in his journalism studies and it was a means of striking up a conversation with the locals and improving his language skills. He had intentionally taken a handful of photos of the four Canadian seasons including one displaying an array of orange, yellow, and red, autumn leaves, and one of an apple orchard where pickers were on ladders harvesting the fruit. But the most awesome and intriguing ones were of the winter ice storms and winter scenery. The children especially, were interested in viewing the one of the ice fishermen on the St. Lawrence River, an island in the background.

"You mean to say that these men can walk on the ice? Were they apostles who could perform miracles just like Jesus walking on water?" asked a young boy, who was stunned at the very thought.

"It is so cold that the water freezes until it makes ice so thick that you can actually drive your car on it in some places," replied Phil.

He showed the group of children another photo as they gathered around. It was a summer scene with a water skier behind a speedboat in front of the same island where the fishermen had been. They were amazed at the difference and would laugh and chuckle and ask questions. Phil had a natural way of drawing the children to his attention. He especially enjoyed performing magic tricks for them using a deck of cards, coins and other little trinkets he had stashed in his bag. He told John that children's laughter was a universal language and that it was contagious and should never to be ignored. This was a side of Phil that John had not known until he stood on the sideline observing his interaction with the local youngsters.

Phil stood peeling a mango with his Swiss Army knife a few feet away from the tent. He was deep in thought admiring the keen blade with his initials etched upon it. Valerie had given it to him on his eighteenth birthday, a gift he used and treasured. He was thinking about how fortunate he was to have remembered at the last minute before checking his luggage through customs, to transfer it from his coat pocket to the side zipper pocket of his backpack. He had seen the large square glass box containing hundreds of items that the customs officers had confiscated from passengers, nail files, hammers, screw drivers, scissors, walking sticks, and all kinds of knives.

The woman ahead of him had to forfeit her nail clippers and was very upset, not at the fact that she wouldn't have them, but because of the way the custom officer treated her. The power trip was evident to Phil who was observing the disrespect he showed to the passenger.

His thoughts were broken with the sputtering and spurting of the twin engine in the distance. Distracted, he dropped the mango along with his knife and scanned the sky hoping to see something. John was in their two- man pup tent rolling up his sleeping bag, oblivious to any action outside. Then he heard Phil's voice.

"John! Hurry up! Come here! I think there's an aircraft coming our way! It sounds close but I can't see it." Phil was excited and yelling.

John flipped the canvas door back and poked his head through the opening. He didn't seem too concerned.

"It's probably just some rich tourists."

But his buddy was convinced there was something wrong.

"No! No! It sounds like they're in trouble! There it is! Get the binoculars!"

John unbuckled his knapsack and found what he was looking for. Phil was pointing westward when he emerged and handed over the Busch binoculars. Phil zoomed in and followed the course of the faltering aircraft. He held his stance, paralyzed by what his eyes beheld. He seemed to be in a state of shock as he witnessed the fateful event. Suddenly the plane hit the ground. Chunks of dirt and debris appeared simultaneous with the sound of the crash. The belly bounced. The tail dragged and bounced off. The right wing tipped, hit a boulder, and flew into the air. The belly bounced again, skidded, then slowed and came to an abrupt stop.

"Holy shit John! Take a look! That plane just crashed!"

He shook his head in disbelief. It happened so suddenly. John stood impatiently beside Phil, wanting to view a piece of the action. He'd have to see it to believe it, although right now he had no doubt Phil was telling the truth. He squinted and thought he could see a part of the dead plane with his naked eye. He turned to his friend whose eyes were glued to the binoculars. He was intrigued and wanted to see for himself what was going on. It wasn't fair to deprive him of the excitement.

"Let me see those binoculars."

Phil passed them over and John brought them into focus. John stood gawking at the sight. His mouth dropped in awe. He could see the passenger door swing open and a small man jump to the ground.

'Thank God there's no fire and the body is at least intact.'

He was about to drop the binoculars and run to help, but then he witnessed the little man scurry around to the pilot side. He then attempted to open the door. Then he stepped back swinging his arms and appeared to be yelling. John was too far away to hear what was being said but he could only guess. Someone was in trouble or perhaps didn't survive the crash. They had to do something. John dropped the binoculars and started running toward the crash site. Phil was right behind him.

"What did you see John? Is anyone hurt? I thought I saw someone. Are they okay?"

"Yes. There's a man outside the plane. He seems to be okay but I'm not sure if there are any other passengers. The man appears to be trying to help someone who might be trapped inside."

The backpackers continued over rough terrain, maintaining their pace, making a beeline for their destination. The only sound that followed them was the thudding of their boots hitting the hard packed terrain. John was mentally recollecting his course in first aid in case he needed to use it. Although he was very fit, Phil was trying to keep up with John. He was sorry that he drank more coffee than he should have under the circumstances. They were now running uphill which was the most direct approach.

CHAPTER 5

The impact stunned the two occupants. It took a few minutes for them to absorb the shock before the Cessna, or at least what was left of it, came to a full stop. José had lowered his head and braced himself shielding his face with his arms. He felt them smash against the dash, which helped cushion the impact. When he raised his head, he was thankful that it had been somewhat protected and he couldn't believe he was still alive. It was a miracle! He turned his attention to the pilot who was bent over and José shook him.

"Señor Murray! Señor Murray! Wake up! Wake up!"

The pilot was unresponsive. Fearing the worst, José opened his door without effort and immediately jumped to the ground. He ran around to the opposite side and looked around. '*What should I do?*'

Malcolm Murray was regaining consciousness and was groaning. His head felt like it had been hit with a sledgehammer. He was disoriented until he heard a familiar voice. José was about to abandon the Cessna when, from the corner of his eye he detected movement in the cockpit. He began yelling as he tried to get the pilot's attention.

"Señor Murray! You okay? You alive?"

Malcolm Murray opened his eyes and glared down at José, blood dripping from his forehead.

"Of course I'm alive el stupido."

That's what he often called him. He tried in vain to release the door handle. He wanted to get out of there. With each attempt, he felt a stabbing pain in his head. He turned to José for help.

"Open the fucking door an get me out of here," he commanded.

After several tries, José made one last effort while Malcolm heaved against the door with his shoulder ignoring the pain. Finally, the door flew open and the pilot tumbled out and landed on the hard packed terrain with a thump as he cursed and swore.

"You okay Señor Murray?" asked José trying to express concern, all the while not really caring.

"Do I look fucking okay?" Malcolm fumed with sarcasm. He pointed to the cockpit.

"Get in there and throw me down that bag of cash. We've got to get out of here. The authorities will be on our tail in no time. Hurry up!"

He doubted that the authorities would be there so soon but he didn't want to take any chances. Besides, the threat would motivate José to move a little faster. Without hesitating, José scrambled into the cockpit and located the bag to which Malcolm was referring. He grabbed it and handed it to Malcolm who slung it over his shoulder.

The pilot's vision was a little blurry before he brought it into focus. He figured that he was suffering from a minor concussion but he had to move on, no matter what. He looked around and tried to get his bearings. He knew that there was a dirt road not far to the west that he wanted to avoid. He might even be able to spot it if he headed for the large hill to the east where he was pointing.

"We go that way. Move fast and follow me," he commanded José.

The pilot hated to abandon his cargo. From now on he would be a fugitive. He was more worried about the fact that he couldn't afford to take the time to wipe his prints from the plane. But he was thankful that his prints were nowhere on record. Maybe he would have plenty of time, but then again he didn't want take the risk of being caught. In his business he quickly learned that minutes counted. He would have no problem getting out of the country. He was good at that, having several false passports stashed away. But he didn't want to do that right now. He would make his way to the capital and lay low for the time being. There was a slight chance that his cargo wouldn't be found for days. As soon as he would reach the nearest phone, he would make a call to someone who would know the facts first hand. That would help. Maybe that person could send another out to snoop around for him. There were a few gofers in the operation. You never know. He could get lucky. His thoughts turned to another problem at hand.

This would be the end of José's career. Malcolm didn't want it to end here. It was too risky. José had served him well but he was disposable and could be easily replaced. He would pay someone else to do his dirty work. In the meantime José wouldn't have a clue about what he was planning.

José feared the authorities with reason. Although he knew that he was a good guy at heart, he had his weaknesses. He would never resort to being the hardened criminal that his boss was. He had more respect for life. He followed Señor Murray around like a puppy dog on a leash. After this episode he would be glad to be rid of him. Once he reached civilization he planned to disappear from Malcolm Murray's sight forever. Ironically this would be his last mission with Señor Murray.

CHAPTER 6

Mauricio Paredés and Eduardo Ramirez were two law enforcement officers in this area with a vast jurisdiction. Mauricio was fifty-six, tall, his square face slightly pocked. He was broad shouldered and looked like he could lose a few pounds. Eduardo was just a few inches over five feet, lean, and much younger, although he had a weathered look about him.

The older of the two was known in the area for abusing his power and his ability to manipulate a situation to his advantage. He was protective of his territory, not wanting to share any of his confiscated booty with a scrupulous newcomer. The few locals who lived there were law-abiding citizens and avoided associating with the older officer. He was pleased that he had a certain amount of control over his partner since he caught him cheating on his wife. He had Eduardo right where he wanted him.

Eduardo swore that it only happened the one time in a moment of weakness, when a beautiful young lady from the city took a liking to him and it was *she* who had seduced *him*. He had helped her with her luggage when she couldn't manage it getting off the bus. She was visiting her aunt for a week when one thing led to another. He was sorry he had ever met her. He had a wife and four beautiful young children whom he loved and treasured. He would do anything to protect them from finding out about his one night affair. Unfortunately for him, he felt trapped. But this was nothing. Mauricio's control over him would eventually get him into deeper trouble than he could ever imagine possible.

With little excitement occurring lately, they eagerly responded to a report that there had possibly been an accident involving a small aircraft. It was somewhere north of Santa Inés, somewhere near the only dirt road that existed which ran north south. They happened to be on that road after settling an early morning dispute among workers in the valley below. They were winding their way back up the mountain when they received the call.

It was a long and difficult to drive back down into the valley to speak with the person who had seen and reported the aircraft in trouble. Since they were returning from the valley, they were disappointed that they hadn't seen nor heard it themselves. But then again, that was understandable, given the distance they had traveled and the many mountainous obstructions around every hairpin corner. Peruvian music blared from the cassette player, which wasn't permitted in an official police vehicle. But no one really cared. Most people minded their own business and kept out of trouble.

Scattered about in the surrounding highlands, few local inhabitants lived in thatched roof huts eking out a living by tending their small herds of llama and alpaca. The children would usually accompany a mother or a father. It was their traditional way of life for many generations. When the children were old enough, they would be well trained to shepherd the herds on their own.

During their search, the two police had stopped along the way to question the herdsmen regarding the reported accident. A few had heard it in the distance but hadn't seen it. It wasn't long before a twelve- year- old boy told them that he had seen the plane. He pointed in the direction to where it was heading. The officers estimated would be in close proximity given the information the boy had divulged. Apparently the aircraft was flying at a dangerously low altitude. They anxiously headed in that direction. It would be an eventful foreboding day. A day they would regret for the rest of their life.

CHAPTER 7

Malcolm led the way. José tailed behind in bewilderment. He was grateful to be alive after the close call that could have taken his life. José smiled to himself and whispered a prayer of thanksgiving.

"Thank you Jesus, Mary, for saving me. I promise that from now on I'll be good."

It was a true act of contrition. He sincerely meant it with all his heart. He would mend his ways. No more visits to the shaman!

He looked up and noticed that Malcolm had stopped and was looking around. He had guessed correctly about the road. From where he was standing he could see it clearly. Malcolm wanted to disappear out of sight of that road as quickly as possible. José glanced back to take a look at the wreckage for one last time. As he did so, a moving vehicle suddenly appeared from around a curve in the road in the distance. He paused with curiosity. He squinted and noticed a logo of some kind or maybe it was printing on the side of the vehicle. With further concentration he thought he could perhaps identify it. He increased his pace, running to catch up with his partner in crime.

"Señor Murray! Señor Murray!" he yelled at the top of his lungs.

"We in big trouble! We in big trouble!" His fear was becoming a reality.

At first Malcolm ignored the little guy and kept his pace, aware of the fact that he should get out of the area as soon as possible. But José kept running and shouting at him at the same time. His voice carried a ring of panic. Malcolm finally lost his cool, stopped in his tracks, and was ready for a confrontation. He turned his back to face José and see what all the fuss was about.

"I don't have the patience for this you little worm! What the fuck is the matter with you? What's your problem?"

Then the pilot was shocked and understood when his eyes strayed and caught sight of the approaching vehicle in the distance. His first impulse was to reach for is gun and shoot José on the spot and run with the money. Despite the fact that he had just decided otherwise, José would be a burden now. He could be the cause of a major threat if he were to be eventually caught by the National Police. He would not hesitate to strike up a deal with them in return for squealing on the pilot. Malcolm reached for his gun which he kept hidden away, tucked inside his belt. Suddenly, his heart skipped a beat.

'Where the hell is my gun?'

He continued to feel for it, patting his hand around his waist.

'Damn! It must have fallen out during the impact of the crash.' He was annoyed with himself for being so careless. *'How stupid of me, I need my weapon.'*

José knew Malcolm well enough to realize that when he saw him reach for his gun he was in real danger.

'I wouldn't put it past him if he were gunning for me. I must get away from him. He'll kill me with his bare hands at the first opportunity.'

His boss was much more fearsome than the authorities at the moment. He began running. He could feel his heart pounding in his chest. He thought that it would burst right through his ribcage. His nimble legs carried him at top speed ahead. He heard the familiar angry voice call out behind him.

"Stop! Or I'll ...."

Despite Malcolm's long strides, he was unable to catch up. José was getting away.

All the while the two culprits were escaping away from the crashed Cessna, the two tourist were approaching it. Little did they know that their paths were about to cross. Preoccupied with the chase, neither José nor Malcolm noticed a tall young male and his companion running towards them, coming from the distance. But as soon as their heads appeared from behind a nearby mound, the pilot became aware of them and he suddenly stopped for a few seconds. The tall, fair-haired young tourist also paused, surprised at the unexpected encounter. The intensity of the moment was just long enough for Malcolm's cold black eyes to lock with John's bright blue eyes.

John couldn't help but notice the big ugly scar across the bridge of his nose and the gash above his left eye exposing dry blood. It was obvious that this man was one of the survivors.

"Remember that face!" Malcolm said to himself.

John called out to him, "Hey mister! Do you need any help?"

But a split second later, the man rushed off in his buddy's direction. Phil, who was lagging behind John, slowed his pace, taking the opportunity to catch his breath. They stood perplexed, watching the chase disappear into the distance.

"That's strange. They didn't even stop. It's as if they didn't even see us or didn't want to acknowledge us. They must be running for help. Someone must be hurt," exclaimed Phil with concern.

"Oh, they saw us alright!" John said suspiciously, then added, "Why are they running away from the road instead of towards the road where they might have a better chance of finding someone? It doesn't make sense." He shook his head from side to side.

"I don't know about that! So far we've only seen a couple of pickups carrying produce on this road and maybe the odd car," replied Phil. "There isn't much traffic. Maybe they flew over a house somewhere down there in the valley and are heading down there for help."

"We've got to check it out. Let's go!"

John began to sprint. The two proceeded towards the wrecked plane. It didn't take long before John grabbed the handle of the open pilot door and pulled himself up. As he placed his hand on the seat for support, he felt a sharp sting on the palm of his hand.

"Damn! Be careful Phil! I just cut my hand on something."

Phil had grabbed the handle of the passenger door on the opposite side and was about to enter the cockpit but decided to step back down after hearing his friend's warning.

"You go ahead and search inside John. See if there's anyone in there."

John looked around. The windshield was cracked and buckled. Splinters of glass from a broken beer bottle were strewn over the seat. Several drops of blood were seen on the dashboard. When John looked down, the floor revealed several drops of blood as well. The compartment behind the cockpit was intact except for a rope that held the cargo in place. It had broken with the impact and some of the brown duffel bags were scattered in disarray. One bag revealed a shard of metal piercing the canvas exposing a snow-white powdery substance that had spilled out. John was relieved to find no one who required medical attention.

Finding himself alone in the cockpit, his passion for flying overcame his logic. Without thinking of any possible consequences, he took hold of the controls and allowed his imagination to run away with itself. He was like a little boy with his favorite toy. He soared over the mountain peaks and dipped through the valleys, a free spirit in the wind, one with nature.

Phil had one too many cups of coffee for breakfast and took the opportunity to relieve himself. Then he stood outside impatiently awaiting the results of the search. John's daydream was rudely interrupted as Phil called to him through the side window.

"Hey John! What's taking you so long? Quit playing around in there and tell me what's going on."

When John glanced around he suddenly awakened to the incredible reality of their situation. As he jumped from the cockpit, he missed the step twisting his ankle with the impact of his foot hitting the ground. Ignoring the pain, he regained his balance and looked at Phil, hesitating to speak. He was in a daze, his mind reeling.

" Well come on! What did you find? Is anyone in there?"

"'This is not good!" was all John could say as he stared past Phil.

"What do you mean by, "This is not good"?

John began focusing on Phil.

"I think the plane belongs to people who deal in drug trafficking. That's why those two guys were running away. They didn't want to get caught."

Phil's eyes widened in amazement.

"You're kidding me right?" he said as he scrutinized John. John often pulled stunts on him, trying to get at rise out of him. He thought this was one of them. With knitted brows, John bit on his lower lip and pointed his index finger at the wreckage. Apparently his friend didn't believe him.

"I'm not kidding you Phil! I'm *telling* you! There's cocaine in that plane, lots of cocaine if I'm not mistaken! Do you think I would kid about something like that?"

As soon as Phil recognized the expression on John's face, he knew. He was astounded, given the severity of the predicament in which they found themselves. This was a trip in a lifetime and he feared that it would be totally spoiled if they stuck around. He was not willing to do that. He was also concerned for their safety.

"What do we do now? I think we should get out of here. They've seen us and we've seen them. They'll figure out that we could identify them and when they do, they'll come looking for us. We can't afford to mess with those guys. They're dangerous. Let's finish packing up our stuff and get out of here, right now!"

At first, John believed that his friend was over-reacting.

'It's highly unlikely that anyone will come looking for us. They will be more concerned with running and getting as far away as possible, save their skins. On the other hand I shouldn't be so narrow-minded. Phil could have a point, however slight that possibility.'

He began to assess the situation. "Let's consider our options," he began.

"If no one knows about this accident, I mean, under such clandestine circumstances it could take days before someone stumbles across the wreckage, then it would be safe for us to leave. But if someone saw and reported it right away, then they'll likely conduct a search by air. We'd definitely be seen in that case. Take a look around."

He twisted at the waist and extended his arm, moving it across in an one hundred and eighty degrees arc. The landscape was barren of trees. The only foliage that covered the mountains were patches of moss, lichen and low lying grasses, the odd sparse shrub, among other small forms of plant life.

"There's no place to hide except maybe in that lone, squat, ancient, stone church we passed on the way here, but that's kilometers away. We could search for a temporary spot to hide ourselves, maybe a cave or something, but who knows how long we would have to be holed up before there would be an opportunity to leave? If we packed up and walked away from here now and if anyone stops us and questions us, we have a choice. We could either tell them that we were looking for help or we could act as if we know nothing. If we would stay here and wait for the authorities we would become involved in their investigation."

John realized that he was talking in circles and right now he was confused as to what course of action to take. He wanted to get on with their adventure but he also knew that it would be unwise to run. Phil was adamant and knew what he wanted to do.

"I really have no desire to hang around here. Do you remember the horror stories in the past, about tourists in foreign countries accidentally getting involved in situations like this, situations beyond their control? Some of the unlucky ones were thrown into jail without a trial. Don't you remember the media coverage just before we left? About the older Canadian woman who was being held in a Mexican jail for two years before even a trial and besides, what about our trip? It will be spoiled. Do you want that to happen?" He flung his arms in the air in frustration. He didn't want to be here.

John *did* remember and could see Phil's dilemma. But that scenario was different. He didn't think that the unthinkable could happen to them. He would soon find out otherwise. John began to respond. " I think it best that we should........" but he didn't have a chance to complete his sentence. Phil was on high alert and suddenly pushed his friend aside as if to protect him. The two had been standing near the nose of the plane and now they were further behind, beside the passenger door.

"Hey! What are you doing pushing me around like that?" John laughed and raised his voice to playfully mimic annoyance.

"Quiet John! I think I hear voices!"

Phil squeezed his buddy's arm as a warning. His voice sounded like a raspy whisper of panic. John suddenly wiped the smile off his face and immediately became serious. He attentively strained his sense of hearing. He now could hear the faint voices that Phil was referring to in the distance. He had mixed feelings about what to do next because he had heard that in this country, a person was presumed guilty until proven innocent. The law was incredibly backward but it was true. Right now, they were in a precarious situation.

'What to do?'

The two Peruvian police were keenly on the lookout. They happened to spy the broken plane from one of the very few points of vantage as they proceeded down the road. When their jeep could no longer carry them over the rough terrain, they were forced to go the last leg on foot. They walked briskly towards the plane as their voices became louder and louder with excitement.

John and Phil were standing on the opposite side, hidden from view of the approaching officers. They had procrastinated for too long. They crouched down and peeked around to determine to whom the voices belonged.

"I should have listened to Phil," thought John. "We should have taken off when we had the chance. But now it's too late."

He looked around to verify a fact that he already knew. There was nowhere to run and hide temporarily until they could decide on what to do next. The two young tourists easily identified the uniforms that were quickly approaching. They were the Peruvian National Police and they didn't look too friendly.

John was prepared to approach them with what little information he knew and to describe what he had seen. At this point, he didn't think there was any other choice. They would have to take their chances and hope for the best. Otherwise if they were caught trying to evade questioning, they would look suspicious. Besides, their belongings weren't too far away. The officers would surely take time to go over to the camp and check out their alibi. John exhaled a sigh of relief because his decision was made and he was just about to act on it.

But little did he know what was going on in Phil's mind and what he was about to do next. Phil was pondering over the contents of his conversation with John. He was frightened when he saw the uniforms. He sensed danger and subsequently he did a very foolish thing. He panicked and ran away as fast as he could without thinking. He turned around and beckoned his friend to follow. John's eyes widened in disbelief.

'What in the hell is he doing?'

Phil didn't get far before he stumbled on a rock and landed flat on his face, arms spread, dirt in his mouth. John limped to help him, his ankle hot and swollen. He crouched beside his friend. When Phil looked up he was as white as a ghost. John spoke in a hushed voice.

"Are you okay? Let me help you up and we can explain everything."

So far they hadn't been seen. One officer was standing on the opposite side of the aircraft while the other one was busy searching the plane, totally unaware that anyone else was around. He expected the pilot to be long gone given the circumstances. At the moment, his attention was focused on the amazing contents in the wreckage rather than his duty in trying to apprehend the criminals responsible for dumping this valuable load at his doorstep. The officer who was searching the plane was calling out excitedly in Spanish to his partner.

Phil's eyes were beseeching as he whispered to his friend.

"Are you crazy? What if they think that **we're the** ones who crashed that plane? They wouldn't hesitate for one moment. They'd haul us in and throw us into jail in a flash and throw away the key."

That remote possibility was beginning to register with John. How would it look if they were caught fleeing the scene? It was an unsettling thought. His eyes were close to ground level and he could see a bolder ahead of him and to his left. It was quite large and it just might be enough to conceal them for the time being.

'And then what?'

He pursed his lips and raised his index finger to them indicating to Phil to remain silent. His heart was pounding and the sweat poured from his brow. He pointed to the bolder that was about ten to fifteen feet away, and the two began to crawl quickly towards it where they could possibly hide. John's ankle was killing him but he dare not groan. They were within a few feet of being out of sight when the piercing echo of a gunshot ended their flight. When they turned their heads and looked up, they both knew that they were in trouble.

The officers approached them, pistols drawn. The young Canadians scrambled to their feet. The officers ran in front of the two campers placing Phil and John between the aircraft and themselves. One of the officers barked an order at them. John, not understanding turned his head with a puzzled look to Phil who was placing his hands behind his head.

" He wants your hands behind your head," he told John as he stared at his captors. John slowly obeyed, perplexed that Phil was not making an attempt to explain. Phil was too stunned to say anything.

" Say something Phil!" John's voice quivered.

" Somos Canadienses. Estamos acampando. Alla! Alla !" (We are Canadians. We have a camp over there.)

He was continuously pointing his chin in the direction of the tent and repeated himself trying to explain in Spanish. The bulky officer turned his head and briefly looked in that direction. Phil was certain that the cops could understand but they didn't seem impressed with his explanation.

" Search them," Mauricio commanded in his native language.

Eduardo placed his handgun back into the holster and stepped towards Phil.

"What are you doing?" cried Phil.

He felt violated as Eduardo removed his travel pouch that was snapped around his waist containing his passport, credit card, and a few soles. Then the policeman searched John and removed his travel pouch.

"You can't do this! We haven't done anything wrong!" John cried out in anger.

Eduardo shoved the pouches into his jacket pocket. Mauricio studied the suspects then asked them, "Hablas Espanol?"(Do you speak Spanish?")

"Poco," replied Phil. (A little)

"Americanos?" asked Mauricio Paredés.

"No, Canadiences, Touristas."

"Narcotraficantes?"(Are you drug-traffickers?) asked the older officer accusingly.

"No! No es verdad!" (No! It's not true!)

That was all Phil could reply. He was too petrified to say anything else.

Mauricio Paredés turned to his partner. He had decisions to make.

"You watch these two. I'm going to take another look inside that plane."

Eduardo withdrew his pistol and guarded the two captives while Mauricio proceeded to the plane. As he was climbing into the cockpit, he noticed the handle of a gun sticking out from under the seat. He reached into his pocket, took out a pair of leather gloves and pulled them over his big hands.. He picked up the gun and examined it. It was a 9mm.Glock. He smiled. A plan was beginning to form in his mind.

When he returned, he consulted with his fellow officer. It was obvious to the hostages that they were having some kind of an argument. Eduardo was shaking his head from side to side objecting, "No! No!" He was looking at Phil with frightening eyes. Phil tried to understand what the argument was about but they were speaking too fast for him. In the end, the younger of the two seemed to give into the older man's wishes.

The older Mauricio reached into his jacket pocket and produced the gun he had retrieved from under the seat. He checked the chamber to make certain that it was loaded. He checked the safety. Then he walked up behind Phil and removed the right hand from the top of his head. He stood so close that Phil inhaled the acrid odor of body sweat. The large man then firmly placed the revolver into Phil's hand griping it with his own. When he raised his arm forcing it to point straight ahead, Phil's whole body tensed then began to tremble.

"What is he doing?" he called out to John praying that he'd somehow intervene.

John began speaking but the emphatic move of his captor's gun warned him to be silent and keep still. Mauricio forced Phil's index finger over the trigger, held it there and fired. The llama and alpaca herds scattered as the echo pierced the valleys below. The laborers who were stooped over on the distant slopes lowered their piques and stood upright, perturbed at hearing this for the second time. Then the big man shook Phil's arm and ordered him to let go of the gun. Phil released it into Mauricio's hand.

John flinched. "This man is crazy!" he thought as he witnessed the bazaar behavior, his ever mounting fear increasing. Little did he know that what the gunman was about to do next would be a crime, one that would haunt him for the rest of his life. The law officer stooped and picked up the empty cartridge and slipped it into his jacket pocket along with the Glock. Then he pulled out his own revolver and waved it indicating that he wanted John to separate from Phil. They had been standing side by side.

"Step aside, further away from your friend!" he commanded.

"John, he wants you to move further away," translated Phil.

John reluctantly did so. He was terrified.

"We don't have to do this," pleaded Eduardo who wanted no part of the scheme. But he had no choice and he knew why.

"Why must we do this?" he begged a second time.

"He's the one who understands our language. We have to eliminate one of them to make our plan work as I said before. It would then be only one foreigner's word against ours. Don't argue with me! It will happen as was discussed," replied Mauricio raising his voice.

Then the gunman motioned for Phil to turn around and ordered him to start running. Phil pretended that he didn't understand. He began experiencing momentary vertigo. He was so petrified that he thought his knees were going to buckle. Moments passed and it was evident that the policeman was getting impatient. He repeated the order and ever so slowly Phil turned his back fearing the worst. A momentary premonition flashed before his vacant eyes.

"Oh my God! He's going to shoot me!" he cried out.

John took a quick step forward, impulsively wanting to attack the terrorist. His wide set blue eyes met those of his controller as he instinctively yelled,

"Wait! Please wait! Don't shoot! What are you doing? You can't do that!"

Mauricio instantly turned his head and took his eyes off Phil, looking intently at John. At that moment Phil took advantage of the distraction. He charged as he zigzagged toward the Cessna that was his only cover, if he could make it in time. Maybe John could hold the gunman's attention somehow for a little longer. It was his only hope. His entire being was focused on reaching cover.

His heart pounded heavily with every stride he took. Suddenly, he felt an agonizing sting on the back of his thigh. He grabbed at the injury as he screamed in pain and fell to his knees. The pain was excruciating. He began to rise. He was determined to make it. He wasn't going to die. He began to pray. "Hail Mary full of….." but his prayer was cut short.

A second shot was fired. He arched his back but didn't feel a thing. John ran over to his best friend and ignored Eduardo. The guard lowered his gun allowing John his time and space. Tears streamed down John's face as he knelt beside Phil's lifeless body. He lowered his head into both hands and bawled like a baby. The devastation was unbearable. He raised his head toward heaven with his eyes closed tightly and released a sharp anguished cry at the top of his lungs.

"Oh no! Why? Why? Why?"

When he opened his eyes he was gazing into the eyes of a murderer. Mauricio was standing over him. His piercing black eyes radiated an evil presence that John had never experienced before. He was momentarily gripped with fear but his fear suddenly turned to anger. He clenched his teeth.

"You son of a bitch!" he lashed out.

In an instant he was on his feet, fists drawn. Before he could strike, arms grabbed him from behind and threw him to the ground. His arms were forced behind his back and he was handcuffed. Then Mauricio carefully slid the pistol from his pocket and placed it a few inches away from Phil's right hand. He dropped the empty cartridge with it. Then the heavy officer grabbed John by the arm, pulled him to his feet and pushed him ahead. John had no idea what the cop was doing or why, but his anger turned to resign. As soon as the prisoner was cuffed, he had him where he wanted him. John couldn't understand why he had been spared from a sudden death. He was a witness to Phil's murder so why let him live?

'*Where are they taking me? Are they going to kill me too? Maybe they plan to torture me. But why would they do that? For pleasure?*'

His heart raced as he imagined what could happen to him. He thought that he was at the mercy of a couple of sadists. They could toy with him and bury him somewhere out here where he would never be found. No one would ever know what happened to him. His family and Phil's family would always wonder and search, but never find them. They would constantly be tormented at the thought of their son's disappearance. There would never be closure.

All of a sudden, John felt cold and was shaking uncontrollably. He was in a state of shock. His teeth began to chatter. As he licked his lips he could taste his salty tears streaming down his cheeks. He sniffled and tried to calm himself.

"Dear God," John prayed, "Please just let this be a nightmare."

But somewhere deep down inside he knew it was an evil reality.

Mauricio led the way back to the jeep. John hobbled behind, his head hanging in despair. Eduardo took up the rear and within minutes the jeep was in full view. Eduardo positioned himself in the driver seat. Mauricio opened the rear door for John, shoving him into the back seat. Then he seated himself beside the prisoner. By this time John was a little calmer. He couldn't help the repetition in his head.

'I'm sorry Phil!. I'm so sorry Phil! I'm so sorry!'

John was two years older than his best friend Phil. He was overwhelmed with guilt. *He* was the seasoned traveler and *he* was the one who suggested they take this trip together.

'I just stood there and watched. It happened so fast. Please forgive me.'

At this point he didn't care what would happen to him. Everything was his fault.

The engine was running and he felt a jerk forward. He closed his eyes hoping for oblivion but the bouncing over the ruts and potholes prevented that from happening. It began to drizzle. By the time they reached their destination it was pouring.

About a dozen dilapidated houses stood in the hamlet on the huge high plateau. Half of them looked abandoned but actually were not. They looked abandoned according to John's standards but they belonged to families who worked together, pooling their resources, eking out a living in whichever way they could.

A scrawny Hairless Mexican dog greeted them wagging his tail. It belonged to no one and yet it belonged to everyone. It was a shared pet that automatically went from house to house every day at the same time looking for table scraps. There weren't many rodents around here. The cats took care of that. But by the same token, there weren't many cats either. The dogs took care of that.

John was escorted into a tiny concrete building with two rooms. The small office contained a messy desk and a chair, with another chair opposite the desk. A small rusty wood stove stood in the corner along with two stools, one on each side. The holding cell was within the office, the cell door facing the desk. A low door stood off to the side for a small washroom. Dirty white paint chipped and peeled throughout.

Eduardo lifted the cell key from a nail on the wall and swung the door open. John was shoved into the eight feet by eight feet cell containing a single cot, a sink, and a urinal. He was thrown an old pair of coveralls that were hanging behind the door and told to strip and don the coveralls. The cell door creaked and squeaked as it was swung closed. Edurado frowned as he placed the large key into the lock and secured the door. Then he placed it back on the nail. After John changed, he was told to pass his clothing through the bars and they were shoved into a black bag with a pull string. When he felt this unjust and demeaning treatment, his despair turned to anger.

"I won't allow these murders to intimidate me," he told himself. Then he bravely addressed them.

"You can't do this! I'm allowed one phone call! I want a lawyer I demand a phone call to the Canadian Embassy! I am a Canadian!"

He spoke loudly and with confidence with the intent of letting them know that he was a foreign tourist and not a common criminal. He chose his words carefully, knowing that they could understand certain words like tourist, Canadian, and embassy.

"My uncle works for the Canadian Embassy here in Peru," he lied, "You can't keep me here forever!"

His knuckles turned white as he stood grasping the iron bars of his cell. His head tilted backwards and his watery eyes stared beyond the dull gray ceiling. He cried out,

" Can you hear me Phil? Are you with me? I swear justice will be served! These bastards will pay the price for gunning you down in cold blood!"

The two officers had had enough ranting and raving from the prisoner.

"Silencio!" yelled Mauricio, narrowing his eyes and raising his truncheon.

John recognized the cruelty in his voice and quickly stepped away from the bars, sat down, and raised his leg, resting it on the cot.

Eduardo was rocking back and forth on the two back legs of the grungy chair with filthy stuffing breaking through a tear in the up-holstery. His feet rested on the edge of the desk but he was not com-fortable. Mauricio was pacing the floor in small circles, his hands behind his back. He was worried about something. He confided in Eduardo.

"I've been thinking. The man I shot, he pointed and mentioned something about a camp. Could it be possible that he was telling the truth? That in fact those two were camping somewhere out there?"

Eduardo decided to tell his partner what he wanted to hear but also gave him a piece of his mind at the same time.

"I don't think so. I think that this man here behind bars sustained his injury during the crash. It doesn't make sense otherwise. But you didn't have to shoot his buddy. He was unarmed and posed no threat to us."

Mauricio was only half listening and continued his train of thought.

"But it puzzles me as to what may have happened to the pilot. Would he have escaped or did those guys make him disappear and then plan to run with whatever they could pilfer? If that's the case, then we must immediately locate the camp and eliminate all traces of it having been there."

Eduardo had been skeptical all along. He was in a bind and was desperate to protect himself if this prisoner was a Canadian tourist and not a drug trafficker. He should have been more assertive, but his partner wouldn't have listened to him anyway. He never did.

"That's possible. Who knows? But if that's the case we must act quickly. There's not much time. We had better find out. You should have listened to me in the first place."

Mauricio took command and began giving orders to Eduardo.

"Since this case is drug related, I'll call police headquarters in Lima and notify them. By the time they arrive, we'll be ready. In the meantime, you go up there and confiscate a portion of that shipment. Don't be careless or greedy. Leave enough behind. We don't want to raise any suspicions if most of the cargo is missing. Take a shovel and some plastic with you and bury it. Cordon off the area and call me on my private cell phone when you are finished."

Eduardo grumbled to himself as he left. Although the rain had abated, it didn't improve his mood.

' *Why must I do all the dirty work? He's had me under his thumb for too many years, ever since he caught me cheating on my wife. I'm sorry I ever let it go this far. I can believe some the corrupt things he's done in the past, but this killing…..? I had no choice. If I hadn't agreed with him, I think he would have killed me with that gun and have blamed it on them.'* He shook his head in disbelief.

When he arrived at the plateau his eyes avoided looking in the direction of Phil's body. It had been lying there in the cold, wet gravelly mud and the thought made his stomach churn with the lingering aftertaste of death. He felt nervous and rushed.

'*There's so much to do, where do I begin?'*

He looked in the direction in which his captive was pointing. He would soon discover whether he was lying or telling the truth. He began his fast walk, and after a time he was ready to give up but kept going just in case the camp was really there. He was both surprised and disappointed when, within a short distance thereafter he spotted the two- man pup tent behind a high hill. He was surprised because he was half expecting not to see it.

'*This complicated things. If our superiors find out that we have arrested the wrong party, how are we going to explain things?*'

He was disappointed because he had more work to do. It was too late to change his mind. He looked around for clues.

'*I've got to move quickly*'

The small Primus stove and a couple of tin cups were all he could find at first. Then he spotted the binoculars lying on the ground. He picked them up and shoved them into his pocket. He would keep them for himself. Everything else was neatly packed away inside the tent. He tossed his findings inside and hurriedly pulled the pegs and tossed them inside as well. He pulled the tent corners together and tied them into a knot. He stood, his eyes searching the terrain for a disposal place. Along the side of a steep downhill slope was a con-cave depression. With an effort, he attempted to heave the collapsed tent with its contents over his shoulder. When he realized it was an impossible task, he dragged it to the spot he had chosen and packed it in tightly with his hands. There was plenty of room for the gear. He looked around just in case he was being watched. It didn't hurt to be a little paranoid.

Then, using his shovel he covered it with a combination of wet mud and gravel and tampered it with his feet. He stood back and examined his work to make certain that the evidence was well con-cealed with a natural fit into the landscape. Satisfied with the results, he used his boots to scuff up the drag marks he had made.

Then he ran back to perform his second task. He haphazardly cordoned off the area.

'*It doesn't matter how I do this. There is no one around to keep out.*'

When he climbed into the cockpit his disposition changed. He became aware of the   illegal cargo behind him. He stood and ran his fingers through his thick black hair expelling a low whistle. He was amazed. He remembered when he and Mauricio had confiscated a small amount of cocaine once before. Mauricio kept the coke and let the man go free with merely a warning. But he had never seen the stuff on this large a scale before. His heart skipped a beat at the thought of the profit he would make. Then, almost instantly, as if he had been hit with a ton of bricks, he became aware of what he was doing. The temptation was great, but the regret was overwhelming.

'I wish I didn't have to do this.'

But he knew it was too late to change anything. He felt ashamed because he allowed himself to be intimidated by Mauricio and even more so, he was frightened of him after what had happened earlier. He had to do what he had to do. He hauled the duffel bags the short distance and carefully piled them into the jeep and placed the shovel across the floor in the back. Then he drove slowly towards Santa Inès keeping his eyes peeled.

'I've got to find a good place to hide this.'

His eyes continued roaming over the vast terrain until he was satisfied with the spot he had chosen. When he completed his task he used his cell phone and called Mauricio.

"Good work! You'll be well rewarded."

The call took thiry seconds. " I've completed the job."

CHAPTER 8

Officer Mauricio Paredés stared at the phone for a few minutes. He was very pleased with himself when he picked it up and dialed. Just after lunch Lieutenant Francisco Amaya was sitting at his desk at police headquarters in Lima when his phone rang. He had worked for the National Police for fourteen years and was highly respected by his colleagues. He was a family man with a wife and three children.

"Lieutenant Amaya, this is Officer Mauricio Paredés. I'm calling from Santa Inéz. Early this morning we received a report that a small aircraft had crashed north of here. We have since discovered that this plane was being used to smuggle cocaine out of the country. We do not have the proper technology here to conduct a thorough investigation. Since this is a drug related matter, I am reporting it to you."

When the lieutenant heard this, he was upset. Time was of the essence.

"You mean to say that a plane full of drugs crashed early this morning and you've waited this long to contact us? This is incredible!"

Officer Paredés didn't expect to hear an angry voice at the other end of the line barking at him and he was taken aback.

"But Lieutenant Amaya, I've been trying to contact you but couldn't get through. Communications are difficult in this remote area and sometimes we cannot get a signal. It has something to do with tower failure," he lied.

"We were quick to respond and have already apprehended one suspect fleeing the scene. Unfortunately his partner will not be available for questioning. He was shot and killed in an attempted escape."

Lieutenant Amaya was upset when he heard this.

"What! Was it really necessary to shoot him?" I assume you weren't alone. You could have pursued him on foot. He may have been able to provide us with valuable information. Aren't you aware of how difficult it is to penetrate these narcotraficantes? We needed him alive."

Officer Paredés interrupted in an attempt to defend himself.

"It was unavoidable. The suspect had a gun and fired at me. I had no choice."

Lieutenant Amaya traced his finger over a large map on the wall behind his desk and located Santa Inés.

"Well, all I'm saying is, that it's very unfortunate that he wasn't captured alive. I'll dispatch a helicopter to the area with our investigators and forensics team immediately. What are the co-ordinates?"

Officer Paredés wasn't prepared for this question and didn't have an exact location per se. He tried to give him a good estimate.

"The crash site is approximately twenty kilometers north of here. You can easily spot the road from the air and it's just east of the road. You can't miss it."

"What information were you able to extract from the suspect you're holding?"

"We were unable to interrogate him as he only speaks English. Although he does not possess any ID, he claims to be Canadian. He says his name is John. That much I understand. We have him in our temporary holding cell."

"I'll send a chopper along with an escort to transport him back here for questioning in the morning. In the meantime keep him there overnight. Have a copy of the police report ready to send back with the escort."

Before Mauricio could respond, the line was disconnected.

After he hung up, the officer was in no mood to write up a police report. He sat at his desk pondering the contents of the conversation. He was sulking like a spoiled child. Here he was, co-operating with police headquarters and what thanks does he get? A reprimand from his superior for performing his duty! After all, he couldn't allow an armed criminal to escape. What did he expect? But then again, the lieutenant wasn't there so what did he know? He would find out just exactly what kind of danger his subordinate was in once he read the police report. Then he would have to apologize for jumping to conclusions. Delighted with the scenario that he had created, he took out a form and began composing his report. He would have to be cautious about its accuracy, not make any mistakes. Somewhere in his demented mind he was beginning to half believe himself.

He was finished by the time Eduardo arrived back at the station. He slammed the door after entering, wanting his partner to know that he wasn't pleased. Mauricio noticed that Eduardo looked haggard but he didn't particularly care. That wasn't *his* problem. Besides, his plan was going to make them both rich soon and his partner should be grateful for that. If he wanted his share he would have to pull some weight and earn it. He looked up at his partner.

"I've finished writing up the report and you're just in time to witness it."

When Mauricio handed his report to Eduardo, Eduardo scowled as he read it. He could see that it was full of lies. He reluctantly signed it and handed it back to Mauricio who then opened the right hand top drawer of the desk and placed it there to be picked up in the morning. Then he reminded his partner.

"I hope you realize that this is an opportunity of a lifetime. I trust you've done a good job because remember, we're in this together and if you screw up...."

His sentence ran off into mid-air without finishing. It was another one of his threats. Eduardo was sick and tired of his partner's threats and for the first time in their relationship he realized that he could afford to reciprocate. He didn't have to be afraid of Mauricio

41

any longer, now that he actually witnessed him murder someone. But he would have to be careful or he may be his next victim. He looked Mauricio in the eye.

"Yes I'm perfectly aware of the fact that we are in this together and if I screw up we both go down. So don't think for one moment that I'm not aware of the consequences."

Mauricio heard him loud and clear but if that comment shook him up a little, he didn't let on. He pretended to ignore the remark and continued his orders.

"I've contacted headquarters in Lima and they are on their way. You stay here and guard the prisoner while I go and meet them."

He looked up at the clock on the wall.

"They sent a helicopter and I want to be there when they arrive. If I leave now, that'll give me plenty of time."

He was looking forward to join the big shots from the big city. He deserved credit for taking down these foreigners who were creating havoc in his country. He left without saying another word. Eduardo sat there and tried to eat his lunch but hunger evaded him. He sat observing the prisoner who was sitting on the cell cot staring into space. He felt sorry for him. He didn't deserve this. Eduardo felt like he had suddenly transformed into an evil person. He felt like a monster. He wished away the dark cloud that was looming over him. He picked up his lunch, walked over to the cell door and offered it to John. John felt like throwing it back in his face but he also knew that he needed it to sustain himself. So he took the lunch and nibbled away at it wondering what was going to happen to him. It was going to be a long day and a long night.

CHAPTER 9

Lieutenant Amaya placed the receiver in the cradle and immediately punched in Detective Walter Diéz's extension number. The detective was young and relatively new to the department. He was a sought after bachelor and very much so, with all the charm and appeal of a handsome Latin American, but his work was his passion. He loved a challenge and was good in public relations. He also spoke English.

"Detective Diéz, would you kindly report to my office immediately."

"Yes sir. I'll be right there." *'I wonder what is so urgent?'*

Walter Diéz had been in his cubicle finishing up a report. He placed it in the 'out' shelf above his desk and headed for the office down the hall. When he knocked on the door and entered, Lieutenant Amaya greeted him.

"I have an assignment for you," he said looking up at Walter Diéz who took a seat opposite the desk.

"There's been a small plane crash just north of Santa Inéz. It was carrying cocaine and I want you to lead the investigation. They have a suspect in custody and another suspect was shot and killed when he tried to escape. You need to get there as soon as possible. I'll arrange for the suspect to be picked up and taken back here tomorrow for questioning. For now, concentrate on the crime scene. Given the remote location, the fastest and most efficient means of transportation is by helicopter. I'll arrange for one while you notify our team of forensic scientists, detectives and E.M.T. Are there any questions?"

His superior hoped that he wasn't sounding too blunt. He was discouraged because these criminals needed to be put behind bars where they belong, and so many were eluding the law. Only a small percentage of them were being caught. He was assigning Detective Diéz to the case because they shared the same passion when it involved drugs.

"If you have no objections I'd like to escort the suspect myself tomorrow. I'll have a chance to interrogate him where he's most comfortable, in the air. Maybe if we're lucky I can extract some pertinent information from him and hopefully a confession. At least I'd like first crack at it."

He raised his brows waiting for a response. He anticipated that the lieutenant would approve. Lieutenant Amaya softened his voice.

"That's fine with me. If there's anything else at all you need, just let me know. You are the one in charge from now on."

Lieutenant Amaya had complete faith in the detective. He had proven himself in the past and if anyone could crack the case it would be Detective Diéz. Diéz rose from his chair and was ready to leave.

"Thanks, I'll keep in touch."

The detective left the office and immediately notified everyone. Then he went to his locker to collect the belongings he needed for the trip. He would need his jacket and raingear. It was bound to be raining where he was going. Then he remembered that it would probably be late when he returned. He had been invited for dinner at a friend's place. He would have to call and postpone the engagement until another day. She wouldn't be happy but that was part of his job. He had to deal with, and be prepared for the unexpected. In this case, he was eager to participate in what might be a major breakthrough. It was imperative that the government succeed in quashing the drug trade, not only for the reputation of the country but on behalf of its people and for the sake of all the victims. If they could capture anyone who could divulge information that would lead them to the source, the drug kings, then they could penetrate and finally put an end to this illegal trade. He was a soldier among soldiers trying to fight a perpetual war on drugs.

The team was gathered and loaded their equipment into the chopper. Detective Diéz waited for everyone to board before he did. He could tell that the crew was a little excited although they pretended not to be. It wasn't often that they were summoned to the heart of the highlands. It was a change and a brief escape from the big city crime scenes that they had grown accustomed to.

The helicopter lifted off as they headed southeast. When they were well into the interior, it began to rain. The pilot turned his head and raised his voice above the din of the engine and the repetitive rhythm of the windshield wipers.

" The weather is not in our favor."

"No it isn't, but then again, it's to be expected. At least we came prepared for this."

"The rain is going to make it difficult for us to collect evidence. Hey Ricardo! Did you bring your rain gear?"

They joked among themselves teasing Ricardo because the last time they were in the highlands on a case, he had forgotten his gear. His thick ebony hair had curled tightly when the rain had washed out the straightening gel and he looked like a black sheep. The pilot knew that they were approaching their destination when he caught sight of the road and followed it southward.

"Everyone keep your eyes peeled. The road is just ahead. I anticipate that we should be near the site shortly."

It wasn't long before the co-pilot pointed to his right.

"There it is!"

Everyone craned his neck and leaned towards the window for his firsthand glimpse of the wreckage from the air. They could see the broken wings and scattered debris. The experienced pilot chose a safe landing spot within a short distance of the site, enabling a short walk for his passengers. The team disembarked, hauling their cases and equipment with them. When the engine had died and the rotors had stopped, the silence of their environment was deafening. They were anxious to get started.

Their first encounter was the yellow crime scene tape surrounding the perimeter. Mauricio Paredés, who was patiently awaiting their arrival, approached them with a strut to his bulky frame. With an air of self- importance, he reached out to shake the hand of the man in the lead.

"Good day! I'm Officer Mauricio Paredés and I apologize for the absence of my partner. He is presently occupied guarding the prisoner."

"I'm detective Walter Diéz. Did you touch anything?"

They continued walking.

"Yes, we had to go inside the plane in order to search for possible survivors. We also draped a plastic sheet over the victim because of the rain."

"Did you search the body for I.D.?"

" No I didn't. I wanted to wait for you," he lied.

As he was being further questioned, Officer Paredés could detect the occasional flash in his peripheral vision and was aware that a technician was documenting the crime scene. The medical examiner had determined the approximate time of Phil's death. Criminologists were dusting the plane for prints and taking samples from the blood for D.N.A. testing. Detective Diéz sensed that Officer Paredés seemed uneasy during the questioning.

'But then again he's just been through a very harrowing experience. He's probably not used to this. Even in his line of duty, a situation like this would be a rarity.'

When the detective was finished his questioning of Officer Paredés, he would have to make a request. It would be the first time in his career that he made such a request but he had to do it. He reached out his hand and said in a soft voice.

" I'll need your gun."

Mauricio was unprepared for this but hid his emotions well.

"Of course! I understand it's necessary."

He reluctantly withdrew his pistol and handed it over to the detective.

The detective then walked toward the medical examiner. He was just finishing his examination of the body. One of the crime scene investigators held up a zipped plastic bag containing the 9mm. Glock and showed it to the detective.

"We found this a few inches from his hand. It looks like there was a lot of action going on here."

"Yes," replied the detective, "there certainly was! It's such a shame, he's so young."

When Detective Diéz noticed the position in which the body was found, he wanted to question Officer Paredés further. He would have to locate him. Diéz looked around and spotted the officer then walked in his direction.

"I have one more question," he said as he drew near, "You previously said that the deceased was trying to escape. From the position of the body, it appears that he was running towards the plane and not away from it. What precisely happened?"

The detective was not suspicious. He was merely looking for an explanation. When he first arrived, he wanted to question the arresting officer, examine the crime scene, and then if he had any further questions he would pursue them.

The arresting officer had been vague at the time of questioning, deliberately failing to provide exact details. He had reason enough to be nervous and he figured the less said the better. Officer Paredés was forced to think quickly in order to conjure up a feasible story that would cover up his error of omission.

His eyes searched the landscape as he tried to appear nonchalant. Without hesitating, he pointed toward a nearby bolder, the one that Phil and John tried to reach without being noticed.

"We were searching for the suspects and they appeared from behind there when we were in that area. I don't think that they were expecting us so soon and they probably saw us coming at the last minute. They hid behind there where we couldn't see them from here. At first we searched in the other direction and had our backs to them. They probably thought that they could avoid us by backtracking. When we decided that we had gone far enough, we turned around. If we hadn't, we probably would never have seen them running back to the plane for cover.

That sounded logical enough to Officer Paredés after he spoke. He was relieved and smiled covertly when Detective Diéz appeared satisfied with his answer.

"Thank you. I just want to put things into perspective while I'm here but I know that all the details will be in your police report," said the detective. "I'll be back in the morning for the prisoner."

To be thorough, he would check out the area a little later before leaving the scene. The rain had soaked into the ground. Puddles of water and mud had formed making it almost impossible to detect any footprints left behind. Phil's corpse was placed into a plastic body bag and zipped up and carried on a stretcher to the awaiting helicopter. Before they left, the detective wrapped things up.

" It looks like we're finished here. Detectives Blanco and Martinez, I'm leaving you in charge of guarding the plane. I want a full report of the inventory. I've already called for assistance to clean up this mess and they're on their way. In the meantime, I needn't remind you not to let that plane out of your sight."

He strolled up to Officer Paredés who tried to blend in and appear to be of help. The officer's mouth twitched nervously when he saw the detective approach but he quickly brought it under control before Diéz had a chance to notice. The detective extended his hand in a professional manner.

"Again, thank you for your help. I'll be returning tomorrow to take the prisoner back to Lima for processing. I'll contact you later if we have any further questions."

Officer Paredés firmly grasped the detective's hand.

"I'm happy to co-operate."

The policeman forced a smile but he was not happy at all. The whole investigation had been swept from under his nose. His smile evaporated as he stood and watched the chopper lift off. But now that they were gone, he relaxed his shoulders and breathed a sigh of relief.

He stood there for a long time staring into space, watching the chopper disappear in the distance but not seeing it. His mind was focused on something else. He was meticulously concentrating on the details that Detective Diéz had brought to light. The corners of his mouth turned upward. He was confident that the detective had no misconceptions about what had happened. According to him, the evidence was clear. The officer was thankful for the input. He would have to draw up a new police report making the changes in order to correspond with the version he gave to the detective.

'I really pulled it off this time! To think that this time yesterday was just an ordinary boring day!'

He pulled up the collar of his jacket, turned, and proceeded to his jeep. It was getting late. He wouldn't need to return to the station because he had plenty of empty forms at home. He would fill in a new police report after dinner tonight and have it ready to hand over to Detective Diéz when he arrives tomorrow. It would be perfect.

CHAPTER 10

John had estimated that he had slept fitfully for less than six hours. He tossed and turned reliving the nightmare of the previous morning over and over again. The thin hard mattress reeked of mildew. At times he found it difficult to breathe. He resisted the urge to vomit. He relieved himself once during the night, having to inhale the putrid odor of urine that remained in the pipes.

By dawn he was sitting on the edge of the cot staring at the cracks in the concrete wall facing him. He thought about his parents. His mother was apprehensive about his decision to backpack through Peru but he recalled his father's words to her.

"Laura, the two most precious gifts we can give our children are roots and wings."

Laura had looked at her husband and smiled, knowing what he had meant and knowing that he was right. His sixteen- year-old sister Ruth, and his eighteen-year-old brother Steve, envied John because he was so free and adventurous. He was their idol.

Memories of the fun and laughter he had with Phil crept into his mind. They had grown up in the same neighborhood. John had dated Phil's sister for a brief period of time in high school. Valerie was charming and lively but was soon captivated by the advances of a popular football player. John's mind began to recede back in time. All the fond memories of his childhood came rushing into his head. At least it was a way to escape the madness of his situation but he had never felt so alone.

After what seemed like forever, the office door opened, allowing a rush of fresh air to enter. John took the opportunity to inhale deeply, permitting oxygen to fill his lungs and rejuvenate him.

Eduardo Ramirez did not recognize the man who entered but was told that he would be arriving. He didn't expect him to be so early. He had just finished cleaning up and mopping the floor before the visitor from headquarters arrived. A tall handsome man wearing a multicolored sweater and dark trousers introduced himself.

"My name is Detective Walter Diéz. I'm here to escort the prisoner back to Lima. We need to question him and I'd like to get back as soon as possible."

When his greeter shook hands with him, the detective noticed the red circles around his eyes.

"I'm Officer Eduardo Ramirez. Officer Paredés isn't in yet, but I'll call him right away and let him know you're here."

He reached for the telephone sitting on the desk. The loud ring at the other end of the line awakened Officer Paredés with a start. He had a problem sleeping last night. It wasn't because of a guilty conscience. It was a combination of getting the police report just right and where to spend all his money once this was all over. He panicked when he found out that he had overslept and told his partner he would be there shortly. He would have to rush.

While the officer was on the phone, the detective studied John who was on his feet peering through the bars. John had been observing the meeting between the guard and the new face. He had no idea of what was happening or what was about to happen.

Walter Diéz was surprised at how young and innocent looking John was. He had been expecting a much older prisoner. John had his attention and was about to get more. He called out louder than he expected.

"Hey mister! Do you speak English?"

"Yes I do."

John's hopes soared as he continued to keep his tone loud for effect. He pointed a finger at Eduardo.

"That man stole my passport and my credit card. He held me at gunpoint while his buddy killed my friend. He shot him twice in cold blood! Where is Phil? Where is he?" he pleaded. " Why am I here? Please get me out of here!"

John's eyes began to water. His throat was parched and it was sore. He held up his painfully swollen ankle and pulled up his pant leg at the same time.

"Look at this! I need medical attention! I need to see a doctor!"

Detective Diéz was confused by John's nonsense. He had grown accustomed to prisoners' ranting and raving but what he heard just now sounded absurd. The prisoner was probably incoherent because of the traumatic situation he was in. Maybe the young man deserved to be here but the detective wasn't inhumane.

"I'll see what I can do for your ankle temporarily until we can get you to our clinic in Lima. A medic will take a look at it."

He turned to the officer who was now off the phone.

Officer Ramirez heard the brief conversation between the two speaking in English. It was killing him because he couldn't understand a word.

'I wonder what they were discussing?'

The officer with a conscience was uncomfortable and he felt the perspiration built up. He scratched his chin nervously and attempted to control his imagination regarding the contents of the brief conversation between Detective Diéz and the prisoner.

"Officer Paredés is on his way. He'll be here any minute."

Detective Diéz only half heard him. John's ankle was badly swollen and he felt compassion for the prisoner.

"Why hasn't this young man received First Aid treatment? Can't you see that he needs a tensor bandage on that ankle of his? Where is your First Aid Kit?"

He would have preferred an ice pack but he knew that ice was unavailable since the electricity was insufficient to power an electric refrigerator. Propane refrigerators were available in the larger cities but were very expensive. In this temperature it was a luxury and not a necessity.

Eduardo appeared somewhat flustered as he opened the bottom drawer of the filing cabinet and withdrew the kit. He was actually very concerned about the precarious predicament that he was in. So far the detective hadn't mentioned yesterday's events. He was thankful for that. But if the subject were to be brought up, would he be able to lie without arousing suspicion? He wasn't as good at deception as his partner was. He was turning into a nervous wreck as he passed the kit to the concerned detective. He was aware that his hand was visibly shaking and tried to cover up the reason for it.

"I'm terribly sorry. You are right. I should have been more attentive our prisoner's needs."

'More than you'll ever know.'

Walter Diéz opened the kit and found what he was looking for He took out the tensor bandage and turned to John who was still standing, gripping the cell bars.

"I'll put this on you before we leave. In the meantime keep your foot elevated,"

Their eyes met.

" Where are you taking me? You're getting me out of here, right?"

The detective read the anxiety on John's face.

"I'm taking you out of here. We are going to Lima where you will have an opportunity to explain things to authorities there."

He turned to Officer Ramirez.

"Do you have the police report?"

"Yes, of course." The officer walked around the desk and reached to open the right-hand top drawer of the desk.

At that moment the office door flew open and Officer Mauricio Paredés entered with a sealed brown envelope in his hand.

"Ah! Detective Diéz," he said extending his hand.

His voice was surprisingly jovial for not sleeping well the night before.

"I've been expecting you. It's nice to see you again." He smiled a fake smile.

The detective shook hands with the officer that he didn't particularly like for some strange reason. He was good at reading people and the officer had bad vibes about him. Perhaps it was that charm he was attempting to project, but Diéz didn't buy it.

" Oh! By the way, you haven't yet received the police report?"

It was a question rather than a statement. Mauricio Paredés was testing to see whether or not he was too late with his revised copy. He was worried because he forgot to tell Eduardo not to hand over the old one before he got there. The stress was getting to him no matter how much he wanted to deny it. His fate would depend on Diéz's response.

"No, I don't have it. I expect it's ready?"

Mauricio was extremely relieved to hear this.

"Of course it's ready. I'm sorry I'm late. Here you go."

He handed him the envelope.

John was getting impatient with all the seemingly formalities.

"What's going on? Am I leaving now or not?" he asked.

" We'll be leaving shortly, as soon as these officers release you into my custody," replied the detective from Lima who then turned and spoke to Eduardo and Mauricio in an authoritative tone.

"I'll take charge of the prisoner now, along with his belongings. I'd like to get going. I have an important meeting to attend and I don't want to be late."

Eduardo quickly took out a pair of handcuffs, grabbed the keys from the nail on the back of the door and opened the cell door. As John was being cuffed he asked for a drink of water. Walter Diez translated the request and Officer Paredés readily obliged. He handed John a bottle of water that was sitting on top of the filing cabinet. John gulped it down without taking his eyes off the arresting officer.

'Read my mind. Nobody frames me and gets away with it.'

"Let's get that ankle taken care of before we go," said the detective.

John sat quietly while Detective Diéz wrapped it neatly with the tensor bandage. As he rose to leave, John silently cursed the two corrupt police officers then the detective whisked him through the door, leaving them behind in the room. Mauricio was relieved to see them exit. He didn't like the arrogant, big time, city slicker cop, but would never admit to his jealousy as he stood akimbo and mimicked the man after he left.

'I'll take care of the prisoner now along with his belongings. Oh! He has an important meeting to attend and he'd better hurry or he'll be late. Who in the hell does he think he is?'

He hoped to never see the man again. But never mind, soon he would become a rich man. All else forgotten, his thoughts immediately turned to a plan that would make that happen. He had connections. People owed him favors. There would be no problem.

Eduardo was quiet for a long time and wanted to leave. He had been there all night and was tired. He was also worried. He had to get something off his chest before he went home.

"What if the prisoner tells the truth about what happened? And what if Detective Diéz believes him? Then what!"

Mauricio was irritated. He couldn't believe his ears.

"Don't be so stupid! Of course he'll tell the truth but who is going to believe him? *Why* would anyone believe him?"

Then it was Mauricio who was worried. He narrowed his eyes suspiciously and gazed at his partner.

"What did you tell the detective before I arrived? You didn't tell him anything, did you? Did he ask any questions? What did he talk about? Tell me!"

Eduardo blurted out defensively,

"I didn't tell him anything. I promise. He was more concerned about the prisoner's ankle. We talked about nothing until you got here."

Mauricio believed him. He wouldn't lie. He raised both hands and raked his big fingers through his thick hair pushing it back. He had to educate his partner.

"Okay Eduardo, listen to me. You have nothing to worry about. Like I said before, it's his word against ours. That's why we did what we had to do. No one is going to believe a single young foreigner over us. No one will question our authority. And besides, all the evidence points in his direction anyway. There's absolutely nothing that would implicate us. Now go home and get some sleep. Things will be much clearer once you get some rest. We can discuss the whole thing later."

Eduardo said nothing. He just shook his head in agreement. He appeared to be in a daze and his partner sighed with resolution.

"Am I getting through to you? Is any of this sinking in?"

Eduardo raised his tired eyes and mumbled, "Yes it is and I'm going home now."

Eduardo placed his hand on the door handle ready to leave. At the last minute Mauricio almost forgot.

"Wait! Before you go, I need to know where you buried the cocaine?"

"Don't worry. It's in a safe place. I couldn't mark the spot. It would be too obvious but I have it in my head. I'll show you the first chance we get."

His partner wasn't too happy with this but it would have to suffice.

"Okay, you can go home now. But I want you to show me the spot first thing tomorrow morning when we are out on patrol. I just want to know where it is. We can dig it up later when all this has died down."

Eduardo managed to mumble "Ya! Ya! Whatever!" as he went out the door.

CHAPTER 11

When John stepped out of the building, he squinted and was happy to see the light of day. He never thought in his wildest dreams it would be something to get excited about. He had always taken the outdoors for granted. As he was being led away, the Hairless Mexican dog suddenly appeared from out of nowhere, yapping, wagging his tail, and playfully nipping at his bandage. At the moment, John wished he could trade places with the animal. At least he would have his freedom. Normally he would laugh and respond to the animal's whims but this was no laughing matter.

Walter Diéz's assistant climbed into the chopper that had landed a short distance from where John had been held. John followed suit with Walter's Diéz's help and was surprised that he couldn't remember hearing the helicopter earlier when it arrived. But then again his mind was preoccupied with other things. Within minutes they lifted off.

John sat quietly looking out the window, his eyes searching below. He was hoping to view the small tent that he and Phil had pitched a few days before. He wanted to point it out so that he could explain everything. As time and distance passed he realized that it was not going to happen. He shook his head deep in thought. He wanted desperately to turn back the hands of time.

" How can this be happening?" he thought.

He continued to peer through the window marveling at the vastness and beauty of the valleys below. A sudden feeling of spirituality and peace embraced him as he prayed,

'Dear God, please don't leave me alone.'

Detective Diéz was occupied reading the police report. He read it over several times wanting to absorb every detail. Occasionally he would look up at John. Finally he spoke in a loud but friendly manner breaking into John's meditation.

"So John, you and your buddy were caught red-handed. I'm sincerely sorry about your loss. Do you want to tell me about it?"

John pursed his lips, turned his head to face his inquisitor and thought for a moment. He was reluctant to open his mouth. He knew that sooner or later he would have to explain what happened but whom should he trust?

"What is your name? I at least have a right to know who I'm speaking to." Detective Diéz smiled to himself, not because he was malicious but because he recognized a likeness of himself in John. He couldn't pinpoint what it was but he admired his forthrightness.

"Forgive me," he said, "My name is Detective Walter Diéz. I'm leading this investigation. There are other things I could be doing right now but I wanted to give you the opportunity to tell your side of the story before the tough guys at the prison in Lima get a hold of you for questioning."

Actually there was something that was bothering him but he wasn't at liberty to disclose that information to the person he was transferring. But he wanted to see if John could verify a small detail for him. He thought that something Officer Paredés had said yesterday during his questioning didn't quite mesh with what was written in the report. It had to do with the sequence of events during the search.

John's face and neck turned red. The scare tactic was working but not in the way in which it was intended. John turned his head away.

'*I can't trust this man. He is probably as corrupt as the rest of them. He will twist my words and create his own version to coincide with whatever is in that report.*'

When detective Diéz wasn't getting a response from the suspect he continued coaxing in his smooth voice.

" Come on John! Give yourself a break! You don't want to take the wrap for someone else, do you? You will serve a minimum of thirty years in prison for drug trafficking. That's a long time, thirty years. Make it easy on yourself. Co-operate with us and we may cut you a deal. Tell us who you work for."

The more detective Diéz thought about it, the more involved he wanted to become in infiltrating the drug ring that was expanding in his country and destroying more lives.

John was developing a headache as he sat deep in thought about how he could prove his innocence. Finally he spoke not recognizing his own voice.

"You have my things. Those two cops gave you my personal belongings in that bag." He pointed his chin to the bag on the seat beside them.

"I have receipts in there that will prove where I've been. They are with my passport. You have the wrong person you'll see. Take a look."

Diéz reached for the bag and examined the contents that were soaking wet.

"The only things that are in this bag are your clothing and nothing else. Can you explain why your passport is not here?"

"Those bastards!" thought John "Why was I so naïve to think that they wouldn't keep my I.D. papers?" Then he answered the detective.

"I can prove we were camping out there. I can show you exactly where if you will just let me. If you find our tent, my diary is there inside it, along with the rest of my stuff. It has a record of where I have been every day since I've been here in Peru."

John's head was throbbing as he looked into the detective's eyes.

"I'm telling you the truth."

Somewhere deep down inside detective Diéz wanted to believe him.

"Alright," he said, "You can tell us where your camp is and we will find it if it's there. But if you are lying, you are in big trouble."

59

He reached under his sweater and into his shirt pocket then took out a stubby little pencil. He opened his briefcase and found a detailed map of the small area. He had thrown it in at the last minute as a spare. It was officially necessary to use one for their investigation to mark the exact location of the crash.

"Here," he said, "mark an X where you say you were."

John took the map. He wanted to make certain that he was as accurate as he could remember. So he handed it back and asked the detective to place an X where the wreckage was. After doing so, he was handed the stub of a pencil and he placed an X precisely where they were camping. He handed the information back to the detective.

"There! Look right there and you'll see that I'm not lying."

The detective took the information hoping that John was right, but that was unlikely. He had read the police report.

'How could it be just a coincidence that he happened to be running away from the Cessna when the police arrived? If he were innocent, why would he run? And who was piloting the plane? Where was he? People just don't disappear into thin air. No! It doesn't make sense. He's fabricating a story. He's trying so hard to be convincing but I'll give him the satisfaction of the doubt anyway.'

"Don't worry! We'll soon find out whether or not you're lying."

John relaxed a little and let out a sigh of relief. They would find his tent for certain. He would be free. But that wouldn't be the end of it. He would then concentrate on bringing justice to Phil's murderers. John was glad they did not speak during the rest of the flight. He was exhausted. He closed his eyes and dozed off.

A voice awakened him and it wasn't long before the city of Lima came into view. As they approached the airport, the pilot radioed for clearance to land. John could see the expanse of the vast Pacific Ocean in the distance. A dozen old obsolete Peruvian military helicopters were parked haphazardly on the pavement in one area, as were several huge military cargo planes. Further to the left, national and international airline jets were lined up at different terminals.

The chopper hovered above the helicopter pad and then made a smooth landing. The pilot waited a few minutes then switched off the engine. When all was clear, he gave the signal to disembark. The assistant opened the door and jumped out onto the pavement, his hair in disarray, his shirt and pants blowing in the wind caused by the blades that were still rotating. He motioned for John to follow, reaching for his arm to help him maintain his balance. Walter Diéz followed closely behind John. The balmy dry air was a welcoming change as he stepped out onto the cement. This was the same airport that he landed in when he first arrived in Peru. He would never have believed that he would be taken back here by helicopter in hand-cuffs. But here he was. The detective left John instructions as he was preparing to leave.

"From here on, you're to go with this gentleman."

He nodded toward the assistant.

" He will take care of you. I will be seeing you later."

"Later when? I thought you were taking me yourself? Don't leave me?"

For some strange reason he hated to be abandoned by the detective. Maybe it was because at least he had somebody he could communicate with. The assistant hadn't said a word in English and it was obvious he couldn't speak the language.

"Later on today. I need to get your statement."

"You mean my confession," thought John, "Well good luck! Because you won't be getting any confession out of me!"

Detective Diéz spoke briefly with his assistant then removed his cell phone from his pocket and made a call. While he was speaking, the assistant took John by the arm and led him towards an awaiting vehicle. Before climbing into the back of the police car, John glanced back and witnessed Detective Diéz open the driver side door of a dark green sedan. He climbed in and drove away.

John was immediately taken to the precinct. Once inside, he was surprised. It was a clean, modern building, unlike the one he had just come from in Santa Inéz. The floors were waxed and polished and there were washrooms off the corridors. He was first taken to the processing room. The man who had been escorting him said something in Spanish to his colleague. Then he left the room leaving John with two other policemen.

"Please state your full name," said the man taking the information.

It was a basic question in Spanish and John understood but he was angry and in no mood to co-operate. His behavior was totally out of character but under the circumstances, who could blame him?

"You have my passport. You already know my name," replied John obstinately. Another cop who stood by listening smiled menacingly at John.

"I wouldn't give them a hard time if I were you. I've seen what happens to people who don't co-operate. State your name, date and place of birth, and your nationality."

His tone was serious and John immediately volunteered the information to the man with the unfriendly face. When he was being photographed and fingerprinted like a common criminal, John had never been so humiliated in his entire life. He had no reason to feel ashamed but nevertheless, it was demeaning. He was grateful that there were no others present to witness the process. But then again, this would never have happened if he had been in Canada.

Then he was taken into the interrogation room and told to wait there. John paced the floor in circles with an overwhelming feeling of naked fear. He was alone and helpless and imagining all kinds of bad things that could happen to him when he wasn't in control of the situation. He hated not being in control. He recalled Phil's warning and Phil was right. He was going to be thrown into jail.

His train of thought was suddenly interrupted when the door opened and the interrogation officer, the one with the menacing smile, entered. He must have recognized the look of terror in the prisoner's eyes earlier because he roughed John's shoulder and shoved him down into one of the straight-back chairs at the table.

"Sit down!" he commanded, "Make yourself comfortable."

In a standing position he bent over and leaned his elbows on the tabletop. His face was inches from John's.

"Who do you work for? Who is your boss?"

"It's not what you think! You have it all wrong! I don't work for anybody!"

"You were caught hauling a load of cocaine in that nice little Cessna of yours."

"It's not my plane!"

"That's called illegal possession and drug trafficking. I don't know about in your country but here in Peru it's intolerable. You must have a lot of money tied up in that operation! Where were you going? What was your destination? Who were you going to meet?"

When the interrogator had raised his voice to almost a yelling pitch, John had had enough. He counter challenged and spoke up with vehemence.

"What are you talking about? I want a lawyer. I demand a phone call to my lawyer."

With that, the man exercised caution. He wanted desperately to succeed in intimidating the suspect to the point where he would break down and confess to anything, but he decided to let up, now that the prisoner had requested a lawyer.

"Okay," he said, "have it your way for now."

Just then someone knocked on the door, it opened, and a man poked his head into the room.

"Excuse me," he said, "Can I speak with you for a moment?"

The interrogator stepped outside the door and closed it, leaving John relieved to be alone. He had been badgered enough and thought that for the first time since he was arrested, he may have won a round.

"What is it?" asked the interrogator.

"Our prisoner has a visitor in the next room. I know this is highly irregular but he has clearance."

The messenger gave the interrogator a blank look and shrugged his shoulders. John was still sitting when the door opened.

"Okay we're done here. I guess today is your lucky day. You have a visitor next door."

There were three identical rooms side by side, used when necessary to question different people individually at the same time. John followed them out as instructed and was shown into the room with the visitor.

"He's all yours!" The door closed behind him.

A young Caucasian man sat at the table and stood up when John entered. He was wearing a navy blue business suit with a white shirt and blue striped tie. He introduced himself without a handshake.

"My name is Paul Forrester. I'm working here in Peru for the Canadian Embassy." He flashed his official Embassy I.D.

"Lieutenant Amaya was kind enough to contact me on your behalf. Although I have never met the man, he seems reasonable and fair. Let's sit down. Maybe we can help one another."

John let out a huge sigh of relief when he heard this. Finally he was being rescued.

They each took a chair at the table, sitting opposite one another.

"How long am I going to be here?" John eagerly blurted out. "And what about Phil? His family must be notified and my family as well. They have no idea what has happened to us. I shouldn't be here. Why are they keeping me? I haven't done anything wrong."

The man from the embassy held up his hand as if it would stop John from speaking.

"Wait a minute! Please understand. I am here in a very limited capacity. The Canadian Embassy has no desire and no intentions of getting involved with the case against you."

John's eyes widened in astonishment and disbelief.

" I can't believe you're saying that! What's the point of having an embassy here if you either can't, or refuse to help Canadians who are in trouble in this country? Why are you really here?" he asked, uncertain about trusting him after what he had just heard.

Paul Forrester felt sorry for the young man who was sitting with him. He also was embarrassed because he thought he didn't have an appropriate answer for John. Like other government employees he was just doing his job. To a point, he agreed with the prisoner but his hands were tied. Then he had an idea. Maybe he could help after all.

"Listen," he said, "I'm just performing me duty but off the record, I can maybe help you by recommending a good defense attorney if you don't mind. I know him well and he's one of the best."

John wanted to know more.

"How do you know him?"

"I met him through a friend. He was born in Peru. His Canadian father came to Peru from Montreal as a missionary. That was before Carlos was born. His mother is Peruvian. His family returned to Canada when he was fourteen. He continued his education and studied law. After he graduated, he opened a practice in Quebec. After his father died, his mother became very homesick and so he came back with her to her homeland and has been looking after her. Now he continues to practice law here in Lima. His name is Carlos Aguillar."

Paul Forrester hesitated a moment before volunteering.

"I could speak with him if you like. However," he continued, "you are under no obligation. You are perfectly free to retain a lawyer of your own choice."

John raised his eyes to meet his adviser's.

"I have to trust someone," he thought. He was relieved to hear this offer and almost smiled, for it was the first time since his capture that he possessed a glimmer of hope.

"Yes. Please do as soon as possible. Today!" he heard himself say.

"Okay, I'll see what I can do."

There was an awkward silence while the man from the embassy stared at the wall beyond John as if his mind was somewhere else. He was hesitant to approach the subject for which he had been summoned. Finally he spoke.

"The embassy received a phone call from Lieutenant Amaya who works for the National Police. He had an unusual request. Apparently there is a John Doe at the morgue. The lieutenant has reason to believe that you may know his identity. Please forgive me if I sound cold and callous, but I have never had to do this kind of thing before."

John's breathing became shallow. "Where is he? I want to see him!"

"I'm terribly sorry but you can't."

Paul Forrester deplored what he had to do next.

"I was given a photo. Are you ready for this?"

He reached inside his pocket and was about to pull out a large envelope.

"No! Wait!" said John, " Please, just give me a minute!"

It seemed to take forever before John thought he was prepared and strong enough to face the truth, that his friend Phil had been killed. At times, somewhere in the back of his mind he wanted to believe that Phil was in a hospital, miraculously recovering from the gunshot wound. A state of denial was his defense mechanism substituting for the guilt he felt.

"Okay I'm ready! Let me see it!"

The bearer of bad news solemnly removed the envelope from his pocket and placed it on the table. "There's no easy way of doing this," he thought. Then he carefully slipped the photo out of the envelope and placed it on the table so that it faced John.

"Do you recognize him?" he asked.

At first, John avoided looking down at the image, fearing the worst. He forced his eyes to take just a quick glance then he looked away. He needed to look a second time in order to make certain.

"That's him!" was all he said as he placed his hands on his forehead, shielding his face. Large teardrops fell, marking the tabletop. He sniffled and swiped the back of his hand across and beneath his nose. Paul felt cruel having to ask his next question. It was an intrusion on the prisoner's right to mourn for his beloved friend and the man from the embassy hated having to extract information under these circumstances.

"Who is he? What is his name?"

"He's my friend Phil, Phil MacAllister."

"I'm so sorry. I will personally make arrangements to contact his family and your family immediately." Paul Forrester was a gentle and compassionate man.

"Please, how may I get in touch with them?"

John inhaled in several short shallow breaths, the kinds that are produced when someone has been quietly sobbing. He then relayed the necessary information that was required, while his visitor wrote on his notepad. When all had transpired and Mr. Forrester was ready to leave, John became dismayed and blurted out without reserve,

"Must you leave now? Can you please stay longer? I really need to talk to someone this very minute. What is so urgent that requires your immediate attention?"

John was desperate to keep him there for as long as possible. Anything to delay having to go to prison. He searched the man's eyes for an answer. The man from the embassy had been there long enough and was trying to think of an excuse to get out of there.

"Like I told you before, we don't get involved in legal matters in this country. I must get back and contact your family and your friend's family as well. I want to make that phone call to Mr. Aguillar as soon as possible.

"Phil is dead now. What difference would half an hour make?" John retorted.

Paul glanced at his watch.

"Okay! Half an hour," he said, "but this is totally off the record."

'I'm surprised that they have given us this much time!'

John took his time to relate the sequence of events that led him to this point where he was in prison. He had his listener's full and undivided attention and the man from the embassy interrupted with the occasional question. In the end, John had no way of knowing whether Mr. Forrester believed him or not. He could only hope.

"Please," he said, "I'm telling the truth. You have to believe me."

"I have no reason not to believe you. It certainly sounds like an interesting case for my lawyer friend Mr. Aguillar. I don't want to get your hopes up but I am sure he will have no problem clearing it up in no time. Lieutenant Amaya seemed quite concerned about you during our telephone conversation, although I spoke with him only briefly. When I inquired about your friend's death, he seemed to be very annoyed with the police in Santa Inés. Although he didn't say it outright, I could detect it in the tone of his voice.

John was happy to hear this. Maybe he had a chance against them after all. Suddenly the two were startled when a loud knock sounded at the door.

"Time is up!" It was the guard's voice and the door opened.

"Thank you," was all John could say to the man from the Canadian Embassy before be was handcuffed, escorted from the room, and whisked down the hall. For John, this was only the beginning. The worst was yet to come.

The penitentiary was located in a desert area on the outskirts of Lima. Two guards opened the main gate after speaking with the driver of the paddy wagon. The vehicle proceeded toward the inner wall. After stopping a second time, the back door was opened and John, along with two other prisoners jumped out. They were instructed to go with the guards who escorted them inside.

Once inside, John was led to a common area containing showers. He was given a small bar of soap and clean prison garb. Although he was exhausted, the shower felt somewhat refreshing. He actually welcomed it after having spent the night in a squalid holding cell. He washed under the tepid low-pressure water, dried off, then climbed into the blue jumpsuit.

He was taken through a short corridor with a heavy steel door at the end. The guard removed a large metal ring from his belt that held numerous keys. He found the one he was looking for and inserted it into the keyhole. The door opened and John was further escorted down the lengthy hall, cells on each side, the odd one vacant.

Prisoners were hissing, whistling and shouting something about `bonito gringo`. Arms reached for him through the bars. He thought he felt a slight brush of flesh over the hair on his arm and he cringed. He was relieved to see the guard open a door to a vacant cell. He had no desire to share a cell with a cellmate, as some of the others contained two prisoners. He reluctantly entered his cell and immediately sat on the hard cot. He sighed deeply and began to mentally review the events of the day. He was exhausted but his mind was reeling with questions.

How sincere was Detective Diéz? Would he really search for his campsite like he promised? And why didn't he show up today to take his statement like he said he would? Was it because he had asked for a lawyer? Or was he just busy? How long would it take for Paul Forrester to contact his family? Did he do the right thing by telling him to go ahead and contact a lawyer for him? Maybe that was a mistake. And how good *was* this lawyer that Mr. Forrester had recommended? Could he get him out of here tomorrow? Was he *that* good?

Thoughts of Phil would pop into his head but he deliberately ignored them. Wishing them away was another defense mechanism. He always thought that he was a strong person. He could handle anything. But in this case, the pain was too unbearable. He would gladly trade his emotional pain for physical pain. But that wasn't going to happen. He spent the rest of the day being tormented with feelings of anger, guilt, and frustration. He paced the small area in circles while racking his brains trying to figure out a way, some clue that would prove his innocence. The rowdiness of the other cellmates got on his nerves. There was constant yelling between the guards and the prisoners.

He longed to see his family. His feelings of nervousness and tension increased with the thought of his family. He imagined the worry and the heartache his parents would incur with the news of their son's fate. He sat on the bottom bunk covered his face with his hands, closed his eyes and bent over with his elbows in his lap. He withdrew himself from the chaos and din of his environment in an attempt to maintain his sanity. He was experiencing the epitome of torture within, when he finally allowed the thoughts of Phil to enter his mind.

"Dear God" he prayed "It hurts so bad. Please help me."

CHAPTER 12

Keith Emerson was in the state of shock when he received a phone call from Paul Forrester at the Canadian Embassy in Lima. He was working in his office and was grateful that he had been home to answer the phone. Laura was out meeting with her bridge club and the kids weren't home from school yet, so he was the only one there to take the call. He grasped the receiver tightly in his hand as if it were the only lifeline between himself and his son. He was full of questions. He wanted to know all the details of what had happened.

Paul Forrester had given him as much information as he could, but Keith was frustrated at what little information that was. The man from the embassy didn't want to become too involved by giving out details that might be inaccurate but he *did* say that he believed that John was innocent and that he was going to contact a lawyer for him. Even though Paul Forrester was unable to answer most of his questions, John's father was thankful that the man could at least recommend a good attorney for his son. That was good news. He grabbed a pen and wrote down the number where he could be reached. He would contact Carlos Aguillar as soon as possible. Then Keith pounced with the question that Paul Forrester was hoping he wouldn't ask.

"Is there anything you can do in an official capacity that would help my son?"

He waited for the man at the other end of the line to answer.

"Hello! Are you still there?"

"Yes, I'm here."

Paul Forrester was inwardly cowering as he spoke into the mouthpiece. He was glad that it wasn't a face to face conversation like it had been earlier with the son.

"I'm sorry but the best I could do was put him in touch with Mr. Aguillar, the defense attorney. There is nothing more I can do."

He didn't give the reasons why. He didn't even want to go there because he tried to persuade his superior to help in John's case. But foreign diplomats had their policies and regulations to dictate accordingly. It was not their place to become involved and that was that, end of story. Finally John's father thanked the man from the embassy for being there for his son.

After he hung up, he experienced a father's worst nightmare. He envisioned his son totally alone and helpless, behind bars in a foreign country where heaven only knows what was happening to him. His stomach churned and a wave of dizziness crept into his head. He was shaking and had to sit down in order to compose himself. He inhaled deeply and ran his agile fingers through his hair. Laura was due home any minute now. How was he going to tell her that John was in prison and that Phil had been killed?

Without time to prepare, his wife barged in the door announcing that she had made a 'grand slam' today. She was ecstatic until she saw the look on her husband's face.

"What's the matter honey? You look like you just saw a ghost! Is everything all right?"

Her husband took her by the hand and led her into the kitchen where he thought she would be more comfortable. This was not normal behavior and Laura suspected right away that there was something wrong. Keith proceeded with the uneasy task of informing his wife. There was no delicate way of breaking the news.

"Sit down honey," he said, then hesitated.

His heart sank. His wife looked so vulnerable. He loved her more at this moment than the day he married her. Laura sat at the kitchen table and Keith sat beside her with his arm around her shoulder.

"Tell me! What's wrong? Is it Mom?"

Laura's mother had just been released from the Intensive Care Unit at St. Joseph's Hospital. She had had a heart attack and was slowly recovering. Laura's greatest fear was that her mother's health was failing.

"No, your mom is fine. It's John! He's in trouble!"

Keith took a deep breath and began telling her about the phone call he had just received. At first, Laura was in a state of denial.

"There must be some mistake! It can't be!"

But then her husband took her firmly by the shoulders and looked her square in the eye. He hated to do this.

"Listen to me Laura! There's no mistake! We will be there for him! We will help him! We have to face this together,"

Her denial turned to shock, as reality began to sink in.

"What are we going to do Keith? How can we help him?"

Keith hadn't had time to think of a plan and was slow to respond. Laura paced nervously back and forth on the kitchen floor as she kept talking. A lump was forming in her throat.

"We must book the next available flight to Lima. John must feel abandoned. He needs us. I can't imagine what the MacAllisters must be going through right now. My God! I can't believe that Phil is dead!"

Tears streamed down her cheeks and Keith approached her. He gently wiped her face with his caring hand.

"Yes, John needs us and we are going to book a flight to Lima," he reassured her.

Laura was a petit woman with fair skin, blue eyes, and blonde hair. She always took pride in her appearance. Keith put his arm around his wife of twenty-three years and squeezed gently trying to comfort her. He was tall with a lean body of an athlete. He taught gym part-time at the local high school and coached hockey during the winter season. It was a supplementary source of income when the family business was slow. He was more worried than he wanted his wife to believe.

"We'll get through this somehow Laura. I'll give Stella a call right away. If anyone can help, she can. Then I'll arrange for us to leave as soon as possible."

He pulled his wife closer and tenderly wrapped both arms around her. Laura buried her head in his chest and sobbed. He was her rock. He held her until she could sob no more. Then she heard the car door slam. She lifted her head and stepped back blinking.

"Ruth and Steve are home. We have to tell them. Should you do it or do you want me to?"

They usually shared responsibilities when it came to dealing with their children.

Keith placed his hand on her arm as if to hold her back.

"No, it's okay, I'll handle it. Just give me a little time. I need to think."

When they broke the news of John's fate to their other children, an argument ensued.

"I need to go with you," insisted Steve, "he's my brother."

"You need to stay here and look after your sister. And besides, you have your education to think about. You can't just drop out of classes and leave," replied his father.

"He's my brother too," cried Ruth who had been in tears.

"I need to go too. He needs us all," she continued.

"Listen to your father!" Laura snapped, "He knows what is best. Please honey, don't give us a hard time, not now."

Ruth realized she was being selfish and sensed her mother's anxiety. Against her will, she decided to conform to her parent's wishes.

"Okay," she said, "But call us every day. We need to know what's going on and how you're holding up. Please promise me that you'll do that."

She looked at her brother for approval. Laura hugged her daughter.

"I promise we'll keep in touch in a daily basis. Check your e-mail every day just in case we can't get through."

By this time, Steve was anxious to escape the company of his family. He was choked up over Phil's death but tried desperately not to show any emotion for his mother's and sister's sake. His strength was dissipating and he just wanted to be alone to mourn.

"You're right Dad! "he said, "We'll do anything you say. There's nothing else I can do now, so would you mind if I went out for a while? I need some fresh air."

'*And I need to be alone.*'

He was out the door before he heard an answer. His father understood, but his sister Ruth went running after him.

"Wait Steve! I'm coming with you."

CHAPTER 13

The next day Detective Diéz didn't waste any time. When he arrived at his office he pulled two rookies aside and instructed them.

"I have a job for you. You've probably heard about the plane crash and arrest of the drug smuggler a couple of days ago. Apparently, according to him, he and his buddy were camping near the crash site and were merely innocent bystanders who wanted to help. I'm not so convinced, but I want you to go there and search the area. See if you can find his tent. I'll give you a map of where to look and if you happen to see any of the locals, ask around and find out if they saw any strangers there recently to confirm his alibi. Be ready to leave in an hour. There'll be a chopper ready and waiting for you."

"Yes sir! We can do that! Is there anything else you want us to do?"

"No. That's all. If you find any evidence, call me right away, don't leave the site and don't touch anything."

The two rookies were only too happy to oblige. It was an unusual duty for them and it made them feel like an intricate part of the team. They were eager to get started and intended to perform well.

The lead investigator produced the map and gave it to them. He hated to send them on a wild goose chase but at the same time he wanted to cover all his bases. He not only felt obligated to do so but he was also curious. He felt obligated for two reasons, because he gave his word to John and because if John happened to be right about being an innocent bystander, then arresting him was a terrible injustice. And if John *was* right, then how did it come about that he was arrested? And who really was the guilty party?

76

He didn't want to speculate just yet until he had the facts. He would know more at the end of the day when the rookies return. Half of him hoped they would find something. He liked John. He didn't seem to be the typical hardened criminal that he was accustomed to dealing with. The other half hoped that they had their man and could use him to get some information that would lead to more arrests.

While the search was in progress, Detective Diéz was at the crime lab examining the large photographs of the crime scene that were spread out on a large glass tabletop in front of him. The forensic team was busy processing the evidence. He decided to pay a visit to the medical examiner's room downstairs.

The cool air was a change when he opened the door. Immediately, his nostrils sensed the pungent odor of antiseptic. Equipment and bottles of chemicals stood on shelves against the wall. On the opposite wall stood a deep sink, a lab table and a computer. The coroner was swamped with work and was behind schedule. He held a hose in his hand and was about to wash down the body. Detective Diéz donned a white lab coat from the hook on the wall and approached.

"Is this our victim? What did you find?"

"Well, he took a shot to the leg but the bullet that killed him was the one to the back. It traveled through the heart and killed him instantly. Take a look at the trajectory of the bullet."

He adjusted the florescent light that was suspended above the lab table. The assistant gently rolled the body onto its side and held it there. The M.E. probed a rod through the wound, which displayed the angle of entry.

"The shooter would have to be a giant with that angle. Either that or the victim was down on one knee or both knees when he took the fatal shot"noted the M.E.

"Maybe he dropped his gun and was picking it up when he was shot in the back."

"It was at fairly close range. What does the police report say?"

Diéz had no problem recalling what was written.

"According to the police report the suspect tried to escape. Officer Paredés fired a warning shot into the air and ordered him to stop. When the suspect continued to flee he shot him in the thigh to try to stop him. The suspect fell to his knees but then produced a gun and fired at the officer. That is when Officer Paredés shot him in the back."

The detective was focused on being thorough.

"Is there anything else I should know?" inquired Diéz.

The medical examiner looked at the detective.

"The victim has calluses on both hands and there's gun shot residue on his right hand and wrist which indicates that he did fire the gun. The toxic report came back negative. There were no drugs in his system."

"Thanks Bernardo, you've been a big help."

Diéz's next stop was the ballistics expert who had his eyes to the microscope when Diéz entered.

"How's it going?"

"Everything matches," he said, "The only problem is that we'll never know who the 9 mm. Glock belongs to, the one found with the victim. The serial number is filed off and we can't even get a trace etching using the acid."

"That's too bad. I was hoping that we could get a trace on it, but under the circumstances I'm not surprised. These guys cover their tracks well. Thanks anyway."

With that information, he exited through the glass door hoping to have better luck in the print lab. One of the technicians was sitting at a computer desk when he entered. He walked up behind her looking over her shoulder at the screen.

"Any luck with the prints?"

She had been concentrating on her work and didn't hear him approaching. She nearly jumped out of her chair when he startled her.

"Sorry! I didn't mean scare you." He smiled broadly as he apologized.

"Not yet, I've just started. I've got my work cut out. There were six sets of prints found in the plane. I thought I'd start with the known ones first. Officer Mauricio Paredés's and Officer Eduardo Ramirez's prints will be on record. I'm entering them now."

She typed in the information. Within a few minutes she was able to match up those two sets of prints.

"Now I was able to get the deceased victim's prints. Let's see if we can get a match."

She fed them into the computer. It didn't take long to match Phil's prints that were found on the passenger side door when he was about to climb into the cockpit but changed his mind at the last minute.

"It makes it easy when you know ahead of time what you are looking for."

She continued to press the keys on the computer. John's prints were now in the police database for comparison and also turned up a match.

"We have two unidentified sets left. These may take a little more time depending on whether or not they are in our database."

The screen kept going in fast forward until finally it stopped when it had found a match. The criminal's photo and information popped up on the screen.

"Here it is. The prints belong to José Peres, age 38, born in Iquitos. He has a record of small time felony charges. He's been in and out of prison several times."

The detective was elated. It was the first real lead that he could pursue.

"Can you print that one out for me please?"

"I sure can."

With the touch of a key, the printer started and spit out a copy for the detective. "One set of prints to go."

After waiting for some time and hoping to identify the last person who was a mystery, the results were negative.

"No match for these. Five out of six isn't bad " said the technician as she turned in her seat and looked up with pleasure.

"Not bad! That's wonderful. Good work! Sorry but I've got to run now."

He sensed her attraction to him, winked at her and hurried out the door. He had one last piece of evidence to check out. He walked into the D.N.A. section of the lab. He had put in a 'rush order' for the results and was able to get away with it only because he had asked Lieutenant Amaya to pull some strings for him. A young male and a middle age female were working. Their backs were turned from him as he entered.

"Were you able to get a match on the blood found at the crime scene?"

The young gentleman who was presently working on it responded.

"We have two different D.N.A.'s taken from the blood samples at the crime scene. One is a match to the suspect. It matches the blood found on the seat. The other one doesn't match the suspect's or the victim's. So the blood found on the dash and on the floor and belongs to someone else."

"Interesting," thought Diéz, "So our suspect does have something to hide. I think it's about time we get a statement from him. I'd love to hear his explanation."

Before leaving, he put a rush on the paperwork. Although the processing was done, some of the paperwork hadn't yet been completed. He wanted it to be sent to his office as soon as possible. He knew that a trial date hadn't been set as of yet, but he had plenty of evidence for a conviction. He was prepared now to confront the suspect.

He desperately wanted to penetrate the drug syndicate that John was involved in. He was just a pawn in the larger scheme of things. But with his testimony, he could eventually lead them to the leaders of the syndicate and break it wide open. This was a chance in a lifetime. He might not get another opportunity like this. With this thought in mind, he headed for the prison.

While he drove, he imagined the crime scene and the series of events that had occurred. He couldn't fathom why Phil MacAllister would risk his life and run away. *'What was he thinking? He was so young and I suppose he thought he was invincible.'* He shook his head from side to side. It was a shame that the Officer Paredés had to kill him. But he supposed that he didn't have much choice under the circumstances. He might have done the same thing had he been in the officer's shoes. He would soon have a chance to question John again and this time he had better cooperate if he wanted to help himself.

CHAPTER 14

At the end of each day Carlos Aguillar routinely collected his messages from his secretary. He had spent the day in court defending a man accused of larceny. It was a difficult case because one of the witnesses testifying against his client was a member of the client's family. The attorney also knew that his client was struggling for his family to make ends meet, so he agreed to take on the case 'pro bono'. That was the kind of man Carlos Aguillar was.

Today he was tired and planed to retire early. However, when his secretary handed him the list of messages, he happened to glance down and saw the name Paul Forrester. He was curious. This was a personal call and not a business call. Should he phone Paul now or should he wait until tomorrow? He hadn't spoken with his friend for some time. It would be good to catch up on the latest news. He decided to pick up the phone and punch in the numbers beside his name.

After a lengthy conversation with his friend, he had already made up his mind about taking on the case. He would re-schedule his ten o'clock and eleven o'clock appointments in the morning and visit John Emerson.

Sitting at his desk he mentally reviewed the information Paul had given him. He pondered the devastation and destruction of drugs on people's lives. He had a nephew, his sister's son, who got mixed up with the wrong crowd and ended up killing himself with a drug overdose. It was ruled accidental. That was two years ago but the memory remained indelible in his mind.

"I'll take my time and see what this man has to say," he thought, "Paul must have believed him somewhat or he wouldn't have called."

He knew that if John was guilty he deserved to be behind bars for a very long time. But if he were innocent, he would do everything in his power to prove it. He stood up from his desk and walked into the reception room where his secretary was gathering her belonging and getting ready to leave for the day.

"Maria, I know that it has been a long day, but before you go, I have just one little favor. Could you please reschedule the tomorrow's appointments from ten o'clock until two o'clock? Try to fit them in later on in the afternoon. Something has come up and I'll have to leave."

Maria was a dedicated employee since the office had open and Carlos was good to her. He appreciated her loyalty and they always got along well.

"No problem," she said with a smile, "I'll do that right away."

The next morning Carlos Aguillar maneuvered his way through the relentless barrage of traffic. Lima was the second largest desert-city in the world, with a population of over eight million, and the streets were chaotic. Ahead of him, a bus driver was yelling out his window arguing with a taxi driver concerning who had the right of way. With few traffic lights and no stop signs at intersections, the rule of thumb was, whoever got there first had the right of way. As a result, the majority of vehicles had bent fenders or dents and scratches or both.

The defense attorney was looking forward to meeting his new client. Finally he reached his destination, found a parking space, and locked the doors of his white sedan. He climbed the steps of the building hauling his briefcase. He walked through the spacious lobby, through a glass door, and into the reception area. The deputy asked for his I.D., searched through his briefcase and had him walk through the metal detector.   Then he was escorted through a short corridor with an intercom announcing his arrival. The heavy metal door was unlocked electronically.

He proceeded to a contact-visiting room for a face to face meeting with John. He peered through the one-way window for a first hand glimpse of his client. John was sitting with hunched shoulders, head down, staring at the floor. He was so exhausted that he was numb. The guard opened the door and pointed to an intercom on the wall.

"Press that orange button when you're finished."

John jumped in his chair. His heart skipped a beat when the door opened. He looked up at his new attorney and summoned the strength to perk up. He couldn't afford to be indifferent. This was important. He had to be alert. He had to make a good impression.

Carlos Aguillar was dark skinned with thick wavy gray hair and a handsome broad face. He had always looked younger than he actually was. But lately he was beginning to show his age with long working hours and visiting his mother regularly at the nursing home. Unlike her, he was tall and lean, inheriting his father's steel gray eyes. He wore an expensive dark suit and John relished the fragrance of his cologne simply because it reminded him of the outside world. John stood up.

"You must be my defense attorney. Thank you for coming. I really appreciate Mr. Forrester for sending you."

Meeting his lawyer face to face gave him renewed energy. He was keen to tell his story to someone he could finally trust, someone who could help him. Carlos Aguilar immediately took a liking to John.

"My name is Carlos Aguillar."

He reached out his arm and they shook hands. The two automatically took a seat and the attorney continued speaking.

"I've spoken to my friend Paul Forrester who has filled me in on some rather interesting details regarding your situation. Do you still want me to represent you?"

"Yes I do. I trust Mr. Forrester's judgement in recommending you. At least we have something in common."

Carlos Aguillar looked puzzled. John understood immediately and clarified himself.

"You lived in Canada for a while."

"Yes I did. It's a beautiful country. I've always said I would return for a visit and I will some day."

Carlos then got right down to business.

"Now, we need to get some facts," he said to John.

John sighed deeply before responding. Getting the facts was not a problem. Proving the facts was going to be the problem, a real challenge as far as he was concerned.

"I'm in quite a mess and not of my own making. I don't know where to begin," he said seeking some direction. The interview was under way.

CARLOS:

"Let's start at the beginning. When did you arrive in Peru and what was the purpose of you visit, and where have you been staying?"

JOHN:

"We landed in Lima on the first of January. We checked into a hostel and spent a few days touring the city. Then we flew Aero Condor to Iquitos. We booked a six- day tour with P.V. Amazon Explorer Company that took us up the Amazon by boat. We stopped at villages along the way, met some natives and explored the jungle. We returned to Iquitos and spent three or four days sightseeing. We wanted to see the majestic Casa De Fierro. It was designed by the famous Eiffle in Paris and shipped piece by piece to Iquitos. We wanted to see remnants of the rubber boom days like the elegant mansions and the Portuguese art. Then we took a return flight back to Lima on January 12th and spent another couple of days hanging out at the beach."

John paused for a moment and stared at the floor deep in thought.

'That was a long time ago. How did I end up here?'

The attorney was aware of the fact that his client was rambling but for some reason he didn't mind. If his client could provide a detailed account of where he had been and what he had done, it would be easier for both of them. Easier because all air, bus, and rail companies required by law to have a record of all passengers' names and their designated seats. When buying a ticket, the purchaser, including the locals must produce an I.D. Foreigners must use their passport for I.D. Every passenger must show their I.D. once again upon boarding whatever means of transportation they are using. This practice was implemented due to the many fatal accidents that occur in the precarious Andes.

CARLOS:

"Then where did you go?"

JOHN:

"We decided to head for the Central Highlands."

CARLOS:

"Did you go by air, train or bus?"

JOHN:

"Originally we were going to take a bus south along the Pan American Highway down the coast and follow the Gringo Trail. We would arrive in Puno on Lake Titicaca, spend a few days on the islands on the lake, then we would head for Cusco. We would tour the Sacred Valley then take the four-day expedition climbing the Inca Trail to Machu Pichu. Then we would fly back to Lima. But at the last minute we decided to do the opposite. We figured we had lots of time, so why not veer off the beaten path? Very few tourists take the time to experience the real Peruvian culture in the heart of the Andes. So the four of us split the cost and hired a taxi."

CARLOS: "What do you mean by the four of us? Who was with you?"

JOHN:

"Phil and I stayed at the Home Peru Hostel and we met an American couple who were staying at another hostel in Mira Flores. They were fed up with the transportation system and were looking for someone to share a taxi with to go to Tarma. So we joined them."

John's new lawyer was very thorough. He preferred to trace John's steps in the hope of being able to produce a witness to vouch for his whereabouts. He continued prodding John's mind.

CARLOS: "Can you give me the names of this couple?"

John realized that he knew them on a first name basis only. He had met many different backpackers on his trips but he kept in touch with only a few. Unfortunately he didn't bother to get their full names.

JOHN:

"Peter was the guy. Marion was the girl's name. They didn't say what their last names were but I think that they were staying within a few blocks from where we were staying. We bumped into them several times on the street and at the local supermarket. If you need their names you could check it out."

CARLOS:

"Do you know the name of the taxi driver or the company that he worked for? They all have their I.D. in full sight somewhere in the front of the cab."

John pursed his lips, closed his eyes and tried to recall that morning.

JOHN:

"I remember seeing his I.D. dangling on a string from the rearview mirror but I wasn't really paying attention because the scenery was so awesome and I was sitting in the back seat."

CARLOS:

"How long did you stay in Tarma and where did you stay?"

JOHN:

"Peter and Marion knew about a bed and breakfast farmhouse just outside of the town, so we spent three nights there with them. It was very informal. We were the only guests. I don't even know if it was a real bed and breakfast because they didn't ask to see our passports and two of the family's children were sleeping on the couch every morning when I went to the kitchen. I think that we took their room. We left on the third morning."

John was getting impatient as he was trying to remember every-thing.

"How long is this going to take? I have a diary that can account for each day I've been here. Can you get my diary and personal be-longings? I can't tell you exactly where they are. The cops took our passports. I don't even have a passport."

CARLOS:

"I'll look into it as soon as possible. I promise. Right now I'm interested in the events leading up to your arrest. I need to know whether or not you took any public transport from Tarma to where you ended up near Santa Inès. And I need to know where you stayed in between."

JOHN:

" Phil and I had had enough of noisy hostels and shared rooms. We were itchy to do some serious trekking. We hitched rides most of the way in the back of pick-ups with the locals and their produce. We'd be dropped off at markets and spend the daytime hours tour-ing the town. In the evening we headed for the outskirts and pitched our tent where we could have some peace and quiet and our own space. A couple of times we were invited to stay at a worker's home. They looked hardworking and impoverished, so we accepted the of-fers from those we thought we could trust, figuring that it would help them out. We'd give them a few soled for the stay. Believe me, they appreciated it and we had no problems doing this.

We had no trouble at all until we were in Huancavelica looking for a ride to Ayacucho. We found out that there were no connect-ing buses and there was no direct route. When we referred to our Peru travel guide, it referred to this stretch as 'The Missing Link'. I guess we should have checked it out ahead of time, so much for foresight. Anyhow, a man overheard Phil's inquiries in front of the Tourist Information Office and offered to take us for sixty soles. The offer was too good to resist but we didn't know what we were getting ourselves into.

We ended up hopping into the back of an old pickup, preferring it to the front seat because of the 360 degrees panoramic view. After about an hour, it began to rain. It poured. We had our raincoats but there was nowhere to sit without getting wet. We banged on the back window and tried to get the driver's attention but he ignored us. We were cold and shivering. He wasn't going very fast and we talked about jumping out, but we had all our gear and decided not to risk it. At one point we even thought he was trying to kidnap us. Then suddenly he stopped the truck in the middle of nowhere and told us to get out. We thought that he finally realized we were getting soaked and that he would let us get into the front seat with him. But as soon as we climbed out, he took off and left us stranded. It was weird. We were totally bewildered. He didn't even collect his 60 soles.

It was cold and windy so the first thing we did was look for shelter. We walked toward the hills and found the ideal location to pitch our tent. We changed into dry clothes and made ourselves a cup of hot tea and joked around about how we were such great survivors."

John took a deep breath and sighed. Deep sorrow engulfed him. He stared blankly at the tabletop in front of him.

'That was the last place on earth where Phil took his last breath. We had so much fun together. Why did this have to happen?'

CARLOS:

" What about the driver, can you describe him?"

JOHN:

" He was wearing an colorful old wool sweater with holes in it. His skin was dark and unshaven. He was maybe fifty years old."

CARLOS:

"Can you describe the truck? Did you get the license plate number?"

JOHN:

"It was just an old junker, a battered up white and green mixed color, so old that I didn't recognize the make or model. I remember when I saw him drive away. It didn't have any plates on the back."

CARLOS:

"Was anyone around? I mean could anyone have seen you, any houses nearby that you can recall?"

JOHN:

"I doubt very much if anyone saw us. We passed the odd person walking down the road and there were a couple of children walking in the distant hills tending the llama and alpaca herds. I remember seeing an old thatched roof lean-to up the road but it looked deserted. The countryside was so scantily populated that we met only three vehicles all the way there."

CARLOS:

" How long did you stay there?"

JOHN:

"We spent one day and two nights there. The rain had stopped and we slept well the second night. The next morning was cloudy but beautiful. I had some catching up to do in my diary. It was Phil's turn to light up the burner and make the coffee. The air was fresh and the view was absolutely spectacular. I laughed when Phil......"

John suddenly stopped. At that moment he was unable to continue. His attorney could see how choked up his client was becoming at the mention of his deceased friend. He gave him some time to compose himself.

"I know how difficult this must be for you and I'm terribly sorry that I must put you through all this. You're doing very well so far. Do you want to take a 5 minute break and stretch your legs?"

Carlos stood up and John followed suit. A few minutes later they were ready to continue.

CARLOS:

"So it was morning and you were camping somewhere near Santa Inès. How long had you been there before you saw the plane crash?"

JOHN:

"It was on the second morning. Phil saw it first. Or I should say, he heard it first. It approached over the crest from the southwest. It was west of us when it crashed. I saw with my own eyes. The two guys got out of the plane. The same ones that ran past us."

John was getting ahead of himself. Carlos held up his hand as if to stop John.

CARLOS:

"Hang on a minute. What do you mean by 'the same ones that ran past us?'

JOHN:

"Well, we were running towards the plane and the two men were running towards us and away from the wreckage. I thought that they had spotted us and needed help but they avoided us and ran straight past us. It was weird at the time. We thought that someone else must be hurt so we kept running to the plane crash.

CARLOS:

"How far away were they from you? Would you recognize these two men if you saw them again?"

JOHN:

"I certainly would. The bigger one anyway. I'm not exactly sure about how far away we were. It happened so fast. It was completely a surprise meeting. I stopped in my tracks. The big guy was just as startled to see me. I didn't get a good look at the little guy but he was about 5' tall, lean, dark hair, in his thirties."

CARLOS:

"Then what happened?"

JOHN:

"We reached the plane. I climbed in to see if anyone was hurt, but there was nobody inside. After I looked around and saw what I saw, I realized that I didn't want to be there. Phil and I debated a little about what we should do, but then we heard voices. I guess we just panicked and ran. I know it was a stupid thing to do."

CARLOS:

"I can certainly understand that it would arouse suspicion."

Hearing this remark prompted John to flare up in anger. He thought that his new attorney was siding with the cops.

"You don't believe me? Do you think I'm making all this up just for the fun of it?

The vein on his forehead visibly protruded.

"If you don't believe me I'll find another lawyer who does. Damn it!"

Carlos was on the defense.

"Look John," he said, "I'm merely attempting to learn all the facts leading up to your arrest. I'm not accusing you of anything. Please. It's my job to probe. Trust me, I believe you."

John recognized the sincerity in his voice.

"Sorry. Forgive me if I seem a little ticked off. I have nothing to hide. If anyone has anything to hide, it's those two cops who chased us."

CARLOS:

"So they chased you and then what happened?"

JOHN:

"We heard a gunshot and the chase was over."

John continued to explain in detail how they were searched, their pouches taken, how Phil was killed, how he met detective Diez and was transported to prison in Lima. When John was finished, his attorney referred to his notes. He had a few more questions.

"Were you explained your rights when they arrested you?"

John thought for a minute before he answered.

"I don't know. My Spanish is very limited. I only know a few of the phrases for tourists. I was rarely spoken to. When they did speak, it was only brief sentences and commands. Phil was the one who was more learned in Spanish."

CARLOS:

"Is it possible in any way that the two officers that apprehended you could have seen the same two persons you saw running away from the plane?"

JOHN:

"I'm not sure. It was a close call but I don't think so. They were out of sight pretty fast. The only way they could have seen them is from the road I guess. That is, if the timing and direction of approach was right."

CARLOS:

"From the time you left Lima for the Central Highlands until the time you were arrested, did you use your bank card or any credit card, use the internet, or make any phone calls?"

JOHN:

"I withdrew six hundred soles from the A.T.M. in Lima before we left so that I'd have enough cash until we reached Cusco. That is the last time I can account for using my bankcard. As for correspondence via the Internet and phone calls, I made my last contact with my family the morning we left Lima and told them I would let them know when I arrived in Cusco. Neither Phil nor I used the Internet after we left."

CARLOS:

"You say that Officer Ramirez took your money belt. What did it contain?"

John gave him a list of items.

"My passport, my credit card, my bankcard, some soles, my driver's license, my pilot's license and a copy of Phil's passport. We carried a copy of each other's passport as a precaution against loss or theft."

CARLOS:

"Your pilot's license, you 're a pilot?"

The attorney was surprised to hear this. It was unexpected. But on the other hand, lots of young men acquire a pilot's license. Unfortunately in this case, it was just a coincidence but certainly not one in John's favor.

"Yes. I've had it for two years now. My grandfather was a pilot in the Second World War. He flew a Lancaster bomber and I'm very proud of him. Anyhow, I took flying lessons at a small airport back home just outside of Ottawa, Ontario.

I took my pilot's license on this trip because last year while I was in Arizona, I met a pilot from Carefree Turf Soaring School, just north of Phoenix. He took me up in his private plane but he wouldn't allow me to take the controls. I missed the opportunity to fly over the Grand Canyon because I forgot my license back home."

John was conscious about how this would affect his position, but he persisted in claiming his innocence.

"And if you think that having a pilot's license will jeopardize my position, once again I swear I had nothing to do with that plane crash."

CARLOS:

"Don't worry, the evidence will lead to the truth. I just have a couple more questions. Did Officer Paredes or Officer Ramirez try to verify the fact that you and your friend were camping in the vicinity?"

JOHN:

"Phil kept pointing to where our tent was pitched, and he told them about it, but I guess they didn't believe him or didn't want to believe him. They weren't even interested in checking it out."

CARLOS:

"Is there anything you'd like to add?"

JOHN:

"I don't think so. I've been going over and over it in my head and that's as accurate as I can remember."

CARLOS:

"If there's anything else you can recollect, any names of people you've met, or a place you've been, for example the name of a café or bar, it would help. In the meantime, the first thing I'm going to do is find some evidence of where you were staying and find your belongings. Leave everything to me."

The attorney placed his notes into his briefcase and snapped it closed.

"Hopefully I will have some good news for you soon. I'll keep you updated on our progress."

He reached out to shake John's hand again before leaving.

"Thank you Mr. Aguillar. I really appreciate what you are doing for me. I have a trust fund that will cover your fees. It was set up for my education but I can assure you that I am good for the money."

"I'm sure you are. I'll need a retainer fee but we'll discuss that at our next meeting. For now I need to find out what evidence has been collected against you and to determine whether or not it's enough to hold you here."

"Do you know if Mr. Forrester was able to contact my parent's yet?"

"Yes. When he called me, he said that he was just off the phone with your father. He said they would be getting in touch with me. You should be hearing from them soon."

The attorney pressed the orange button on the intercom. He was about to have his questions answered sooner than expected. Detective Diez had arrived at the prison while John was being interviewed. The detective was anxious to obtain a statement from the suspect. When the guard opened the door for Carlos Aguillar, Walter Diéz was with him. John immediately recognized Diéz, as well as the officer who was in close pursuit, the one with the menacing smile who had questioned him yesterday.

"I'm Detective Walter Diéz," he said as he entered the room, "and this is Detective Adrian Blanco."

At first glance, Detective Diéz did not recognize John's attorney because he was focusing on John. Then he smiled when he recalled the last time he had seen Carlos Aguillar.

Two years ago, his brother-in-law, who was a teacher, was arrested for assaulting one of his students. Mr. Aguilar was his lawyer. As it turned out, Mr. Aguillar found out that the injury was from a bad fall and the alleged assault had never taken place. There was resentment on the student's part because the teacher had caught him cheating on his finals and reprimanded him. The student wanted to get even, by making false accusations. He was confident enough to think that he could get away with it and almost did. But the attorney had worked hard on his client's behalf and the family appreciated it.

"I see you have a good attorney. You're going to need one," continued Diéz.

Carlos Aguillar silently acknowledged the compliment.

"Hello detective. It's been a long time."

"Yes it has. It's unfortunate that we are not meeting under more pleasant circumstances. Is your client prepared to give his statement?"

The atmosphere was tense. John was just finished explaining everything to his lawyer and was exhausted. He was in an emotional turmoil. At the same time he wanted to get it over with. With a blank expression on his face he turned to his attorney for council. The attorney spoke taking turns looking back and forth at each of the detectives.

"First of all I'd like to point out to you that according to my client, the officers who arrested him did not recite the Miranda to notify him of his rights. And secondly, what evidence do have against my client to keep him here?"

Everyone sat at the table, Carlos beside John, the two interrogators across from them. It was going to be a long harrowing session John thought as he slumped in his chair. *'Dear God please give me the strength'*

The detective responded.

"First, according to the police report, Officer Paredés *did* inform your client of his rights when he was arrested. And second, we've got plenty of evidence against your client."

Detective Diéz began relaying the evidence his team had gathered.

"Your client's fingerprints were found in the plane. We also matched the D.N.A. from the blood found in the plane to your client. Gunshot residue was found on his partner's hand. He had fired the gun found at the scene. He was caught fleeing the scene,"

" It's quite obvious that he is as guilty as sin," interjected Blanco.

John sadly bowed his head and spoke with disappointment in his voice.

"You know I had nothing to do with those guys, the drug smugglers. Like I told you before, we were camping near where the plane crashed. You promised that you would check it out."

The detective was concentrating on John as he spoke. Then he turned and concentrated on the lawyer when he responded to John's statement. He wanted him to know that he had done his job well.

"I sent my guys out on a wild goose chase looking for your so-called camp. There was nothing that even resembled a camp, not even remnants of a campfire."

"We used a stove," retorted John.

Detective Blanco spoke up as he narrowed his eyes and pointed his finger directly at John in an accusing manner.

"You know what I'm thinking! I'm thinking that you had plenty of time to concoct a story with the hopes that we would be gullible enough to believe you. Well, we're not that gullible, so why don't you just give up and tell us the truth?"

Carlos Aguillar sat there quietly. Years of experience had taught him not to display any delight, shock, or any other emotion to his adversaries. But he was dismayed at the fact that no trace of the camp was found. That was a mystery. He also knew that they would do a background check on John and probably find out that he was a qualified pilot. That wasn't in his favor either, along with the fact that he fled the scene. He could understand why the detective would think that he had the right suspect.

Carlos Aguilar's philosophy was that if his client was innocence, he had nothing to worry about. That was because he had never let a client go to prison for a crime he didn't commit. According to his client's explanation, there was obviously more evidence to be collected. The evidence they already had, the fingerprints, the D.N.A., the gun shot residue, logically matched his client's version of what happened. It was just going to take time to collect incriminating evidence against the arresting officers. In the meantime, John's credibility was at stake and so was his future. John had nothing to hide including the fact that he had a pilot license.

The detective reached for the tape recorder and impatiently tapped it on the table. Carlos Aguillar placed his elbows on the table, leaned forward, and steepled his fingers. He spoke on his client's behalf.

"My client is prepared to tell you exactly what happened and after you've heard all the details, I guarantee you'll be prepared to look elsewhere if you're sincerely interested in finding the true culprits. We are willing to co-operate one hundred percent and help you nail the persons who are responsible for the wrongful shooting of an innocent young tourist and the unlawful imprisonment of his friend. My client is also in a position whereby he can assist you in identifying at least one of the narcotraficantes who escaped from the plane."

The aggressive interrogator, Detective Blanco, was pleased to hear John's admission, that he was willing to identify a drug smuggler. He was pumped up and eager to squeeze out a confession from the prisoner. Now he interrupted, deliberately harassing John. He had a stake in the case and it was expedient that he do this. His familiar voice made John cringe.

"So your client *did* lie to us. Now we're getting somewhere. You *are* guilty. I knew it! Now tell us. Who do you work for? If you can identify him, tell us his name. Who is he?"

He glared at the defense attorney with the anticipation that John would disclose the information he needed. He was so wrong. Carlos Aguillar was prepared for a certain amount of hostility from the accusers but he wasn't prepared for this. He was disappointed with the detective and he was in no mood to play games. He bit his lip and gritted his teeth. He was getting nowhere with this narrow-minded man. He stood up, gazed at the two sitting opposite him and abruptly announced,

"This interview is over."

He looked at his client and calmly instructed him.

"Don't say another word until I tell you to do so. Do you understand?"

John was miffed but what could he say?

"I understand," he simply replied.

The attorney and the two detectives left the room together.

"I want copies of all the evidence you have against my client and everything you have collected from the crime scene, regardless of whether or not you think it incriminates my client. And I trust you will include everything. It is very unfortunate that you did not give my client an opportunity to explain himself in his own defense. How do expect to conduct an investigation when you won't allow a key witness to assist you? You will eventually learn that sometime in the future you are going to need him."

"That's absurd!" replied Blanco smugly.

Diéz gave Blanco a sideward look of contempt and then turned to the lawyer.

"I'll have everything you asked for faxed to your office as soon as possible."

Diéz respected the defense attorney and wanted to say something more.

"Again, I'm sorry that we had to meet under such unpleasant circumstances."

After the attorney went his separate way, Diéz pulled Blanco aside and gave him a look of annoyance.

"You asshole!" he said then he walked away before Blanco had a chance to respond.

Detective Diéz turned to his office and contemplated the contents of the interview. He was baffled at the abrupt ending of the interrogation. He suspected that it was the aggressive tactics of detective Blanco that halted the co-operation of the accused. He didn't like Blanco, but he was the only person available who was fluent in English. He was thinking that he should have used a little more finesse. The accused was prepared to give a statement and on the verge of divulging information that they needed, until Blanco opened his big mouth.

Who was John Emerson protecting? What did his attorney mean by proclaiming his innocence? But then, that was his job. And something about the wrongful shooting of his accomplice? He was confounded with all this and then he recalled that the suspect had said something to him from behind bars. He tried to remember exactly what it was. He should have been more attentive to what he was saying at the time and followed up on it. He regretted the fact that he had lost his opportunity to hear what John had to say.

Blanco was right on one point. The prisoner *did* have time to concoct a believable scenario to present in his defense. Diéz's duty was to analyze the evidence and draw a logical conclusion. The interview was puzzling and that frustrated him.

Remembering that he promised to send the requested material over to Mr. Aguillar's office, Detective Diéz gathered what he had in his file. The lab hadn't yet sent the data that was being printed out for him. He would send the attorney everything he had, including the information on José Peres. The attorney would see that the lab had found one set of unidentified prints and D.N.A. of an unknown source.

'Carlos Aguillar is going to have a tough time trying to prove his client's innocence. But he seems convinced. I can't understand it, with all the incriminating evidence we have against him? His client isn't helping himself by withholding the information we need. How can I get him to co-operate?'

CHAPTER 15

As he walked to his car the defense attorney knew that he had made the right decision. He didn't have enough evidence to support his client's story, at least not yet. He needed time. What was he thinking? Who would believe a foreigner as opposed to two experienced law enforcers? His gut feeling told him that his client was being framed. There were too many vivid details in John's account that made his version all the more credible. He suspected that the prosecution was not disclosing everything and withheld certain facts either deliberately or unknowingly, in order to point a finger at the only suspect they had, which was his client.

He sat behind the steering wheel contemplating his next move. He often used the services of private investigator Victor Caballero. Victor had all the attributes of a good sleuth. He was vigilant, witty and had good instincts. Although he was a bit sloppy in his appearance at times and his office and his apartment were usually in a mess, his mind was sharp. But what else would you expect from a bachelor? Everyone liked him. He had charisma and charm. Carlos Aguillar scanned through his personal telephone directory for his number and pulled out his cell phone. There was an answer on the fifth ring.

"Victor Caballero here," boomed a confident voice at the other end of the line.

"Hello Victor, Carlos Aguillar here. How have you been? Have you met the love of your life yet?" he joked.

The last time he had seen Victor, his romantic life was in turmoil when his favorite girlfriend had stood him up.

"Very funny! You know me. I just can't seem to settle down. What's up?"

"Are you busy? I have some work for you."

"I'm just wrapping up a case now. My schedule is pretty much up to date. Yes I can handle some work. What is it?"

"Are you free for lunch? Can you meet me at Mira Flores Café at around noon?"

They had met there on numerous occasions in the past during previous investigative work.

"Sure. It's your turn to buy lunch by the way," he chuckled, "I'm looking forward to seeing you again. It's been a while."

"I'll see you then."

Carlos entered the small café where diners were sitting at the counter. He looked around and spotted Victor sitting at a table in the corner where they usually sat. He strolled over to Victor who stood up and they patted each other on the back, as was the custom.

"Hello Victor! It's good to see you too."

The familiar waitress approached the table with menus and a smile.

"Hi Theresa! What's the special of the day?"

"Cream of asparagus soup, garden salad, and chicken with rice."

"That sounds good to me."

"Sounds good to me too. We'll take two of them."

"Two daily specials coming right up," replied the waitress.

Carlos discussed the case with Victor while waiting for their meal.

"What I have in mind, is for you to go to the Santa Inés area and interview some of the locals, see if any of them have seen a couple of backpackers recently. We need to get on this right away seeing that it's a drug- related matter and involves foreigners. The press will have a field day with this one if we don't put a lid on it right away."

Just then, Victor glanced up at the muted T.V. suspended from the ceiling in the opposite corner of the room. He motioned to the waitress as she set their plates down.

"Could you turn that up please Theresa?"

The screen revealed a female newscaster standing outside an area taped off with yellow crime scene tape, the crashed Cessna in the background.

"One suspect was shot and killed while trying to escape, the other is in police custody. Details are sketchy at this time but we will keep you informed as we learn more. This is Julia Escalante reporting for Channel 7 News, Lima."

The two diners looked at one another and wondered how long it would take before more information would be available to the press. The media had a way of presenting scenarios based on what little they know, which wasn't always favorable to the defense. In some cases, the public presumed that the person in custody was guilty, depending on how the media presented it.

"I also want you to thoroughly search the area. Concentrate mostly east of the plane crash site. See if you can find that tent I was telling you about. Detective Diez sent a couple of his rookies to comb the area for it but obviously they were searching in the wrong place. It will be hidden from the road behind a hill. I will give you a map indicating where it should be. If you find it, don't leave it unattended. Call me right away."

"If it's there I'll find it. Anything else?" asked Victor."

"Well, this is a long shot but there's a stray bullet out there somewhere. I realize it's like looking for a needle in a haystack but you may stumble across it if you're lucky. I don't believe that the prosecution would have found it."

"I'll keep that in mind. What about the two arresting officers? Do you want me to talk to them? Maybe I can snoop around at the same time. You never know what I might find."

"Not just yet. I want to read the police report and go over the evidence first. I should have it later on this afternoon, tomorrow morning at the latest. When it comes to those two bastards, I want to proceed with caution. I want to nail them good. But wait and see what you come up with. I have a feeling that you will find what we are looking for, and then we can act."

Carlos checked his watch. He smiled as Victor stared at the bill left on the table by the waitress.

"You needn't remind me again. It's my turn," laughed Carlos as he picked it up.

They exited onto Avenue Arequipa that was lined with beautiful mansions displaying colonial Spanish architecture. They walked down the pedestrian walkway in the center of the avenue and turned a corner. When they reached their cars that were parked on a side street away from the hubbub of major traffic, they bid farewell to one another. Carlos had to get back to the office and Victor was on a mission.

Victor planned to leave as soon as possible. He would need to pack warm clothing for the highlands. He wanted to get there before anyone had the chance to remove the evidence that would prove the John Emerson's innocence. He had to hurry. Once the site was found abandoned, it could easily be stripped and gone. That could be today, tomorrow, or in a month of Sundays.

That night Carlos Aguillar had trouble sleeping. Earlier, he sat in his study thinking about his new client. He tried to piece together what really happened that day. He believed the incredible sordid story John had told him, but he had so many questions that needed answering. Now, as he lay in bed blinking, he was asking the same questions. Did the cops who arrested John actually believe that he was the pilot? They probably did. But if Phil MacAllister told them otherwise, that they were tourists and had been camping in the area, why didn't they investigate? Why would they ignore him? According to John, he was certain that they understood what his friend was saying. Even if they didn't believe him, wouldn't they want to check it out just in case? Then why did they stage a murder making it look like something else? What would be their motive? Was it a sick power trip? Did they do it for attention, wanting to be recognized for their bravery in the face of danger? Did they think they would achieve publicity, crediting them for their part in capturing and killing the drug smugglers?

It was certainly an elaborate scheme. But it had to be planned on the spur of the moment. It didn't make any sense. They didn't know the plane was going to crash and that the two tourists would be there. He was too tired to think anymore. Maybe tomorrow when his mind was fresh, he would be able to think clearly and look at things from a different prospective. The fax that he was expecting from Detective Diez hadn't been sent that afternoon. He would receive it in the morning. He was sorry that he hadn't at least asked for a copy of the police report before he left the precinct. He was anxious to see how the officers had construed it. Finally he closed his eyes and fell asleep.

CHAPTER 16

A few days later when Carlos Aguillar arrived at his office, Stella Bennett was waiting for him. She didn't have an appointment and was hoping to see the attorney before his first client arrived. It was imperative for her to meet with him and the sooner the better. She would wait all day if she had to. When she first got there, the door was locked but she could hear someone moving around inside and so she knocked.

The secretary was always there an hour before her boss. It gave her an opportunity to work without any interruptions. Usually she would leave ahead of him at the end of each day. She opened the door when she heard the knock, with the intent of turning away whoever it was, that the office would be open in forty-five minutes. She could return then. But Stella was persistent and explained the purpose of her visit. She would gladly wait inside.

When the attorney entered, he was surprised to see a female sitting in his waiting room with her legs crossed reading a magazine. He didn't think anyone had an appointment this early. Once in a while on a busy day, there would be an early booking. Did he forget to check his appointment book? He didn't think so. But he was glad that he had decided to come in early this morning. Actually, it was because he promised his wife that he would be home early today because they were having guests for dinner this evening. Since he was here, he would have time to see the unexpected client, whoever she was?

As soon as he entered the room, the lady stood up. She was a few inches over five feet, hazel eyes and in her early thirties. Her long auburn hair was tied at the nape of her neck with a multi-colored silk scarf. The only makeup she wore was a tad of peach lipstick that complimented her fair complexion. She wore a plain powder blue skirt and a cream colored blouse. She introduced herself extending her hand. She politely spoke Spanish wanting to get some practice.

"Mr. Aguillar, my name is Stella Bennett. I'm a private defense investigator from Toronto Canada. Keith Emerson hired me on behalf of their son John."

She deliberately forgot to mention that she was Keith Emerson's niece. She didn't want him to know just yet that she had a personal stake in the case. She would tell him later how she was related to his client. Right now, she was here in a professional capacity.

" I hope you don't mind the intrusion," she said with confidence.

"No. Not at all," replied Carlos shaking her hand firmly.

Stella then switched to English.

"My firm has sent this letter of introduction along with copies of my credentials." She handed him the envelope. The attorney was somewhat puzzled.

"You didn't waste any time getting here. This is highly unusual. Please come into my office."

She followed him into a spacious modern office tastefully decorated with top of the line furniture and modern art paintings. She sensed an aura of a very successful professional. The attorney assessed her briefly at a glance. He noticed that she was plain but not unattractive.

"I would like to compliment you on your fluency in Spanish," he said as they both took a seat.

"I'm a little out of practice, but thank you. I worked a case six months ago in Mexico and quickly picked up the language. Then I continued with Spanish lessons at the university. It is very similar to French which is my mother tongue."

Carlos wanted to mention the fact that he had lived in Montreal and was partially of French Canadian decent, but he didn't have the time for a social visit. Perhaps, he would have the opportunity at some later date.

"I've already hired a detective but you are welcome to join us. We need all the help we can get."

"I believe that's what the Emerson's had in mind. They arrived last evening. They were anxious to meet with you but John is their first priority. I volunteered to come here while they visit their son. Once again I hope you don't mind."

Carlos opened the envelope and briefly took note of the contents. When he was satisfied he set it on his desk and looked up at her.

"Certainly not! I welcome your assistance. I'll give you a quick update on where we are."

He walked to his filing cabinet and withdrew John's file. He opened it and reviewed the evidence with her; the lab results, photos of the crime scene, and the police report. It was an unsettling experience for John's cousin. It was one thing working for somebody else, but it was the first time working on behalf of a close family member.

The attorney informed Stella that he had already hired a private investigator to work on John's case. He explained to her that he had combed the area looking for evidence and came up empty handed. When Stella heard this, she was skeptical and had to speak her mind.

"How can that be? Are you certain he searched in the right area? Surely there must be some mistake! Either John's directions were incorrect, he was under a lot of stress and could easily have been disoriented, or the investigator you hired made a mistake."

She inwardly cringed having to say this because it appeared that she was accusing the private investigator of possible incompetence. But what other explanation was there? She observed the miffed look the attorney gave her but wasn't going to apologize for her bluntness. She had every right to ask questions.

At first the attorney experienced a moment of slight annoyance because he knew that there was no mistake, but it was still a mystery.

Then he softened his mood because he realized that he might have asked the same questions if he were in her shoes.

"I understand and appreciate your concern. We were as perplexed as you are so we double-checked with John and he was adamant that he had been accurate in marking the spot. But just in case, we double- checked for ourselves with an air search."

He wanted to reassure her.

"Please believe me, we were thorough. My investigator also looked for witnesses who may have seen some tourists but unfortunately that too was unsuccessful."

"So the investigation is at a standstill now? What about pursuing evidence against the arresting officers?"

Carlos Aguillar was following her line of questioning. He said that he was contemplating his next move. It would be a direct confrontation with the arresting officers. But it was only in the planning stages. He needed more evidence and they had to be very discreet in their effort to obtain it under the circumstances.

Keith's niece took charge of her own assignment. She knew how she wanted to conduct her investigation .She unzipped her large beige handbag and found a map of Peru. She stood, then opened it up pressing the creases over the desk with her hand. She bent over and focused on the Central Highlands. She traced the route with her index finger.

"I'm going to book a flight to Ayacucho and backtrack on highway 24 up to Santa Inés. I'm going to search the area first for evidence and interview the locals. Then, I want to interview the arresting officers under the pretence that I'm a freelance reporter doing a documentary on the illegal drug trade and how it affects the lives of average Peruvian. Perhaps they would be willing to discuss the recent plane crash in their area. Maybe I can persuade them to talk about their latest arrest and lead them to believe that I will expose them as national heroes. Somewhere in the conversation they may slip up. All we need is one little contradiction to what is in their report. What do you think?"

The attorney didn't know what to say or think. Her plan about interviewing the cops seemed somewhat far-fetched but not illegal. He didn't want to offend her by telling her that it was out of the question, in case it somehow backfired. But maybe her plan wasn't such a bad idea. He was conscientious about Victor. He was meticulous when it came to work ethics and he didn't want to give his outright approval of her plan without consulting with him first. He thought of a way out for himself.

"Victor Caballero is the name of the private investigator that I hired for this case. I'll give you his number."

He tore a small page from his notepad, and wrote down the number then handed it to her.

"I'll let him know ahead of time that you'll be in touch with him and the two of you can work together on this. I'll try and get a hold of him after you leave. I'm telling you this because as I said before, he has already questioned the locals and searched for evidence without any success. I don't want any conflict of interest between the two of you. I'm sure you can understand my position. We were holding back on questioning the two arresting officers because we didn't want to alert them of our suspicions until we have something concrete. We were hoping to find some incriminating evidence against them. I like your idea if you can pull it off. Give Victor a call and meet up with him. See what he has to say. I'm sure you can come to a compromise. But if you do interview the police, be very careful" he warned. "I don't want to arouse suspicions. You will be dealing with dangerously conniving criminals. I think it will be difficult to pull the wool over their eyes if you know what I mean."

Stella Bennett had no objections to what John's attorney was saying. She understood completely. In fact she was eager to get started. She didn't want to offend anyone by duplicating what Mr. Caballero had already done but at the same time she needed to be thorough and do things her own way.

" I'll give him a call and, like you say, we can work together on this."

The defense attorney smiled. He liked Stella Bennett. She had a mind of her own. She was creative, perceptive, and very professional. She came prepared with a map of Peru in her handbag. That was impressive. But Victor Caballero also had a mind of his own. He wondered how they would get along.

The attorney was getting pressed for time. He wanted to talk to Victor before his first appointment of the day, if he could get a hold of him. Stella noticed that the gentleman before her was glancing at his watch. It was a subtle hint. She reached for the map, folded it, and placed it back into her purse.

"Thank you for meeting with me. I can see that John is in good hands."

She extended her hand and Carlos grasped it.

"My pleasure," he said, then saw her to the door and opened it for her. He watched her exit the reception area, then returned to his desk and placed a call to Victor Caballero. There was no answer. He would try again later.

Before putting John's folder away, the attorney reviewed Victor's notes. The private investigator had conducted an intense investigation tracing John's and Phil's footsteps trying to locate someone who remembered the two backpackers. He was unable to find the so-called bed and breakfast near Tarma because no one that he had spoken with had heard of it. He interviewed many of the locals around the town markets from Tarma to Huancavelica but all tourists looked alike and no one could positively identify John or his friend Phil. He hoped that someone from the tourist office in Huancavelica would remember Phil but unfortunately, he hadn't entered the building. He made his inquiries outside, in front of the office where they were offered a lift. What more could Victor do?

If Stella Bennett could do any better than that, then let her try, all the more power to her. He placed the file back into the cabinet and was ready for his first client of the day.

CHAPTER 17

It seemed like an eternity had passed when the guard announced to John that he had visitors. He could feel the adrenaline rush as his anxiety mounted. He would never be prepared enough to face the crisis of encountering his parents under these circumstances no matter how hard he tried. His cell door opened and he was led down the hall, having to feel humiliated by the shouts and whistles of the other prisoners as he passed by their cells. He closed his eyes briefly and walked blindly.

'Oh my God, I can't stand this! Please get me out of here!'

Laura and Keith Emerson stood in the visitors' quarters anxiously awaiting the arrival of their son. When John was escorted into the room, they were shocked by his appearance, for he no longer stood tall and proud. His shoulders were slouched forward. His smile was replaced by a gaunt expression. Tiny creases were visible across his forehead. They had not been there before. He was thinner and he looked so forlorn.

"Oh John!" whispered his mother as she rushed to hug him. Her eyes were glassy but she suppressed the urge to weep. She vowed to herself that she would be strong for her son's sake. John hugged his mother, unable to speak.

"It's good to see you son," said Keith as he embraced John and patted him with affection on the back. His father was angry and be-wildered, angry at the judicial system, and bewildered as to what had happened? He and Laura had agreed prior to leaving for the jail, not to ask any questions about how John ended up here in prison. Paul Forrester from the Canadian Embassy had provided some details over the phone but was unable to answer any of their questions. They would get a full and accurate account from Stella once she returned from the attorney's office.

John held onto his father, not wanting to let go. He radiated a warmth and a love that seemed never ending. When he finally did let go of his father's embrace, he returned his attention to his mother.

"I'm so sorry Mom! Thanks for coming."

The lump in his throat forced him to swallow as he attempted to hide his emotions.

"I wish I could be here instead of you," choked his mother.

She shook her head from side to side holding him at arm's length as they studied one another. John thought his mother looked ragged and he felt responsible. He would never be able to make it up to her. Laura didn't intend for her comment to spark her son into giving an explanation for being here. He opened his mouth, hesitated, then spoke in almost a whisper.

"I don't know what to say. I didn't do anything wrong. We were in the wrong place at the wrong time. Poor Phil! He didn't stand a chance."

He paused for a moment thinking about his friend's family.

"How are Mr. and Mrs. MacAllister doing?"

John so desperately longed to hug them and console them for their loss. They were like second parents to him. Yet at the same time, he feared his next meeting with them because he had survived and they might blame him for what happened to Phil.

The Emersons and the MacAllisters were good friends and neighbors for many years. As soon as Keith and Laura were informed of Phil's death, they were there for the Emersons. Keith inhaled with deep sorrow thinking that Phil's life was cut off too soon from a future. What would he have done if it had been John's life that was taken? It was a painful question and he felt a pang of guilt because he was relieved that it wasn't John's.

"They are totally devastated and they will be demanding a lot of answers. There's much to be accounted for. Eventually, like us, they plan to get to the bottom of what happened to their son. For the time being they are staying at the hotel with us. They have traveled with us in order to claim Phil's body. They will be leaving as soon as it is released for burial."

At that thought, John's father reached into his pocket and took out a photograph. It was four inches by four inches.

"By the way," he said, " when they were going through his personal belongings, they found this and asked me to give it to you. It was in the inside pocket of his jacket."

He handed it over to his son. The colored photograph was of John and Phil standing in their skates and hockey uniforms, holding their hockey sticks on the ice to form a 'V' for victory. They were wearing grins from ear to ear.

John took the photo into his hands and lowered his eyes allowing them to linger there. He vividly remembered that day and he couldn't help but crack a brief smile. They belonged to a hockey league and their team had won the cup last year. His parents watched in silence. The room was so quiet, you could hear a pin drop. John could no longer contain himself and his shoulders began to shake.

"I can't believe Phil is dead!" he sobbed.

His father instinctively threw his arms around his son and hugged him. He felt like a fool for being so insensitive.

"I'm sorry! I should never have given you that photograph. Please forgive me son. My timing was terrible."

Laura looked on helplessly and regretfully. It was her idea to give the picture to John. She suggested that the good memory might lighten his spirit.

'What a stupid idea! What was I thinking?'

John immediately composed himself. He didn't want to drag his parents down any more than he already had.

"That's okay Dad! You know I'll always treasure this. Thanks."

Laura felt uncomfortable and quickly changed the subject.

"We've arranged for Stella to come here to help," she said.

John quickly turned his head and shot a glance at his mother.

Terror in the Andes

"You didn't have to do that. I've already hired a lawyer. I hope you don't mind. I told him I would look after his fee. I'm sorry. I was desperate and I really needed him. He's the best."

He was looking for his father's approval. His father was always there for him and supported him, trusting that he would make the right decisions as a responsible young adult. So far he had every reason to be proud.

"We know about Mr. Aguillar. Stella is meeting with him as we speak. Don't worry son, we need to get you out of here. There's obviously some huge misunderstanding. Once we explain everything to the judge things will be cleared up. You'll be out in no time once bail is set."

This was a sensitive topic that John had discussed with lawyer a couple days ago and he knew his parents would be as upset as he was.

"It isn't that simple Dad. There is no bail hearing for drug smugglers in this country. And even if there were a hearing, I'd be a flight risk. They stole my passport. I don't know where it is, so I'm not going anywhere before the trial unless I'm cleared before then." Keith was shocked.

'No bail hearing? That can't be true!'

He didn't know what to say. He didn't want to challenge John at this point. He would ask Stella about it later. She would know.

John quickly changed the subject when he saw the incredulous look on his father's face. He inquired about his brother Steve and his sister Ruth and wanted and update on their progress, socially, at school, in sports, etc. The visit continued in a somber mood until it was time to leave.

When visiting hours were over, they promised to return at every opportunity. As they exited the prison, they had a reason to be concerned about John's morale. If they weren't able to keep up his spirits, they feared he would end up in a deep depression. His predicament infuriated his parents. They would have to do something about it.

They discussed it on the way back to their hotel. As soon as they got back, they would call home with an update on John's condition. If Steve would go to the media for support, and if Ruth would ask friends and relatives to write letters, maybe it would pressure the prosecution to be more responsive in pursuing the truth. They would use anything and everything at their disposal to help clear their son. However, they had no idea how long it would take, or even if it would work in the long run. But out of desperation they were willing to try.

CHAPTER 18

Stella Bennett left the office of Carlos Aguillar and walked to her rented car. She was impressed with the defense attorney. She liked him. He was well mannered, genuine, attentive, and he was very concerned for John's welfare. She wondered what kind of a person Victor Caballero was.

'If he's anything like Carlos I'll be quite happy to work with him.'

She drove to her hotel and took the elevator to her floor. She knocked on the door of the adjacent room where Keith and Laura were staying. She was anxious to hear how John was doing. There was no answer. She was disappointed but this would give her time to make a phone call. She inserted her key, opened the door, and entered her room. She kicked off her shoes and pulled open the curtains. She stood at the window clutching her arms around her, soaking in the sun's warm rays. The view overlooked the coastal cliff tops and the eternal mesmerizing waves of the Pacific Ocean. A paraglider was preparing to take off into the balmy sea breeze. Sunbathers lounged on the sandy beach under large colorful umbrellas.

She lowered her eyes to the park below where young children were playing. Some were on skateboards, some on bicycles. This was the more affluent section of the city with beautiful parks, tall buildings, fancy hotels, modern supermarkets, and fast food restaurants.

Her mind wondered, contemplating the contrast between here and the poorer neighborhoods just around the corner where a dirty stuffed animal was a precious treasure to a child, a life of poverty where families lived from hand to mouth, where food was scarce, illiteracy common. The first time she had seen similar poverty was when she was in Mexico and she told herself that if she ever went back, she would travel light and use the room in her suitcases for charitable donations of shoes, clothing and toys. She was sorry she left in such a hurry and didn't think of taking extra luggage full of these items. She shook her head with a lump in her throat and a sunken heart. She wasn't aware of how long she had stood there. It could have been five minutes or it could have been an hour. Time stood still.

Finally she broke herself away and realized that she should call the number that John's attorney had given her. She dialed and was about to hang up the receiver when the private investigator answered on the seventh ring.

"Hello! This is Victor Caballero."

There was a pause and he waited on the other end of the line. Stella was startled. Her mind had drifted. She forgot to ask whether or not he spoke English. By now she hadn't expected anyone to answer.

"Oh hello! My name is Stella Bennett. I'm Keith Emerson's niece."

She didn't mean for that to slip out. She was there in a professional capacity and like with Carlos Aguillar she wanted to tell him later, that her motive for being there was personal. Oh well! It didn't really matter now that it was said. She continued.

"I was referred to you by Mr. Aguillar."

The male on the other end detected her broken accent and briefly chuckled to himself because he thought it was cute.

"It's okay. You can speak English. I just got off the phone with Mr. Aguillar and I was expecting your call. He has informed me that you are quite eager to help with the investigation and you want to get started right away."

"Yes. He's right. I would like to go over things with you as soon as possible, if that's okay with you."

She avoided asking him if they had discussed any of the details regarding her intentions. She hoped they hadn't. She preferred to do that herself in person so she could feel him out. A personal approach was always better.

"Then would you like to meet somewhere and we can discuss things?"

"Certainly! That's exactly what I had in mind. I'm looking forward to it."

The conversation ended on a friendly note. She agreed to meet him for coffee in the morning at a local coffee and pastry shop where she would lay out her plans and hope that he would approve of them. If he didn't, she was willing to compromise.

Later that afternoon she went to the prison to visit John. She didn't know what to expect. She was disheartened when she first laid eyes on him. He looked terrible. The gleam in his eyes had disappeared, replaced by red rims. It was quite a contrast to the beaming, jovial young man she remembered him as. Would he ever be the same? She forced a weak smile and greeted him.

"Hello my favorite cousin. I'm so sorry!" was all she could say with a lump in her throat and hurt in her eyes. John was glad to see her despite his embarrassment. He knew he looked awful and he also was aware of the fact that he was disrupting her life. That didn't help the situation either.

"And hello to you too my favorite cousin! Thanks for coming."

He was trying to put on a good front as Stella kept talking.

"How are you doing? Are they treating you well?"

John became fidgety and Stella could have kicked herself for opening her mouth.

'What a stupid question!'

"The food's not too great. At least I'm in a cell by myself, no one to bug me. It's all right I guess," he lied. "Mom and Dad came today."

He bent his head and raised his hands massaging his face and eyes. It was awkward for both of them. He didn't know what else to say. The momentary silence said everything. Stella took over the conversation.

"I know. I spoke with them briefly at the hotel when they got back"

She didn't want to go into details about her lengthy conversation with her aunt and uncle after they returned to the hotel from the prison. They were totally depressed and devastated but John didn't need to know any of this.

"I also went to see Carlos Aguillar, your new defense attorney. He's very concerned about you and that's a good sign. I'm meeting another private investigator in the morning to discuss our tactics. I'll be working with him."

She wanted to give him some encouragement.

"Don't worry John! We'll get you out of here and you'll be home in no time."

She hoped and prayed it was true.

"I'm impressed with Mr. Aguillar. He seems to be very thorough and very professional."

"What are his plans? How's he going to get me out of here? Did he tell you what happened? Did he tell you everything? How those bastards murdered Phil and framed me? I shouldn't be here"

Her cousin lowered his eyes and swallowed holding back the tears.

"Yes, he told me everything."

Stella didn't want to elaborate further. She explained her plan to John, and John pleaded with his cousin.

"I hope you find something soon. I hope this other private investigator is good. There has to be some way that you can prove that those cops framed us."

John had complete faith in his cousin.

'If anyone can help me, she can.'

During this visit, they bonded more than ever and when visiting hour was over they said their good-byes, reluctant to leave one another's company.

Stella was anxious to return to her hotel. It had been a long day and she needed a break. She intended to call her cousins Ruth and

Steve. Hearing from their parents was one thing, but they wouldn't confide in them like they would with their cousin.

That night, she was late getting to bed. She had a difficult time trying to fall asleep. The events of the day kept haunting her. She had spoken with Steve and Ruth who had their work cut out for them. Tomorrow they would begin their crusade to help right a wrong against their beloved brother. The stress and excitement was exhausting. She kept going over her own plans and she knew she was overtired. Was she doing the right thing? Insisting on doing things *her* way? The last time she looked at the clock beside her bed it was 2:17 P.M. Finally she fell asleep.

CHAPTER 19

Victor Caballero waited and waited. He was not impressed. He wasn't that keen about the meeting in the first place but didn't let on to neither Carlos nor Stella. He was accustomed to working alone. But he understood, since the private investigator was family she wanted to help. He was about to leave when Stella walked in. He couldn't miss her with her auburn hair. She looked like the typical Caucasian tourist. At the same time, she sighted him in his navy blue dress pants and short sleeve pale yellow cotton shirt. He was exactly as he had described himself over the phone. She walked briskly to the table where he stood to greet her.

"You're Stella Bennett?" He reached out to shake her hand.

"And you're Victor Caballero?"

She profusely apologized for showing up late and she was charming.

" I'm so sorry. Please forgive me for making you wait."

She explained that Laura needed to confide in her and it took longer than expected. She had to be there for her. Her family was her number one priority. What could he say?

She quickly joined him as Victor pulled out a chair for her. She thanked him. She noticed that he treated her as his equal but could make her feel like a lady at the same time. 'A *rare quality in North America.*'

The sweet aroma of pastry filled the café but she resisted the temptation. They ordered coffee and Stella wasted no time in getting down to business.

"Do you mind that I'm here? I mean, I'd like to work with you on the case but I'm imposing on your territory. Mr. Aguillar hired you first and here I pop in, wanting a piece of the action."

She didn't mean for it to come out that way. It sounded terrible, as if it were so matter of fact. It wasn't. It was a matter of deep concern for her cousin.

She detected the slight hesitation in Victor's voice.

"No, I don't mind, as long as we can work together and not get in one another's way."

At least he was honest and didn't beat around the bush about anything. Stella liked that quality about him too. She cautiously proceeded with her next statement, watching for Victor's reaction.

"I'd like to explore the crime scene and search for evidence of the camp. It has to be there."

Victor was offended by Stella's intentions of overlapping the work he had already done so meticulously. Carlos neglected to tell him that *'little detail'* when he called yesterday. What else did he omit? He placed both hands down on the tabletop, leaned forward and stared into her hazel eyes.

"Didn't Mr. Aguillar tell you? I've already been there and believe me, there's no camp. I even went to the extent of conducting a search by air after finding nothing, in case there was some mistake about the location."

Stella was tactful and good at finessing.

"I understand that, and I'm not questioning your competence. But couldn't there be a remote possibility that someone in the area happed upon John and Phil's belongings? I mean, the camp had been abandoned. Someone could have seen that it was unoccupied for a couple of days. Whoever it was could have taken the opportunity to remove everything, keeping it for himself. There has to be some logical explanation for John and Phil's gear disappearing and if that's the case, maybe the culprit left some trace behind."

She didn't know how close to the truth she had been about everything being removed.

Victor thought that the lady detective was grasping at straws, looking for something that he knew wasn't there. Victor sat across from her looking her in the eye admiringly. She was good at analyzing.

"That possibility did cross my mind when I was searching and came up empty handed. There was nothing there!"

He shook his head from side to side. She was stubborn. He had to convince her.

"There wasn't even evidence of a small campfire. It is such a remote place and I didn't think anyone would take *everything*. I also inquired around to see if anyone in the area had seen your cousin and his friend. No one seems to have known that they were there."

The waitress brought two cups of coffee over to the table and set them down. Stella was gasping for a drink. She raised the mug to her lips, contemplating. She didn't like what he was implying.

'*So he believes there was nothing there in the first place?*'

She took a sip then calmly placed her cup on the saucer.

"Then what did you think? That John was lying?"

She spoke softly. This wasn't going to be easy. If this investigator was going to be working with her, then he had better have a little more faith in John's story. Was he giving up already?

That suggestion struck a sour note with Victor. She had misunderstood him and was accusing him of, of what? '*This meeting isn't going well at all.*' He felt like lashing out at her, giving her a piece of his mind, but he bit his tongue instead, being the gentleman that he was. He would have to be tactful with his response and explain himself properly.

"What I meant was, that whoever removed his belongings was absolutely meticulous about it. I mean the two campers spent one day and two nights there. They had to eat. There should have been empty tin cans, potato or fruit peals, papers, some kind of garbage because they left in such a hurry. Who would want to take that?"

The female investigator was embarrassed and lowered her eyes. He was right. Who *would* want to take that? They were back to square one. Stella sighed deeply, feeling defeated. She approached the subject from another angle, hoping for some input from Victor.

After all, up until now she hardly gave him a chance. Maybe they could smooth things over.

"Initially, I thought that it would be a good idea to follow John and Phil's trail beginning from Lima to Tarma, then carry on from there. But even if we could find someone who could identify them, that doesn't prove their innocence. In order to do that, we would need to find the driver of the pick-up who last dropped them off. Since we don't have a make or model or even a license plate number, it seems an impossible task."

She sat there and shrugged her shoulders looking bewildered. Victor came to her rescue with a solution.

"I agree with you completely. So, why don't we go back to the beginning? I'm willing to compromise and start again. We'll go back to the crime scene. Maybe there's something I overlooked."

Stella was so adamant about the search that Victor wanted to give her the benefit of the doubt. After all, it was her cousin she was trying to help and if that's what she wanted to do then so be it.

They continued their discussion and in the end, they worked things out. Stella was happy. She convinced Victor that she should revisit the crime scene. She didn't think it necessary that Victor join her. After all, he had already been there and she didn't want to inconvenience him. Victor had convinced Stella that she would be safer if she didn't travel alone, that he should accompany her. Finally she agreed with him. Two heads were better than one. And besides, it would give them an opportunity to get to know one another.

They planned to leave the next day, the sooner the better. They would fly to Ayacucho, rent a car there, backtrack west on highway 24, and then go north to Santa Inés.

After leaving the café, Victor offered to drive Stella back to her hotel but she politely declined his offer. It was a beautiful day and it wasn't that far. She preferred to walk. Victor hopped in his car and headed for the office. As he drove, he thought about his new co-worker.

'*I guess that's what I'd call her, a co-worker.*'

125

In the past he had always worked alone. He liked to be independent, to be in control of things. This imposition was something new for him. He thought it would take him a while to get used to the situation. He couldn't blame Carlos for sending her to him. She had volunteered her services and she was a close relative of the suspect. If he were in her shoes, he would want to become involved too. How could Carlos refuse her?

Victor was hoping that he could adjust. If they didn't get along, he would just tell Carlos that it wasn't working out. He wouldn't mention the fact that he felt a little uncomfortable working alongside a female. He didn't know why, because socially he had no problem relating to women. Maybe it was because like him, she had a strong personality. She was so adamant. But she was here in a professional capacity and he would respect her position. He decided to make the most of it and accept what she had to offer.

He agreed to look after the travel arrangements so he stopped at the nearest travel agency and booked and paid for two airline tickets with his credit card. He booked a six A.M. flight to Ayacucho with Air Condor, via Andahuaylas. It wasn't a direct flight but that was all that was available and he hoped there wouldn't be a problem. He was told that if there weren't enough passengers for the last leg, then that flight would be cancelled, in which case they would have to take a minibus. They would need a place to stay so he also made reservations for two rooms at Hotel Santa Rosa.

That taken care of, he drove to his apartment thinking that tomorrow would be a long day. He had asked for a later flight, but there was only one flight a day and that was at six A.M. So he figured by the time they arrive, check into the hotel, and rent a car it would probably be close to noon hour. But then he realized that it would take another three or four hours by car to reach their final destination. And by then it would soon be getting dark, too late to do any searching. They would have to wait until the next day and set off early in the morning. He wasn't disappointed because he hated rushing. Besides, it would give both of them a chance to get some rest. They would be up at four o'clock in the morning and would welcome some time to get caught up on their sleep.

Victor parked his vehicle and entered his apartment building. His pad was on the third floor and he took the steps two at a time. He was famished. He opened a can of soup, buttered some dinner rolls and thought about Stella Bennett again as he ate. Why did he seem so bothered about her? She wasn't a threat to him but she certainly had an impact on him. He wondered what he had gotten himself into by accepting to work with her on this case. But then again, at the time, he thought he would be working alone. It didn't occur to him that he would be working with someone else and he knew he couldn't back out now. His lawyer friend was certainly put on the spot when she turned up unexpectedly at his office. Was that a good thing or a bad thing? He snipped open a cardboard box of milk and poured himself a glassful. Would she assist the investigation or would she inhibit the investigation? Only time would tell. It was going to be difficult for her to remain objective. He would have to keep her steered in that direction.

In the meantime, he would call her and inform her of the travel arrangements he had made for tomorrow. He would have a cab pick him up at four a.m. then go to her hotel and pick her up on the way to the airport. Was there anything else he had to do?

He might be gone for a few days, so this afternoon he would take care of his paperwork. He had a couple of invoices to send out and a few bills to pay. Then tomorrow he would be on his way.

CHAPTER 20

After the lights were dimmed for the night, John sat on his cot holding his precious picture in his hands. His eyes were lowered, glued to it. He would never forget that day. He and Phil thought they could conquer anything if they won the championship. And they won. He remained deep in thought until he was suddenly distracted. His ears perked up. He thought he heard someone singing. It wasn't loud. It was barely audible. And it was in English. He slowly rose from his bed and took a few steps to his cell door, trying to detect the source of the music. He stood and listened to it for a few minutes. It was a pleasant voice and a pleasant tune. He spied a Caucasian with long hair, diagonally across from his cell. He was sitting on his cot with a stubby pencil and a piece of paper in his hands. John reckoned the he was in his late fifties or early sixties with strands of brown mixed in with his gray hair and speckles of brown dotting his beard. John hadn't noticed the guy before and he was curious, but he dare not talk too loud. He didn't want to attract attention.

"Hey! Psst! You over there! What's that song you're singing?"

The man looked up from his paper and his face broke into a smile. The deep, hardened lines in his face seemed to soften.

"You speak English! Where are you from son?"

"I'm from Canada. Where are you from?"

" I'm from California. Why are you here?"

John paused and didn't know how to answer.

"Let's just say I'm the victim of a corrupt system. I was framed. And you? Why are you here?"

"Ha! You too huh! How ironic! Well, I've been all around the world except for South America and never had a problem either. That is, until I came here. Some thug tried to steal my Enfield motorcycle when I had my back turned for thirty seconds. She was a gem, my pride and joy. When I accosted the thief, he became defensive and violent. He punched me in the head. I wasn't going to let him get away with it so I punched him back. To make a long story short, a cop appeared from out of nowhere. The next thing I know this guy is walking away with my bike and I end up being charged for assault. That was four months ago and I have to serve another two months before they let me go. I've never been inside a prison in my life but let me give you a little advice sonny. If you don't find something to do while you're here, you'll go antsy and lose your mind."

The prisoner studied John trying to guess what his interests might be. He guessed that this young man would be more interested in a mental challenge rather than a physical one.

"You know what I mean? Like I'm composing songs. I mightn't be any good at it but I always did like music. It's kind of like a passion with me. And in here, it keeps me busy. If you don't do something constructive you'll go nuts. I found *that* out. How long are you here for?"

John didn't know how to answer *that* question either.

"I really don't know. It depends on a lot of factors I guess."

He didn't want to talk about himself so he might as well be honest.

"Listen," he said, "Can we not talk about it? But thanks for the advice."

The old man understood.

"Sorry, I didn't mean to upset you. I wasn't thinking and I should have known better."

He thought that John wanted to conclude the conversation so he picked up his paper and began humming in a low voice.

"No! No! You don't have to apologize. You didn't upset me in the least. It's just that the investigation is in its preliminary stage and I don't have any answers. And besides I'd rather talk about *you*."

The old man chuckled to himself. He was amused because he had never heard a comment like that before. What did this young man want to know? That he was a 'Nam veteran? That he was a medic during the war and had seen more suffering in his lifetime than he cared to remember? Did he care to hear about how he tried to rescue women who were being raped and children who were being slaughtered? He didn't think so.

John thought that the old man had closed his eyes sitting up and had fallen asleep. But he wanted to know more.

"I didn't get your name. What's your name?" Tell me about your music. I like music. It lights up your world, especially in a depressing place like this. I really enjoyed your little composition. It was good. Tell me the lyrics."

John had a way of making a man feel good without even trying. The old man was flattered by his compliment and said his name was Mike.

The other prisoners had been whispering among themselves. The resulting sound was like a conglomeration of buzzing insects at a feast. When the echo of footsteps from the guard approached, there was a sudden hush. The old man raised his index finger to his lips. That would be the end of their conversation. John had met a new friend named Mike.

CHAPTER 21

The pair of investigators arrived in Ayacucho without a hitch. The airport was only four kilometers from the town center. Their hotel was within a block of the Plaza de Armas. It boasted twin courtyards and spacious well-furnished rooms including a refrigerator which was a rare luxury in Peru. After checking in, Stella was too anxious to rest. All she could think about was John in that forsaken prison, and her aunt and uncle's terrible distraught. But she knew that she had to be strong and optimistic so she would make the most of her situation. She had the whole afternoon to kill so she decided to check out some of the sights. At least for the time being, she hoped that it would take her mind off worrying about things beyond her control. Victor had offered to go with her but she politely declined. She had always made a habit of separating her social life from her professional life. She was going to be seeing enough of this man, for heaven only knows how long, so why change now? He was not offended in the least because he felt the same way she did. While she was gone he would rent a car for tomorrow and do a little touring of his own.

Stella's first stop was a visit to the seventeenth century cathedral on the Plaza with its art museum. It had beautiful ornate facades of colonial Spanish baroque. Then she took a bus to the local university museum where there were exhibitions of mummies, skulls and other artifacts of the Inca and Wari Empires. She had never heard of the Wari Empire and was surprised to learn that five hundred years before the Inca Empire the Wari Empire dominated the Peruvian Highlands.

Making her way back to the central plaza she stopped to admire the handicrafts and colorful weaving of cloth, unique to the area.

She loved the colonial atmosphere as she strolled through the narrow side streets, a new surprise around every corner. She was aware of the brief but polite stares she was getting from the humble local indigenous people. Foreigners seldom visited this place because it was very isolated and difficult to reach.

As she continued strolling through the central plaza, she read about the history of the city from a pamphlet she had picked up at her hotel. It was here that a major battle was fought in 1824 in the quest for Peru's independence. It was also here that, during the dark days of the 1980's, the Maoist revolutionary movement, the Sandero Luminoso (shining path) became an armed gorilla organization and tried to overthrow the Peruvian government. Most people now wanted to forget the dark days of the civil war where between 40,000 and 60,000 people died or disappeared, most of them from here in the central Andes. Just like any other war, horrible atrocities occurred, innocent people were massacred, leaders assassinated. There was total political, social, and economic upheaval. The armed forces finally managed to capture the rebel leader in 1992 along with top lieutenants leaving behind small broken groups whose resent activities are limited to the drug traffic industry.

When Stella finally returned to the hotel, her feet were killing her. She was grateful that she had her comfortable hiking boots with her for tomorrow. But the walk did her the world of good. She was right. It was exactly what she needed to relieve her stress. She realized that she was exhausted and hungry. *'I hope I didn't overdo it today!'* She entered her room and marched straight to the hot water tap on the bathtub. She was due for a soaking. It would soothe her weary muscles. As she sank down allowing the water to wrap around her, savoring the feeling, she closed her eyes and thought of nothing. It was the first opportunity she had to relax since she arrived in Peru.

Later, she ordered a meal at the hotel restaurant. She was pleasantly refreshed after her bath but her eyes were growing heavy. She didn't see Victor, not that she really wanted to. Perhaps he was snoozing. She was enjoying her dessert when she heard his voice.

"Hello there! How was your afternoon? Mind if I join you?"

She smiled at him as he waited for her approval before sitting.

"Sure you can join me. You just missed a good meal."

"Oh, I already ate. I guess I was hungrier than you were," he chuckled.

"But I'll have another dessert and tea."

As they sat there, they discussed their afternoon and tried to anticipate what was in store for them tomorrow. They enjoyed one another's company.

Early the next morning the two investigators set out and they were winding their way up the mountain and across the altiplano in their rented car. Stella was the navigator and held in her lap a detailed map giving them the location of the area to be searched. The morning sky was a mixture of light gray clouds and large white fluffy ones. The odd patch of blue sky peeked through allowing the sun's rays to bathe the heat -starved rocks.

By the time they had reached their destination it was early afternoon. Victor parked the car off to the side of the road and they headed out on foot. Stella was fascinated with the panoramic view surrounding her. She was awed at the fact that just a week ago she had no idea that she would be here, wandering across an ancient plateau in the Peruvian Andes. Her eyes were alert as she walked beside Victor.

"How could anyone live here? What do people eat? It's so cold and desolate," she commented as she kicked the lichen with her hiking boot.

Victor was pleased that Stella was interested in his country.

"It's so desolate because of overgrazing. The llama and the alpaca are the main means of survival up here. They provide food and clothing. The inhabitants have survived here for thousands of years on these wind-swept mountains. On the slopes, families eke out a living on subsistence agriculture. Corn and potatoes are popular crops. There are over 5000 varieties of potatoes in Peru. People who live near the rivers and lakes have fished, but the fish population is dwindling quickly."

Victor continued explaining.

"Since the arrival of industrial mining, the pristine water has become contaminated. As a result, many of the indigenous people have unknowingly developed cancer by drinking the water and eating the fish. They have since been fighting to have the pollution cleaned up. But the government is reluctant to intercede on their behalf, so they continue to be sick and helpless. The mining companies have done very little to compensate for their losses and the locals need the work in order to support their families.

Stella was aghast.

"How sad! How ironic! And all in the name of progress!"

Their conversation continued as their search progressed. Stella was intrigued.

"Do the traditional abodes have any electricity or indoor pluming? How do people heat their homes?"

"They can't afford electricity and there is no indoor pluming either. As for the heat, that accounts for the leggings and the layers of petticoats and skirts you see the women wearing. The distinctive hats with a flap to cover the ears are knitted with the wool of the llama for warmth. On very cold nights they are worn to bed. There is very little or no source of fuel for the homes so they are acclimatized to these temperatures."

They were approaching the area with the X on the map, but so far there was no tent in sight. They looked around and Stella was disappointed. She was hoping to see something. They continued to look for the exact spot where the tent was supposed to have been pitched.

"Maybe we are at the wrong location. Perhaps John was mistaken and was mixed up with his directions."

She was aware that they had already discussed this and that she was repeating herself but she couldn't help it. She was almost positive she'd find some little thing.

"There's no mistake. I was here before and this is the place. I told you that there was nothing here."

They were standing in the shadow of a cloud when suddenly the shadow moved and was replaced by the sun's warm rays, brightening the patch of ground on which they were standing. A few feet away, Stella thought she spied a piece of tin foil. She stooped down to investigate and then stopped when her fingers were six inches away from it. On closer observation it was something buried.

"Look at this Victor! I think I found something!"

He stooped down beside her, so close that he was momentarily mesmerized by a whiff of her perfume. It was vaguely familiar but he couldn't place it. He opened his case and found a brush. He carefully began to uncover the buried object.

"Ah Ha! What do we have here? It looks like a Swiss Army knife. Let's bag it for prints."

He produced a pen and skillfully hooked it onto the metal loop at the end of the knife, picked it up and dropped it into the plastic zip lock bag that Stella was holding up for him. They looked at one another and smiled simultaneously.

"I can't believe it. What a fluke! It's not much but it's a start. Surely we must be able to find more evidence here."

Stella's hopes were soaring as her teammate responded.

"Okay, we'll give it another twenty minutes. If we don't find anything, we'll call it quits. Is it a deal?"

She readily agreed, but after fifteen minutes of scouring in vain, they were discouraged.

"There's nothing else here. We may as well give up," suggested Victor.

"All right," agreed Stella, "I think it's about time we find someone who can tell us something. Let's hit the road and talk to some of those folks along the way."

They trekked to their car, carrying possibly the only piece of evidence that could save John. They unlocked the doors, got in, and drove away.

Shortly thereafter, a lonely abode could be seen standing in the distance, well away from the road. Between the thatched roof home and the road, a small herd of llama grazed on the scrub. Two children, a boy and a girl, were running playfully across the field swinging sticks in the air.

"Stop the car!" cried Stella when she spotted them.

Victor obeyed her instructions and the two were standing beside the car within seconds. The youngsters were oblivious until Victor called out to them.

"Hola! Como estais?"(Hello! How are you?)

The children stopped running and looked up in his direction, uncertain as to whether or not to approach the strangers. They cautiously and curiously walked toward the man and the white woman who was dressed funny. The boy was in the lead and he smiled when he realized that the object dangling around the woman's neck was a camera. Stella smiled. She was aware of his shyness and tried to coax him into a conversation.

"Hello my friend. I like your hat. It's very colorful. Did your mother knit it for you? Whoever it was is very talented."

He shook his head in the affirmative. Stella guessed that he was about twelve years old. The little girl hid closely behind the boy. She looked much younger as she peeked around him with curiosity.

"Is that your sister? She's very pretty. Would it be all right if I took your picture?"

The little girl revealed herself and stepped out from behind the boy with the anticipation of having her photograph taken. It was a rare occurrence for them. They eagerly posed for her. She snapped a couple of shots and motioned for them to approach her in order to see their image on the screen. Unlike some of their elders, they were not superstitious. The boy had once heard his old great aunt who condemned the magic machine for robbing people of their spirit. She said that it literally stole one's soul when the image was produced but he was more amused than afraid.

Victor stood back observing Stella's interaction with the children and admired the way she conducted herself with such gentleness. The youngsters were delighted to see themselves as Stella bent to show them the screen. They giggled and insisted on seeing the images again and again.

"And now," she said, "I have something for you."

She reached into her handbag and took out a key chain. She unhooked an amulet of The Infant Jesus of Prague and held it out to the little girl. It was the only thing she could find and she hoped that it was appropriate. She didn't want to impose her religious beliefs on them.

"This is for you," she said as she smiled at the little girl.

The girl's face was smeared with dirt. Her thin legs stepped up a little closer, within reaching distance of her precious gift. She hesitated briefly before she curiously took another step forward. She wanted to accept this gift from the friendly stranger.

"For me?" she asked in amazement as she stretched her neck to have a closer look.

"Yes, for you," replied Stella as she reached out, opened the girl's tiny hand and placed it there closing her fingers around the amulet.

"Thank you," said the girl.

Then Stella reached into her purse searching for something to give the boy. She had hair clips, a pen which she thought would be too trivial as a gift, her scarf, and other objects that were only suitable for a girl. She continued unzipping the different compartments. The only item she could find for a male was a small, dull, pocketknife she had purchased from a street vendor in Lima who was determined to sell her something.

"And this is for you."

She gave it to the boy. His eyes widened as he examined the treasure in the palm of his hand. He wasn't accustomed to receiving gifts from anyone.

"Thank you," he said politely.

"Where are you from?" he asked.

"I'm from Canada. People from other countries are very interested in visiting your beautiful country. Do you ever see different people, strangers taking photos or walking around here looking at the animals?"

The children looked puzzled and shrugged their shoulders. Stella squatted in front of them meeting their eyes. Victor was content to remain in the background while his colleague related to the young herders. He was more comfortable working with her now that he was getting to know her.

"Do you ever see any airplanes fly over here?"

"I saw one fall from the sky" proclaimed the boy.

"When did that happen? When did it fall?"

The young lad scratched his chin.

"Let me think. It was two days ago."

"No it wasn't. It was longer than that. It was four days ago," argued his sister.

She stood akimbo and tried to jog her brother's memory.

"Don't you remember? It was the afternoon when the police drove up and down the road, up and down, up and down."

She dramatically waved her arm back and forth as she tried to explain. Victor became more alert when he heard this.

"Are you certain that is what you saw? It was the police?"

The girl looked offended.

"Oh yes! I'm not stupid you know. I can tell the difference between a police car and an ordinary car."

Victor smiled at her innocence and her naïvety.

"You are very smart and very helpful. I am proud of you," he said, as he wanted to regain her confidence.

However the young boy was unable to support his sister.

"I'm sorry. I saw the police car only once that day. It was in the morning. The rest of the day I was preoccupied tending the herd. The animals roam all over the place."

"That's okay. You've also been very helpful. Would it be all right if we came back here again and visit with you like we did today?" asked Victor.

"Sure. You can stop by any time you want," replied the lad who felt important. "Will you bring us a present too?" asked the little girl.

Her brother nudged her. He was embarrassed because of his sister's rude manners.

"Forgive my sister please. She didn't really mean it."

"Oh yes I did."

"It'll be a surprise present," laughed Victor.

The two investigators drove away in silence, each theorizing a motive for the police driving up and down the road. Were they merely patrolling or doing something more sinister? Stella was first to break the silence.

"I have an idea," she said. Then she began to reveal her plan as Victor continued to maneuver around potholes and boulders that had separated from the mountainside and had fallen onto their path. When she finished explaining she asked for his opinion. His answer surprised her.

"Well partner, it's an angle worth exploring."

He nodded his head in approval and continued.

"But we should have a plan B in case plan A backfires for some reason."

When Stella heard the word 'partner' she suddenly turned her head and stared at him. At the same time she felt the knotted muscle in her neck and whispered an almost inaudible 'Ouch!' Victor frowned when he heard her.

"Is anything wrong? Are you okay?"

"No, it's nothing at all. I just kinked my neck."

As they continued driving, Stella observed him discretely. She realized that she knew very little about her co-worker, including his personal life. She assumed that he was married but never thought to ask.

'He's not bad looking. Actually he's quite attractive as a matter of fact. I wonder if he's wearing a wedding band?'

She twisted and kinked her neck a second time in an attempt to see if he was wearing a ring on his left hand that was over the steering wheel. Her curiosity was satisfied as she whispered, "Ouch!" again and massaged her neck.

The driver had acute hearing and quickly responded. His right hand left the steering wheel and reached for her hand tapping it gently.

"Are you sure you're okay? Would you like me to stop the car?"

At the touch of his hand, Stella could feel her temperature rise and her cheeks flush. She reached for the handle on the side of her door and rolled down the window allowing the cool air to rush in.

"Thank you but I'm just a pain in the neck."

Victor laughed before she realized her blunder and could correct herself. His laugh was contagious. She stared ahead and burst out laughing. It had been a long time since she had laughed so hard despite the fact that she was a little embarrassed.

Darkness came quickly. It was late when the arrived back at the hotel. They made it just in time to order a meal before the restaurant closed. Over dinner they decided to make a few preparations for tomorrow if they were going to follow up on Stella's plan. At first they debated on whether or not to go ahead with it. Especially since they had the knife. But in the end, curiosity prevailed. They wanted to meet Officer Ramirez and Officer Paredés at their station and feel them out. The scheme was elaborate but it just might work. In the meantime, Victor planned to get in touch with Carlos and give him an update on their progress.

The following day they set out to round up the equipment they needed. They had to inquire at several T.V. broadcasting stations before they located an audio-video camera suitable for their purpose. It was dysfunctional beyond repair and was about to be disposed of. Since it was only for show, it was a mere bargain for a hundred soles, perfect for the job. All they had to do to make their roles believable was insert a battery that would power the light for the 'on-off' switch. Stella purchased two I.D. nametags. She highlighted them with a small computerized maple leaf emblem to make it official looking. Now they were ready for tomorrow, if they could pull it off.

At the last minute Stella happened to walk past a toy store and remembered the two little herders. She turned back and entered. Five minutes later she exited with a smile and a large stuffed teddy bear in her arms. In her purse was a pocket video game with extra batteries.

The next morning, Stella had a feeling of déjà vu as she and Victor headed out on their little escapade. Neither one of them had a clue how things would go, but they would just have to play it by ear. The sky was covered with a light cloudy overcast so they brought along their raincoats just in case. During the few hours of travel to get there, they kept their conversation on a professional level, discussing their case for the umpteenth time. They were developing a good working relationship. Right from the beginning, they agreed not to talk about politics or religion. They each had strong opinions on these subjects and thought it wise to avoid them. The last thing they needed was a disagreement. They also avoided talking about their personal life, sticking to topics like history, geography, culture and economics, comparing the two countries, Canada and Peru. The time flew by and before they knew it, they were almost at their destination.

According to plans, Victor drove to within approximately three hundred feet of the law enforcement building and stopped. Fortunately for them, they could see the official police vehicle parked near the building, so someone had to be there. Victor opened his door, walked to the front of the car, opened the hood and located the distributor. He fiddled with the wire on the rotor arm and closed the hood. Stella watched as he walked to the passenger side brushing his hands together up and down several times. She wondered if he were showing enthusiasm or brushing off dust.

"Are you ready for this?" he asked as he opened her door.

At first, she objected to having her independence subdued by his gentlemanly gestures like opening the door for her. But she didn't want to offend him by speaking her mind about it. She was glad she hadn't, because upon her observation of others, she soon realized that she shouldn't take it personally. It was something embedded in the culture, a courtesy to all women both socially and professionally.

"As ready as ever," she smiled.

At the last minute she grabbed her official I.D. and pinned it onto the lapel of her fashionable navy wool suit jacket. She patted it as if it were her good luck charm and then they began their short trek to where the jeep was parked. The place seemed deserted but unbeknownst to them, Eduardo Ramirez lived opposite the station and was sitting inside by the window, eating his lunch at the kitchen table.

Before entering the station, Stella stood outside, ready at the door, in case somebody decided to open it from the inside. Victor stood beside the jeep and took a quick glance around. Then he reached into his pocket and pulled out a roll of tape and slipped on a pair of gloves. He slowly pulled on the door handle, careful not to make any noise, and opened it. He bent over and inspected the inside. At first he didn't find what he was looking for. But when he pressed the groove between the seat and the back, his heart skipped a beat.

'*Bingo!*'

Just then, he heard Stella shriek and he froze. Officer Paredés had opened the door and met Stella face to face. She didn't have to pretend that she was startled. In an instant, she heard her own voice of surprise. Before the officer could step outside, she took a step forward forcing the officer to step back, giving her space to enter the office. She couldn't determine whether he was angry or dumbfounded. It was a scary moment. His size alone was intimidating. At least they were inside and he hadn't seen Victor snooping around in the jeep. Stella immediately composed herself although it was difficult not to be distracted by the dank odor and mess of the place.

"Oh! Thank God you're here! I had no idea there was a police station in this area. I need to use your phone. It's an emergency!"

She wasn't supposed to be playing *this* role. Instead of being a levelheaded journalist, she was forced to portray the role of a damsel in distress.

The officer stared at her.

'*Where in the world did **she** come from?*'

Her blunt manner surprised him. He was unaccustomed to such bold behavior from a female. He quizzically examined the nametag on her lapel, which of course wasn't her real name. He recognized the Canadian symbol but the writing was in English.

'*That would account for it. She's an American.*'

To the majority of the Central and South American population, one was referred to as an American whether from Canada or the United States. It was the same difference. His pause gave her a moment to think.

"You need to use the phone? You say it's and emergency?" he repeated after her. He seemed stunned by the unexpected visitor.

"Yes. I'm terribly sorry to intrude on you like this, but our car broke down and I need to call someone. I left my hotel in such a hurry this morning, Tsk! I forgot my cell phone."

She feigned disappointment and annoyance with herself.

The office door opened and Victor popped his head inside.

"Is everything all right Elizabeth? I thought I'd better check on you. So far I haven't found the trouble with the car. I'm still working on it."

Stella was relieved to see him, and also relieved that he remembered to use her alias. She didn't like being alone with this man but wouldn't be alone with him any longer, now that Victor was here. She scanned his jacket looking for his nametag but he wasn't wearing it. She had to think fast and couldn't for the life of her, think straight.

'*What was his name?*'

143

"Come on in Jerry! Everything is okay. This fine young officer should be able to help us."

She smiled at the officer. Her charm was working but not the way she intended. She thought that she detected a glimmer of lust in his eyes and it gave her the creeps, but she would play along.

"Of course I can help you."

He grinned at Stella and gave her a sideward look.

'*For a small price that is. Nothing in life is free my dear.*'

"You don't need the phone. Where is your car? Let's have a look at it."

He took her by the arm walking close to her and escorted her through the door. Victor followed closely behind and passed them along the way. He wanted to get to the vehicle and pop the hood before they did. He quickly did so, unlatching and bracing it open. He asked the officer if he would get in and try the ignition. Officer Paredés was pleased to comply, but nothing happened when he turned the key. Victor pretended to fiddle with the engine.

"Try it again."

When nothing happened, Victor fiddled for the last time and fixed the small problem. He then poked his head around from behind the open hood and looked at the officer.

"One more time!"

The officer beamed as the engine turned over.

"See! We fixed it! No problem at all!"

Stella, right on cue, smiled broadly at the officer who sat there pleased with himself. She laid on the flattery hoping to keep his attention.

"Oh! Thank you so much. You're a real sweetheart."

When Mauricio glanced up into the rearview mirror, he spied Eduardo walking down the middle of the deserted road, nearing the car. By the time Mauricio had gotten out, his partner was standing beside the female visitor. Stella gave Victor the eye and ever so slightly nodded. It was time to lift the curtain for scene two and

Eduardo gave them the opening they needed. He looked at his partner and smiled.

"I see we have company. Aren't you going to introduce us?"

"Oh! I'm sorry. My name is Officer Paredés and this is my partner Officer Ramirez," he said as he motioned to shake hands with Stella.

"And I'm Ssst ah hem! " Excuse me! I must have something caught in my throat, Elizabeth Mercier. I'm very pleased to meet you. And this is my cameraman, Jerry Springer."

She didn't miss a beat and almost choked on her own words.

'How ridiculous! I hope they don't watch American television!'

She still couldn't remember what Victor's alias was supposed to be and she blurted out the first name that popped into her head. She had called him Jerry by his first name in Officer Paredés' presence and she couldn't afford to stall. Even Victor wasn't able to see the irony. But nevertheless, the officer took the bait and that's what counted.

"I'm pleased to meet you! Your cameraman?" he said eyeing Victor.

Victor remained silent and nodded to Stella who was doing all right so far.

"Yes. Oh! I didn't tell you? I'm a reporter for the C.B.C. that is the Canadian Broadcasting Corporation and I'm here doing a documentary for them. I've finished with my interviews in Colombia. Now I'm here in Peru interviewing. We've already done our city interviews but we though it would be a good idea to get some input from the country folks as well."

She didn't push by elaborating any further. Instead, she hoped their curiosity had been peaked enough to inquire about her work. Officer Ramirez turned to her. He had his own reasons for asking.

"Oh? That's a very interesting profession. What exactly is your documentary about? I'd like to hear about it."

145

Stella didn't hesitate to open the door. This was the opportunity she had been waiting for. She addressed the issue hoping they would bite.

"Our government is very concerned about the escalation of drug abuse in Canada, especially among our youth. We must educate them, and part of that education includes knowing where the drugs are coming from. We know that your government is having the same problem and we are interested in learning how your people feel about it. Is it really as rampant here in this country as we are led to believe, and if so, what is your government doing to eliminate it? Do the Peruvians think that their government is doing enough? How much funding is allotted to fighting the war against drugs?"

Stella realized that she had said enough and was getting carried away. She waited, hoping to hear what she wanted to.

Officer Paredés was intrigued by what he heard and wanted a piece of the action for himself. He took advantage of the opportunity.

"That sounds very interesting. As a matter of fact, coincidentally just last week there was a plane full of cocaine that crashed nearby and I was first to reach the scene. I arrived just in time. Unfortunately I was forced to shoot one of the smugglers who was trying to escape, but I arrested the other one," he gloated.

"Perhaps I can make a contribution to your documentary. It makes for a great story and you would be getting it first hand."

Stellla was fuming internally. Here she was in the very presence of Phil's murderer and could do absolutely nothing about it. Victor was equally upset as he stood on the sidelines observing the act as it was unfolding. He thought he was going to kill the man if he hung around any longer. His attention moved to Officer Ramirez who seemed to be perturbed after Officer Paredés had volunteered his services.

"I need to talk to you please, in private."

He tugged on his partner's sleeve and pulled on his arm.

"Please excuse us for a minute," he said to his company.

Mauricio was extremely annoyed at this intrusion but wasn't about to create a scene in front of the people who had the potential to make him famous. He stepped aside apologizing profusely. His partner insisted that they go further away than necessary because he wanted to guarantee not being overheard by these strangers.

"What is it? What do you want? Do you realize what you're doing? Can't you see that I'm in the middle of an interview?" Mauricio was exasperated.

"Listen to me!" exclaimed Eduardo emphatically.

He had never spoken to Mauricio with such harshness and he wasn't going to stop. This was too important to ignore. He had to say something quickly in order to hold his partner's attention.

"I think I smell a rat! I didn't think it was important then, but I do now. When I was having lunch at the house, I happened to look up and I could see the cameraman through the window. He was snooping around our jeep. I'm not sure how long he had been there before I noticed him. At the time, I was going to go out and confront him, but then I watched him enter our office. I couldn't figure out what he was up to. But I thought that whatever it was, he would have mentioned it to you. Do you really think that it's just a coincidence that they are here? Think about it.

Eduardo studied his partner intently.

"What? You idiot! Why didn't you tell me this sooner? You mean to say that all along you knew that these people could be imposters and you didn't say anything? What did you think the man was doing snooping inside our vehicle? Weren't you the least bit suspicious?"

Mauricio was sweating bullets. He turned his head and could see the man and woman chatting. They looked innocent enough. Should he confront the stranger? What was he looking for?

"I only saw him when he was closing the door then he went inside. I just thought that he was interested in maybe buying a vehicle like ours. Why else would he be there? I assumed that he was going to ask you about it. And besides, I couldn't tell you before. You wouldn't let me. You were too captivated by the lady's charm."

He refused to take the blame for being negligent when he was doing just the opposite. He was alerting his partner to the possible danger that he hadn't foreseen.

Mauricio tried to calm down. Maybe he was overreacting. Maybe everything was legit and these people were who they said they were. He did notice equipment in the back seat, and now the cameraman had the back door open. But what if it was just a ploy for show? Was it worth taking the risk discussing his role after the plane crash? But how could he back out without looking suspicious? The answer suddenly dawned on him. He walked back with a purpose now to face his company.

While the two officers were conversing in private, Stella and Victor had removed their equipment and had it set up ready to go. When they saw the two coming back after their discussion, Stella opened her mouth to say something but Officer Mauricio Paredés was one step ahead of her. In a way, he hated to say what he was going to say. He might be forfeiting his opportunity of being recognized as a hero.

"I'm terribly sorry," he said "but I have to renege on my offer. I just discussed it with my partner and he has reminded me that the investigation is still ongoing. He has every right to be concerned. I don't want to overstep my bounds and jeopardize the investigation in any way by talking about the case before it's been closed. I'm sure you understand."

Officer Ramirez was standing beside him shaking his head in agreement. He was relieved to see how smoothly his partner handled the situation.

"I'm sorry to hear that," said Stella looking up at him as he addressed her.

"We were looking forward to this interview since it would have been a chance to expose some real action in fighting crime. Isn't that right Jerry?"

Victor got right in there hoping they would change their mind.

"It certainly is. I'm very disappointed because I have my camera set to roll. Oh well! We'll just have to find somebody else but I can certainly understand your position."

Officer Paredés held Victor's gaze and changed the subject. The snooping incident was disturbing and he wanted an explanation.

"Officer Ramirez tells me he saw you inside our jeep. I could arrest you for that. Do you mind telling me what you were doing?"

"That's a great vehicle you have there! I love jeeps! I owned one once when I was just a kid. I hate to admit it, but when I'm around those things, I can't resist the temptation to have a look at them inside and out. I didn't think you would mind. Why would you?"

He smiled, raised his eyebrows and shrugged his shoulders. Whether the officer believed him or not was immaterial. He had what he was looking for and he figured the less said the better.

Stella didn't budge or say a word as she observed Victor standing there like the little boy who was caught with his hands in the cookie jar, but this was much more serious.

"Tampering with police property is highly suspicious but I won't press charges because I'm in such a good mood."

Despite the sarcasm, Victor thought he had better show appreciation.

'If he is expecting a bribe, he's not getting one.'

"I didn't touch anything but I sincerely thank you for your consideration."

He was getting anxious to leave. This charade was turning into a nightmare and he expected at any moment, that the officer would ask to see his driver's license.

Stella was disheartened that she didn't get her potential guests to open up. She would have given anything to have the opportunity to trip them up with her questions, and she was convinced that she could have. But she had to wave bye-bye, now that she just lost her chance.

The two officers were no longer comfortable in the strangers' company. The car was fixed and these people had no excuse to hang around. Eduardo silently wished them to be on their way.

"Well, since there is nothing more we can do for you, "he said, "I guess I'll get back to work. I'm pleased to have met our acquaintance."

He glanced at Mauricio.

"Are you coming Officer Paredés?"

With that, Victor and Stella shook their hands, thanked them and packed up.

Walking back to the station, Eduardo had a few questions for Mauricio. He didn't need this extra stress. He wanted some reassurance that everything was going to be okay just like Mauricio said it would be. But it wasn't, not for him anyway. He was having nightmares every night, reliving the horror of partaking and witnessing the murder of an innocent young man. The memory of Phil's body lying in a pool of blood haunted him day and night. His relationship with his wife was strained and he wasn't the same with his children. At one point, he even thought of turning himself in. At times he thought of committing suicide but that would be a last resort. He shared none of these deep dark secrets with anyone.

"What do you think? Do you think they had something to hide, or am I just being paranoid?"

Mauricio was skeptical. He was trying to fit the pieces together. He scratched his head and concluded.

"I think that we can find out for ourselves by contacting the C.B.C. and see if they can verify their story. I don't think that anyone is onto us because so far we have done nothing to arouse suspicion and let's keep it that way."

He gave Eduardo a threatening sideward glare.

"If you know what I mean."

Victor dove slowly away in silence, watching the two men through his rearview mirror as they ambled down the road. He wondered what effect he and Stella had on them. Did they believe the reporter story? It was obvious that Officer Paredes did at first, that is, until his partner showed up. Did they think that it just a chance-encounter or were they onto their investigation? He really didn't care because he had something that might put a nail in their coffin. He continued watching them until they disappeared from sight. Stella didn't look back in case they were watching. They certainly had an impact on her. She had been shaking in her boots most of the time.

"Do you think that they suspected anything? That was a close call when I was nearly scared to death by that creepy cop. I wasn't expecting him to open the door when he did."

She chuckled when her mind replayed the scene, recalling her reaction and the look on the cop's face. She could afford the humor now that it was over. Victor was seriously recovering from the close encounter he himself had experienced.

"That wasn't the only close call. I nearly wet my pants on the spot when Officer Paredés questioned me about the jeep."

Stella looked straight ahead, pursed her lips and suppressed a laugh at the thought.

"That was smooth and cool on your part. You handled it well with your fast thinking. We weren't very successful were we? It was a complete shambles."

"It wasn't a total waste of time. While you were inside entertaining your so-called 'creepy cop', I was busy doing my job."

He turned and smiled at his travelling companion.

"And what did you find? Anything worthwhile?"

She was so riled that she entirely forgot to ask Victor how he had made out.

"I managed to search the jeep and I found traces of the stuff between the seat in the back. We have to get it to the lab first, but I'm sure it's cocaine unless they were going to bake a cake."

He was being facetious, something new for Stella.

"Oooh! You are such a clever detective! That's great! Mission accomplished! You deserve a metal for that one!"

He didn't want to take anything out of context but her raspy voice sounded sexy, or perhaps it was the way she said it. Victor thought he detected a glint in her eyes when their eyes met. Was she flirting with him or was it just his imagination? She was so subtle. She continued speaking.

"I think Carlos Aguillar is going to be very pleased with our findings. We have the knife and we have the cocaine. What more does he need? I think that he'll be able to wrap up this case in no time. I can hardly wait to tell John."

Victor was just as pleased as she was and could hardly wait to see those two cops go to prison. He wanted to be there during the arrest, to see the look on their faces and be able to reciprocate with his own looks of both pleasure and disgust. He knew that would be highly unlikely but he nevertheless took delight at the idea.

Shortly thereafter, Stella's eye caught two children waving their arms and running across the plain toward the road. They must have recognized the car approaching from a distance. With so much on her mind, she totally forgot about them. Victor stopped the car as soon as he saw them. The two investigators got out and walked across the plain to meet them. The little ones welcomed them with open arms and Victor's heart melted. He held the teddy bear behind his back hidden from view. When he suddenly produced the gift and held it in front of the little girl's face, she beamed, jumping with joy, and thanked him over and over again. He then reached into his pocket and pulled out the young boy's present. It was unfamiliar to him but once Victor showed him how to play the hand held video game, the boy was ecstatic. After a short conversation, the children bid farewell and skipped excitedly back to the herd. A warm feeling engulfed the two foreigners as they stood and watched the brother and sister disappear behind a hill.

The rest of the way back to the city was mostly spent listening to their personal private thoughts. Once in a while Victor and Stella would speak to one another, but they were both all talked out and exhausted after three days of constantly being on the go.

After arriving back at the hotel, Victor placed a call to his employer. At first, Carlos was mortified after hearing about their experience with the arresting officers. He envisioned the whole episode as Victor described it. In the end, the two had a good laugh at how ridiculous their whole scheme played out.

Finding the cocaine helped, but it wasn't conclusive, as the attorney would explain later. John's attorney asked Victor to take care of the evidence and to have the lab process it for verification as soon as he returned. He also said that John's parents were keeping in touch with him and wondered how they were making out. Were they safe and did they find anything? After hanging up, Victor packed his suitcase.

CHAPTER 22

The two investigators returned to Lima from Ayacucho via Air Condor the following day. Victor followed Carlos' instructions and dropped off the evidence at the lab for testing. Stella was looking forward to some time alone. She hadn't been in touch with her family for a while and wanted to call them. After that, she planned to visit John. She wouldn't mention anything to him about the knife until after receiving the lab results. She wanted to be absolutely positive that it belonged to either John of Phil before saying anything. She had learned long ago not to make assumptions just in case they were false.

While she showered and changed she wondered how long it would take to free her cousin. That would depend on a lot of things. It seemed that the prosecution had an airtight case against John. Things were so complicated. There were so many factors to consider. She had reviewed them over and over again almost to the point of obsession. Here she was dressed and sitting alone in her hotel room doing it again, but she couldn't help it. She inhaled deeply and started from the beginning.

'*It's impossible to track down the driver of the pick-up. He could be virtually anywhere and there were no plates to trace the owner. So forget about that.*

We couldn't locate anyone who may have seen John and Phil in the area, and it was quite possible that no one indeed saw them. But as a last resort, we could keep looking.

There is an outstanding warrant for the arrest of José Parés whose prints were found in the plane. If they could find him, he would be able to provide some answers. That could take forever.

As far as the unknown suspect is concerned, who is he? How would they be able to find him even if they knew who he was? It's a huge country and he could be long gone by now. Besides, it could be argued that those prints had been there for days, weeks, or even months and that would merely prove that he had been in the plane. It doesn't prove that he had anything to do with smuggling drugs.

It appears that the two arresting officers covered their butts well. They hold the key to solving this case or at least proving John's innocence. We need to get them! They can't be untouchable!'

But then she drew a scenario.

'Back home, if two cops were suspected of being on the take, a search warrant wouldn't be issued on conjecture alone. There would have to be sufficient evidence against them or they would have to be caught in the act itself. It only makes sense. And it must be the same in this country. We can't prove that the arresting officers stole Phil and John's money belts unless the forensic lab went over Phil's clothing with a fine tooth comb and found traces of fiber that matched Officer Ramirez' clothing. I wonder if they did that? Because according to the police report, Phil was never touched. I'll mention this to Mr. Aguillar. If we can find something to disprove their word, then they should be left wide open for investigation. I wish they had talked more about the arrest.'

Just then her cell phone rang. It was Victor.

"Hi Stella! I'm glad I caught you before you leave. I was just talking to Carlos. I stopped by the lab and dropped off the evidence. They said that the results would be ready by tomorrow morning. Carlos wants us to meet him in his office at nine thirty. Do you want me to pick you up? I can be there around nine."

"Sure! I'll be ready. I'll watch for you in the lobby."

The next morning Stella was waiting in the lobby when Victor pulled up. She exited, hopped into the passenger's side and fastened her seat belt.

"Did you pick up the lab results? What did you find out?"

"The lab was unable to pull prints from the outer encasement of the knife but the blades were protected from the elements. Phil

MacAllister's prints were matched to those found on the long blade. The powdery substance lifted from the seat of the jeep tested positive for cocaine."

"I knew it! I just knew it! Now we have something to work with!"

Before long, Stella and Victor soon found themselves in the attorney's office discussing their findings. Carlos was extremely pleased but wasn't convinced.

"I commend you for your excellent work. We now have something concrete to present to the prosecution when the time comes. But let me remind you that it's all circumstantial evidence. As far a s the knife goes, they will argue that between the time of the crash and the arrest, there was plenty of time for the suspects to wander around in the area. The knife could easily have been accidentally dropped. That's what they will argue."

Stella wasn't satisfied with this explanation. She felt like she was being let down.

"That doesn't make any sense. What would be their motive for wandering around then returning to the plane?"

"Initially, they may have decided to abandon the cargo completely, but then they changed their mind and went back to take at least some of the cocaine and that was their mistake. That's when they were caught. I'm looking at it from the prosecution's side. Unfortunately they could also argue that the cocaine in the jeep was transfer from their clothing. After all, both officers as well as the suspect were inside the plane and that would be a logical explanation."

Victor was getting more frustrated by the minute. He could see Carlos's point in presenting the scenarios, but they were untrue. Now he knew why he didn't pursue law school. It was too exasperating.

"There must be something we are overlooking. I *know* those two cops are guilty. But how can we prove it? We need a search warrant for their personal property. We need to find John and Phil's belongings. They have to be somewhere."

He was seething and secretly wished he could physically confront Officer Ramirez while he was alone in some remote place where he could beat the information out of him. He was strongly tempted to do it yesterday, had the opportunity presented itself.

"There's no way a judge will issue a search warrant. On what grounds would he do that? It seems at this point that those cops are literally getting away with murder and we can't let that happen. I'm going to present this new evidence to Detective Diéz and try to convince him that we do need a warrant. There's no harm in trying. But I wish we had more to go to him with."

"Do you know if lab examined the victim's clothing? There could have been some transfer from Officer Paredés' clothing onto Mr. MacAllister's when he was forced to fire the gun or from Officer Ramirez's clothing when he removed Phil's travel pouch. If Detective Diéz knew the truth, he might find some evidence knowing where to look. That would be cause for a warrant."

"You have made a good point Stella and I'll bring it to Diéz's attention. I'll call and set up a meeting with him. I'm really concerned about John. I can't afford to wait much longer."

The attorney believed that Detective Diéz was a reasonable man and he was eager to talk to him as soon as possible. It was the only option he had. He hoped to free his client before the trial. And in order to do that, they should work together to gather evidence against the real perpetrators. By now, Diéz would welcome the opportunity to hear what John had to say. This new evidence would reinforce his story. If Diéz were in the least bit inclined to believe him, it might be enough to convince him to pressure a judge to issue a search warrant. That would be a step in the right direction. Victor and Stella were relieved to hear this. After all their hard work, they felt that Carlos should do something. They didn't have much success with their attempt to interview the cops but at least they came back with something.

"I'm on my way to visit John at the prison. Can I give him an update on what's going on?"

Stella expected the attorney wouldn't object but she respected his position and she didn't want to say anything without his approval.

"Of course you can. If it weren't for you, I'd be going myself. Please tell him not to give up and that we're doing everything in our power for him."

It was important that John have faith in him and he knew that Stella would give him lots of moral support.

As Stella drove away, she thought about Carlos Aguillar. After his explanation of the evidence from the prosecution point of view, she wondered how good the attorney thought John's chances were. When he said that he was really concerned about John, did he mean that he was concerned for his case? or his person? She knew that he cared about his client, but was he optimistic about his case? She was afraid to ask, because he would never admit anything to her if he thought that John's chances were slim at the moment.

She thought about her trip with Victor to the highlands. She was happy that they didn't come back to Lima empty-handed. But on hindsight, she wished that she had tried a little harder to convince Officer Paredés and Officer Ramirez to comment on the arrest and elaborate on it. She could have agreed to drop the interview, and instead, persuade them to speak off the record. All she had to do was regain their trust. Why didn't she do that?

Before going to the prison she would stop at the hotel and inform Laura and Keith of the latest developments. They must be going through hell with their son behind bars in a foreign country. She was their only immediate source of comfort in their distress. The MacAllisters had left and gone back to Canada with Phil's remains. There was no solid support system for any of them. She was very discouraged. When was this going to end?

CHAPTER 23

Meanwhile Detective Diéz sat at his desk preparing for a meeting with his colleagues. He glanced at his watch, stood up, and proceeded to the conference room where they gathered. When he entered, everyone hushed and the meeting came to order.

"Okay, so far what do we know?" asked Diéz as he stood in front of the blackboard.

"Well, the Cessna was reported stolen five years ago. It was registered to a Michael Morris, an orthodontist who lives in San Diego, California. A complete background check has cleared him as a suspect."

"And what about our suspect John Emerson? What did we learn?"

Diéz picked up a piece of chalk and began outlining the details on the board.

"We did a background check on him. He's a university student majoring in chemical engineering. He's a top student and not a user of drugs, nor was the deceased Phil MacAllister. He has traveled to Europe and to South East Asia and this is his first time in Peru. Apparently he is an avid trekker and travels on a shoestring budget."

A female who shared in the research revealed her findings.

"He is a qualified pilot and has no criminal record. He arrived in Lima on January 1st. He spent some time in Iquitos a few weeks before the crash. It could connect him to José Peres who was born and raised there. There's an outstanding warrant out on Mr. Peres but so far, no luck.

Another colleague spoke up giving his opinion based on what he had just heard.

"It looks like these young men happed upon an opportunity to make some extra cash and things went bad for them. Who knows how they became involved, but it appears that it may have been their first drug run."

Detective Blanco interjected agreeing with him.

"I wouldn't put it past them. They had opportunity and motive. I'd say it's an accurate scenario. It's obvious to me that John Emerson is in this way over his head."

The female added her concerns.

"You may be right but we have been receiving mail from Canada, flooding our office, strongly vouching that it is totally out of character for them. And several reporters from the Canadian news media have been requesting interviews. Apparently both suspects were involved in a campaign against drug abuse at their university."

Detective Blanco responded with enthusiasm.

"Anyhow, we have the evidence we need for the prosecution. It's really too bad that we can't find out who our suspect is protecting. Maybe they threatened him with action against his family."

He looked directly at Diéz. It was his way of reminding the lead investigator that he was previously directly involved and wanted to keep it that way. Diéz wondered where he was going with this. He was about to cut him off but he couldn't get a word in edgewise.

"What is baffling is that he was willing to identify an accomplice, but then all of a sudden, he buttoned right up. I'd like to finish what we started, make him talk."

Diéz frowned and scanned the others without looking at Blanco who continued speaking. The lead detective turned sideways and rolled his eyes. When was he going to shut up?

"His attorney said things that didn't make any sense. I think that we should delve a little deeper and try to arrange another interview with our suspect if his attorney is willing to agree. Maybe we can offer him a plea bargain and we can offer him protection."

Diéz had heard enough. The purpose of this meeting was to share information but Blanco had overstepped his bounds when he mentioned the contents of the interrogation, especially the fact that John was willing to identify another drug smuggler. It was premature and totally inappropriate because John Emerson could become a target for anyone on the inside who wanted to shut him up if word got out. Later he would let Blanco know what he though of him in no uncertain terms.

The room was buzzing with questions. Detective Blanco had incited curiosity and was the center of attention. Diéz wanted to promptly wrap thing up and adjourn the meeting before it got out of hand.

"A lot of this is speculation. I'll see if I can set something up and we can meet later to discuss the results. Thank you everyone for coming and thank you for your input. What has been said in this room stays within its walls. I hope I'm making myself clear. I would also appreciate it, if you would step up your effort in trying to find José Peres. I have a feeling he could play a major roll in this investigation if we can apprehend him."

His words were spoken with a ring of truth. José Peres would be the key, but not in the way Detective Diéz was suggesting.

After everyone left, he remained behind. He braced himself onto the desktop and sat facing the blackboard. The pieces seemed to be coming together all right. Despite the righteous character of these two young students, perhaps the temptation was too great. Money was the root of all evil. They might have gotten away with it, but for the plane crash. If he could trace the drug activities starting with John, his chance of busting a cocaine ring could certainly be possible. He would work on that angle. How could he get the suspect to cooperate? He would have to proceed with caution. The death of Phil MacAllister must be taking a toll on John Emerson. And his lawyer wasn't too happy about the outcome of the questioning that took place the day after his arrest. That hot head Blanco spoiled everything. Where in the world was his brain? How did he ever get accepted into the National Police Force?

Diéz was frustrated. He wanted to penetrate to the core the drug syndicate in his country. This was his opportunity of a lifetime. It wasn't a matter of power or recognition for him. It was a matter of justice for the victims of drugs and their families as well as preventing future drug abuse.

He hopped down from the desk determined to succeed. He would call Carlos Aguillar and request a meeting. He wanted a statement *now* and if the suspect were not prepared to give one, he would suffer the consequences. He would lose his opportunity to a plea bargain. This was going to be a one-time offer.

CHAPTER 24

Stella was eager to visit John. She could hardly wait to inform him of the new developments however small they were. She sat across from her cousin and smiled at him. He looked so sad. She hoped to cheer him up a little and in the end she did, even more than she had anticipated, in the most unexpected way.

When she filled him in on the details of her trip, she praised Victor for his quick thinking, understanding, and compatibility. She wanted her cousin to know that they were a solid team.

"We found Phil's knife with his initials etched on the blade."

John's mood brightened at this revelation.

'I knew she would find something!'

"What else did you find?"

He seemed to be distracted and was holding something in his hand.

"What have you got there?"

"Look at this."

He produced the photo of himself and Phil, the one his father had given him .He held it up for her to see and pointed to Phil. He wanted to emphasize to Stella the urgency of serving justice and punishing those responsible for his murder.

"They killed him," he said angrily.

"You've got to help me prove it, if only for the MacAllister's sake.

Stella studied the photo of the smiling young men with their hockey sticks. She hadn't seen John's friend in over five years but she recognized him as that same fourteen year old Phil MacAllister that she knew then. She babysat for her Uncle Keith and Aunt Laura and remembered that the two boys played together. Memories of those days filled her mind. Hoping to cheer her cousin up, she smiled at him and reminisced.

"I remember the time that the two of you came home from school and you couldn't figure out how I knew that you had gotten into the peanut butter jar. You were too young to realize that the smell of peanut butter reeked on your breath from a mile away. And I hate peanut butter!"

There was an awkward moment of silence. This was not a good idea.

Why did I go and open my big mouth? This is the last thing he needs!

Stella's intentions backfired. She could see that John was upset. He let the photo slip through his fingers. Stella's eyes followed it as it landed on the shelf in front of the glass window that separated them. It landed upside down from her point of vantage. She turned her head this way and that as if to decipher a puzzle. Then she looked up in astonishment.

"Was Phil left-handed or was he just posing that way for the picture?"

John responded immediately.

"Yes he was. That's a strange question. Why do you ask?"

Stella placed her elbows on the shelf and cupped her hands under her chin. She was attempting to recall the evidence from the file in Carlos Aguillar's office the day she arrived. When he showed her copies of the crime scene photos, she thought that the gun was near Phil's right hand and not his left hand but she couldn't be positive. Before saying anything to John about this, she wanted to verify it first. But he was too quick for her and had put two and two together.

"That's it!" he exclaimed with jubilance, "What a stupid mistake! He put the gun near Phil's right hand when he is left-handed. Ha! We got him!"

John's eyes sparkled as he carried on.

"He always used his left hand. In grade school everyone called him 'Lefty' because he pitched baseball with his left hand. You can even ask any of his teachers which hand he wrote with!"

Upon hearing this, his cousin immediately cautioned him to use discretion.

"Just a minute John, keep this to yourself for now. It's really a good sign but I don't want you to say anything to anyone. I'll bring this to Mr. Aguillar's attention and he will know what to do with this new development."

They discussed the implication it would have in the investigation and the positive effect it would have for his release. John returned to his cell more optimistic than ever.

When visiting hours were over, the investigator left the prison wondering how much longer John would have to spend behind bars. She hoped that it would be a matter of a day or two. As soon as she entered her car, she called Carlos Aguillar from her cell phone.

"Hello Mr. Aguillar, this is Stella Bennett. I realize it's getting late but I have something important to tell you. I'd like to come over right away if you don't mind. Can you fit me in?"

She didn't think that he would refuse.

"Well, if it's urgent, I can see you after my last appointment which should be in about an hour. Can you come over then?"

"Guaranteed I'll be there. I'd like Victor to be there as well. Is it all right if I call and invite him?"

"Sure. I'll see you then."

She called Victor and informed him of her meeting with the attorney, inviting him to join them. She told him that she had some new evidence. He said he wouldn't miss it for the world, he'd be there in an hour.

She winded her way through the busy side streets taking in the activity. She had plenty of time to kill before her meeting and she took the opportunity to do some more touring of the city. She avoided taking the main arteries because much of the culture was reflected on the back streets that fringed the modern section. Taxi drivers were lined up ahead of her, moving slowly, honking their horns. Finally she crawled past a middle age man who on her side of the street pulling a four feet by four feet cart uphill with sacks of potatoes piled five feet high. His calf muscles bulged with every step. A teenage boy was behind pushing uphill with all his strength. Stella looked on with incredulity. Just like in the highlands, everything was done here was by manual labor. No tillers, no tractors, no lawn mowers, no modern machinery at all.

An indigenous woman was pushing a wheelbarrow full of bananas up the narrow sidewalk to her right. At the intersection, a crowded bus passed by the bus stop where would-be passengers shouted and hailed the driver. But the bus was packed like sardines, no standing room and no sitting room left for other passengers.

As Victor drove to the office, he wondered what Stella had discovered. She wouldn't tell him over the phone. She certainly had a knack for arousing curiosity.

He admired her for her professionalism but was wondering about her personal life. He knew she was single. The information was in her credentials that she had given Carlos when she had first arrived, and of course, his friend deliberately happened to bring it up. But was she in a relationship? He didn't think so because she hadn't mentioned anything about a boyfriend. He was about to find out. As Stella pulled her car into an empty office space, she could see Victor closing and locking his door.

"Just in time!" she thought as she grabbed her briefcase, locked her doors and called out.

"Hey Victor! Wait up!"

At the sound of her voice he glanced around and smiled. The two converged before entering the building.

"Hi amiga! Why are we meeting here?" he asked.

"Ooh! Now it's amiga and not partner," she joked in her raspy voice.

She dared to be flirtatious because lately she couldn't get him off her mind. She wondered if he could say the same about her. She had hoped that one day soon it would be dinner and a movie. As the two pranced down the concrete walkway, Victor looked her in the eye and popped the question.

" How about dinner and a movie some night? You're not married or seeing anyone are you?"

I can't believe he said that.

She smiled at him and was quick to respond.

"Actually I *was* seeing someone but we're not committed in any way. Yes, I'd like that."

"I'm a pretty good cook and I'd like to prove it to you. Do you like seafood?"

"How did you know? I love seafood. It's my favorite," she said as she was thinking about what she would wear.

"Then how about tomorrow night? Do you have any plans? We could have an early dinner then go out to the movies. That would be a different kind of adventure for us."

"Tomorrow night would be great! I'm looking forward to it! But I don't know where you live?" She spoke with a lilt in her voice.

"Don't worry. I'll have a cab pick you up at your hotel, save you driving through the city. Is six o'clock too early?"

" Six o'clock is perfect. But promise me you won't talk about work, okay?"

"Ha! Look who's talking!"

Victor opened the entrance door and followed Stella to the elevator. When they arrived at the office, the last client of the day had just left and Carlos was waiting for them. They greeted one another and immediately got down to business.

"So! You have some good news I hope? What is it that can't wait until tomorrow?"

Victor was just as anxious to learn why Stella had wanted to meet here in the office. His conversation on the way in had gotten sidetracked and he hadn't a clue as to why he was summoned here. Stella smiled ever so slightly, a smile similar to the Mona Lisa. The corners of her mouth turned up ever so slightly, as if she had a secret. Victor wondered what it was. She was so appealing.

"First of all, I'd like to see the photographs of the crime scene and then I'll explain. John pointed something out to me today that I think might clear him but I need to see those pictures."

She was praying that the gun was placed near Phil's right hand, otherwise she was getting all excited for nothing.

Carlos removed John's file from the cabinet. He spread the photos taken at the crime scene across his desktop. Stella found what she was looking for and pointed it out.

"The one photo that interests me is the one of Phil with the gun beside his right hand. This one right here."

The victim lay sprawled in a pool of blood, face down. The image remained imprinted on Stella's mind as she spoke. She tried to remain objective and not dwell on it.

"If you'll look, you'll see that the gun is placed near Phil's right hand. I say 'placed' because Phil MacAllister was left-handed. There is no way he would have voluntarily used his right hand unless he was forced to, and it fits the profile, matching perfectly with John's account."

She looked up and stared at the two men in her presence, waiting for their reaction. They were quiet while they allowed the information to sink in, absorbing the positive impact this would have on the case. Carlos was the first to speak. He gave Stella a quizzical look.

"How did you find this out? I believe you, but how did this come about? I mean after all this time, we didn't know or even think to ask."

"John was the one who pointed it out to me. It all happened by accident when he showed me a picture of him and Phil. Phil was holding a hockey stick in his left hand. When I questioned John, he claimed that everyone knew that Phil was left-handed. I was very tempted to ask him for the photograph so that I could show you, but he seemed so attached that I didn't have the heart to ask him for it.

Anyhow, do you think that we have enough evidence now to prove John's innocence?"

The attorney smiled. The timing was perfect. Along with the knife and trace of cocaine, he had something indisputable to present to Detective Diéz. As he pondered his next move, he heard himself speaking in a low voice.

"When detective Diéz hears what we have to say, he won't be so adamant."

"And let him explain why a person under extreme duress, fleeing for his life, would instinctively reach for his gun with his right hand when he's in fact left-handed. The gunshot residue was found on his right hand, not his left hand," exclaimed Victor.

"And let him explain why Phil's Swiss Army knife was found in the exact location where John had asked him to search," added Stella.

She recalled the day and the moment of the discovery. She would give anything to see the look on Diéz's face.

"We have enough evidence to free John and I think it's enough to persuade Detective Diéz to conduct an internal investigation into the death of Phil MacAllister. I haven't been able to get a hold of him yet. When I called earlier, he was in a meeting. I'll call him right away. Thanks for the good work."

Carlos deliberately looked at his watch. He had a habit of doing that when he was in a hurry but it was getting late and he still had more work to do.

"I think we should get going. Is there anything else you'd like us to do?"

"No, not for now but we'll keep in touch. I'll let you know how it goes."

As soon as they left, Carlos picked up the phone and called the precinct.

"This is Carlos Aguillar I'd like to speak with Detective Diéz. Is he in?"

The switch board operator connected the call.

"This is Detective Diéz. How may I help you?"

"Detective Diéz, this is Carlos Aguillar. Some new developments have come up in the John Emerson case and I really think that in the best interest of everyone concerned, we should meet as soon as possible. You'll be surprise at what we have learned since our last meeting. I promise, you won't be disappointed."

"Mr. Aguillar! What a coincidence! I'm glad you called. I was just about to call you. What new developments are you talking about? I also have some questions for your client. Is he prepared give a statement?"

"My client is prepared to answer all of your questions. He's ready to give you his statement under the condition that you allow him to read it uninterrupted, then you can question him when he is finished."

John was better at expressing himself on paper than orally so his attorney suggested that he prepare his statement in writing. Carlos had already edited it and given his final approval. John would sign it in the presence of the persons assigned to his case.

"That sounds reasonable. I promise he won't be interrupted, but we do have some questions for him. Can we meet first thing tomorrow morning at eight o'clock?"

"I'll see you then."

Carlos Aguillar hung up the phone and leaned back in his chair. He could afford to relax a little. This was the break in the case that he needed. Things were finally beginning to move forward for the first time.

After hanging up, Diéz recalled the last interrogation. He remembered clearly the stark look of confusion on John's face when it ended so abruptly. He didn't blame the attorney for his decision. Detective Blanco shouldn't have been there. This time, instead of having detective Blanco present when John was giving his statement, Diéz would ask Detective Cortéz to accompany him. Blanco wouldn't be too happy, but too bad. He was known to be a tactless at times and Diéz didn't want any screw-ups like the last time.

The next morning, they each sat quietly, full of anticipation. John was prepared to present his statement. He had quietly practiced telling his story to pass the time in his cell. He had placed emphasis in all the right places and had raised and lowered his voice in the appropriate spots for effect. He was now ready. He lowered his eyes and spoke in a pleasant tone. The detectives were captivated throughout the reading of his account. It was just as John had practiced, only this time his audience was real. He had paused and looked up at them at times, just to make certain that they were listening. They were listening all right. What they heard was astounding. When John was finished, he sat back in his chair and gave a huge sigh of relief. He was glad it was over. The defense attorney addressed the detectives.

"There are two things I'd like to point out to you before you question my client. First, a Swiss Army knife belonging to the deceased, Phil MacAllister, was found partially buried in the mud where you sent your rookies to search. The owner's prints were lifted from the blade where his initials were etched.

Second, Phil MacAllister was left-handed. He fired the gun with his right hand with the help of someone who didn't know that. Here's the proof right here."

He placed the photo on the table in front of the detectives. Their eyes immediately lowered and focused on the new evidence before them. John and his attorney sat and watched in silence, awaiting their reaction.

For Detective Diéz, his intuition about John was proving right. There was something about this young man that didn't quite fit the profile of a criminal but he could not rely on intuition alone. The initial investigation was mostly based on the police report. But now, he thought he had good reason to reopen the investigation into Phil MacAllister's death based on the new evidence. This time he would be more thorough.

"It's unfortunate that you didn't tell us this sooner," said the detective.

"We will have to verify for ourselves this new information. The medical examiner should be able to confirm the fact that the deceased was left-handed."

Detective Diéz recalled the conversation he had with the M.E. regarding the calluses on the deceased's hands. He could guess what he was going to say. He intended to get in touch with him as soon as possible.

"I believe that we can work together but I must use protocol. We will have to re-examine the evidence. You stated that you could identify one of the escapees whom you encountered. Would you be willing to work with one of our sketch artists?"

John was encouraged and relieved to hear this because perhaps now the detective was beginning to accept the truth.

"I'll do anything to get out of this hellhole of a prison, "said John.

"Can we go now? Am I free to go?"

"I'd like to release you, but I can't until I verify the evidence to corroborate your statement. Be patient and we'll get to the bottom of this," replied the detective. John was fed up with protocol and procedures. He was nearly in tears.

"Be patient! Be patient! That's all I hear! You're not the one who has to live under these depressing, despicable conditions! Someone get me out of here!"

He was raising his voice and losing control.

Carlos squeezed his arm and spoke in a soft, gentle, voice.

"Please, calm down John. You're making matters worst for yourself. Close your eyes and take some deep breaths. I promise you that I will do everything in my power to get you out of here as soon as possible."

John resigned himself by closing his eyes and shaking his head.

'*How many times have I heard **that** line?*'

The defense attorney gazed at the detective. He was speaking as if to John, but his words were meant for Detective Diéz.

"I'm sure that the detective will go over the evidence again with a fine-toothed comb. He is just as determined to pursue justice and get to the truth as we are."

Carlos phrased his next statement carefully because he didn't want to appear to be telling Diéz how to do his job.

"Maybe he will get a search warrant and find your missing passports. And maybe they will confront the arresting officers with what they know. Then who knows what the results will be? If they confiscate and examine the clothing that the officers wore the day they murdered Phil MacAllister, they might find evidence that will prove your story true.

As for motive in the assassination of an innocent tourist, I'd say there was plenty of cocaine to confiscate and turn into profit."

Then he added an afterthought.

"They will have a sketch of the man who you saw running away. If they would run it through their database they might come up with an identity."

'That will give them plenty to think about.'

The detectives knew what they had to do. Finally things were beginning to register. The attorney could see by the looks on their faces, that he had been successful. He was pleased when he heard the response.

"I'll tell you what," said Diéz as he glanced from John to his attorney.

"I'll check with the M.E. and I'll check with two suitable independent reference persons as well, a coach or professor from his university. If there is proof that the deceased was in fact left-handed, and we can produce incriminating evidence against the arresting officers, I'll arrange for your immediate release. Unfortunately we can't drop the charges until this is confirmed. Then I'll arrange for you to work with our sketch artist for an identity on the unknown suspect and we'll see what we come up with. But you will not be allowed to leave the country because we need you as a witness."

John would have to be satisfied with this for now. He had no other choice. He wasn't pleased at the fact that he would still be a prisoner inside this country since he couldn't leave, but he was willing to make the sacrifice in order to keep his promise to Phil. He would make certain that his best friend's murderers were behind bars before he left the country.

After the defense attorney left, the detectives agreed to meet in the small break room that was often used for informal discussions. It was apart from the main cafeteria. They entered and poured themselves a coffee from the coffeemaker on the counter. Detective Cortez stood rubbing his neck and loosening his tie as he began speaking.

"That was quite an incredible story. What do you think? Is he telling the truth? I don't know about you, but he has *me* convinced."

Diéz leaned on the counter and took a sip of his coffee.

"Up until now there was no reason to disbelieve Officers Paredés and Ramirez. There was no evidence to contradict what was in their report. But on hindsight, something was bothering me. I checked out the place where the suspects were supposed to have hidden. It was merely a low-lying mound of rock. I couldn't see any place where they could have hidden themselves. I wondered how the officers could have walked right past the area without seeing the suspects then turn around and suddenly see them running, doubling-back to the plane.? It didn't make any sense. But at the time, I took Officer Paredés at his word."

He was upset with himself for being so careless. He didn't want to see an innocent man go to prison because of sloppy police work.

"We really need to look into this," said Cortéz who paused and then continued.

"You know, we had the lab look for prints on the gun. I wonder if they found anything else? Like lint from Officer Paredés's jacket. They may have missed it if they were only looking for prints. I'll have them check it out. We also need the officers clothing to check for gunshot residue. I wonder what else we may have missed since we weren't concentrating on evidence that would incriminate the arresting officers. We have to go back."

Detective Diéz made up his mind.

"I'd like you to come along with me to question Officers Paredés and Ramirez. We are going to get some answers and we are going to get the truth. They'll have some explaining to do and I can hardly wait. In the meantime get your gear together. We'll go by car. I don't want to alert them taking the chopper. I want to surprise them."

Diéz stood staring into space. He imagined the events as John Emerson had described them. After having observed his expressions and having heard his detailed account, it was probably true. He was anxious to find out.

CHAPTER 25

Stella felt great. She fantasized the details of her date with a hot Latin American while she showered, blow dried her long thick auburn hair and tied it back neatly. She meticulously applied light make-up, just enough to make a subtle difference. She stood with her closet door open choosing one of three outfits. When she left Canada, she had no idea that she would have need to dress for a special occasion such as this. She had thrown her work clothes, grooming necessities and toiletries into her suitcase. She was in a hurry. At the last minute she grabbed a couple of dresses just in case.

She reached for her sleeveless emerald green dress with a flare. She merrily hummed random notes as she anxiously slipped it over her head and zipped it up the back. The waist was no longer snug like it used to be. She placed her hand on her stomach and examined the fit. It was perfect. She could relax tonight not having to concentrate on holding in her abdominal muscles. That boosted her self-esteem, not that it was ever low. She scrutinized herself in front of the full- length mirror behind the door. Her heart fluttered and her hands were sweaty.

'I've got to relax. This is ridiculous. I'm behaving like a nervous teenager getting ready for her first date. Maybe I should have a glass of wine to calm myself down? No! Not a good idea!'

She decided to turn on the T.V. She couldn't concentrate as she flicked through the channels. After a time, the phone rang giving her a start. Finally the taxi had arrived. She slipped into her matching open toe high heel shoes, grabbed her purse and left closing the door behind her.

Victor lived in an apartment building not far from where Stella was staying. She wondered why he had sent a cab for her. She could have walked the distance. It was a safe neighborhood. But then again, why take any risks? Victor buzzed her in and she took the elevator to his floor. He answered the door with a beaming smile, pecked her on the cheek and bid her entry to his bachelor's pad. She looked ravishing.

"Hi! Come on in! I hope you're hungry!"

Stella smiled. Victor was donned in an apron with a few soiled spots on the bib. It was the last thing she expected to see, a hand- some sleuth wearing an apron.

"You look like you've been busy. I'm starved."

Stella discretely surveyed the living room as she stepped inside. It was small but not cluttered, with a brown sofa and matching recliner chair, a typical male color. The coffee table supported a cluster of mixed house- plants in a hand- painted clay pot. An alluring aroma beckoned her into the kitchen. She followed Victor who stepped over to the stove and adjusted the element. Then he untied the apron, took it off and rubbed his hands together.

"Have a look around. Make yourself comfortable. I'll be with you in a moment."

He stood at the counter chopping the last minute vegetables while Stella browsed around.

 Off to one side was a small alcove. She noticed that it was a din- ing area with a window view of the city lights. The table was set with matching cutlery and a sparkling white linen tablecloth. In the cen- ter, a tall vase held two long stem roses. Two lit candles stood sym- metrically, one on each side. Soft music played in the background.

Mmm! He certainly has a fine touch for romance!

"You have a really nice place here," said Stella, genuinely impressed as she looked about. She also noticed how 'spiffy' Victor appeared. With a fresh haircut, clean- shaven and smartly dressed he looked like he just stepped out of a men's fashion magazine. He was more attractive than ever.

"Thanks. It's not always this neat," he chuckled as he thought about his panic, shoving newspapers, magazines, and pieces of clothing into the closet and hidden spaces before she arrived.

"Dinner will be ready shortly. Would you like a glass of wine while we are waiting?"

He had everything under control but didn't want to rush into the meal before relaxing and spending some quality leisure time with her. In the short time that he had known her, everything had been business, business, and more business. This was different. It was an official date and he wanted it to be a success.

"A glass of wine would be nice. Are you going to join me?"

"Of course I am. I have some fine Chilean wine. It's Casillero del Diablo. I have red or white. Which would you prefer?"

"I'll have some white please."

"White Casillero del Diablo coming right up!"

Victor opened the fridge door and took out the bottle of wine. He set it on the counter. He then opened a cutlery drawer, located the corkscrew and used it to open the bottle of wine. Stella took it upon herself to fetch the wineglasses from the table and set them down on the counter for Victor to fill. Then she strolled over to the table and sat down, deliberately giving her host some space. Victor handed her the glass and sat comfortably across from her, holding his own glass up as if to make a toast.

"Thank you!" she said. "What should we toast to?"

' It would be nice if he suggested something other than 'to our health,' or 'good luck in the future'.

Victor paused and thought for a long moment before he answered.

"Let's toast to the 'delightful evening' we are going to have!"

They smiled simultaneously, clicked their glasses and took their first sip.

"Mmm! This wine is delicious! I must remember the name of it and buy some. I wonder if it's' sold in Canada? If I happen to see it I'll think of you."

"I'm sure you can find it there. It's shipped to countries around the world, one of Chile's main exports."

Victor sat staring at Stella. As she took another sip, his eyes rested on her lips. They were delicately tempting. Stella noticed his stare.

"What?" she asked, wanting to know what was on his mind.

"Did I ever tell you how beautiful you are? I don't think so! You look stunning!"

Stella felt flattered and accepted the compliment gracefully.

"Thank you! And did I ever tell you how handsome you are? I don't think so! You're quite an attractive man and this is already beginning to be a delightful evening. I'm thoroughly enjoying this."

She took another sip and they chatted about this and that, keeping it light. Victor topped up her glass then raised from his seat. By the time he served dinner, her glass was empty.

The meal was superbly delicious. They took their time savoring each and every bite along with each and every glass of wine. They talked about their families and touched on previous romances. Like Stella, Victor had had one serious relationship in the past. Since the breakup he hadn't met anyone suitable enough for a long-term relationship. But that didn't mean he wasn't looking. While on the subject of relationships, Stella tilted her head and expressed her opinion.

"I'm not sure I want to bring children into this world. There are so many kids out there who are neglected and are waiting to be adopted, that I hesitate to think about becoming a parent. I suppose that's why I've avoided getting into another serious relationship. Maybe I'm just plain selfish but that's how I feel."

"I've observed first hand how you are with children. You're a natural and I can see that there's a place in your heart for them. You'd make a great volunteer worker helping children, and a great mother."

She had often thought about that, but this conversation was leading to somewhere she didn't want to go right now. It was getting too serious for her so she politely smiled and continued sipping her wine.

When it was time to depart for the movie theatre, Stella felt a little mellow. She confessed that she wasn't accustomed to drinking wine or any other alcoholic beverage as far as that goes. Then she giggled and said that it tasted good and that she could get used to it.

"As a matter of fact," she said, "let's pop open that bottle of red Castillo del Diablo and give it a try. We don't need to go out to the movies. We can see if there's a good movie on T.V. and sit right here in the living room and watch it."

Victor didn't mind at all. Stella was catching a buzz and he didn't want to spoil it for her. She probably needed to unwind from all the stress in her life lately. He would go along with whatever she wanted to do. He switched on the television and handed her the remote.

"I'd love for us to stay here and watch a movie. That's a good idea. Why don't you see what's on while I open the other bottle?"

Stella flicked through the channels. There were plenty of films to choose from. Neither one of them had seen 'The Mask'. They had heard that it was a good movie so they ended up picking that one. It was an excellent choice because it was outrageously hilarious. Just what they both needed! A good laugh! They agreed that no one could play the role like Jim Carrey. He was perfect. They shared their bursts of laughter along with the bottle of wine, which made a good combination.

On the odd occasion when Stella was captivated by the movie, Victor would steal a sideward glance at her and admire her zest for life. He could see by her reactions to the movie, that she had an out-standing appreciation for comedy. Maybe the wine had something to do with it. He rationed his wine making it last. That was all he had and he didn't want to run out.

When the movie ended, he was sorry it was over. He held his arm around Stella's shoulder and she was snuggled up to him. He felt the scarf that tied her hair in place dangle and tickle his arm. He automatically tugged lightly on the end of it and the scarf slid off. Stella felt his fingers glide across her neck giving it a tingling sensation as he played with long strands of her hair. He drew it closer to his face and inhaled the sweet, intoxicating aroma of her shampoo. Stella turned to face him not realizing how close he was to her. He was so close that she felt his breath on her face and she had difficulty focusing her eyes. It made her dizzy. Or was it the wine?

"You should wear your hair down more often. It becomes you," he whispered.

He slipped his hand behind her head and ever so slowly drew it closer to his. He bent his head and his lips lightly brushed hers, teasing her to respond. As their lips met she extended her arm and ran her fingers through his hair, not wanting to stop. She closed her heavy eyes and her mind was swimming as she melted in his arms feeling feverish. That was the last thing she remembered before she dropped her head and passed out.

Victor carefully rose from the sofa while he supported her, then gently lowered her down to where he was seated. He knew she would have to stay the night. Should he carry her to his room and he could sleep on the couch? No, he had better not. She might be upset when she awakens in unfamiliar surroundings. He raised her head and placed a cushion underneath it. Then he raised her feet up onto the other end and removed her shoes. He went to the closet for a blanket to cover her with. After draping it over her, he stood and stared down at her. God! She was beautiful! He was going to miss her once this was all over. How much longer was it going to last? He had no idea.

He switched off the T.V. and went to bed. It took him a long time to fall asleep because he wanted to be awake when Stella woke up. He didn't want her to sneak out in the morning or even before then.

In the morning when Stella opened her eyes, she was disoriented. She had slept for eight hours without stirring. It didn't take her long to become aware of where she was and how much she had consumed last night. She had a terrible thirst and when she raised her head a few inches off the pillow, it felt really heavy. She wondered what time it was and looked at her watch. She sunk back down and shut her eyes felling more embarrassed than anything.

'*Oh no! What have I done?* **Now** *what does he think of me?*'

She could hear water running in the kitchen and the sound of dishes clicking together. The rich aroma of freshly brewed coffee penetrated her nostrils. She knew that Victor was up.

'*I had better get up now and face the band.*'

She rose slowly and tiptoed into the kitchen. Victor stood buttering breakfast rolls and detected movement from the corner of his eye. When he saw her he smiled.

"Well good morning beautiful! How do you feel?"

"Like I've just been run over by a truck. I'm so sorry Victor. I don't know what to say."

He walked over to her and faced her squarely. Stella stood her ground.

"Well maybe this will make you feel better."

He cupped her chin in his hand, bent his head and tenderly kissed her. He lingered, relishing her sweet taste. Then he let go and stared into her hazel eyes.

"You don't have to say anything. Last evening was truly delightful. And by the way, when I told you that you looked stunning, I meant it, and you still do."

He slipped his hand into hers and led her to the table where he had been drinking his morning coffee.

"Would you like a cup of coffee and some breakfast?"

"I'm dying for a cup of coffee but I'll pass on the breakfast thanks. My stomach isn't a hundred percent."

She joined him at the table where they raved about last night's movie and the fun they had watching it. Stella kept apologizing for drinking so much wine saying that she wasn't used to drinking and that it was the first time in her life that she had ever passed out.

'*If it was going to happen, why did it have to happen here last night? Thank goodness he didn't seem to think it was an issue. Or at least if he did, he didn't let on.*'

They finished their coffee and Stella felt much better after eating a couple of breakfast rolls that Victor insisted she have.

"I think I had better leave now. I promised John I would find out the procedure on applying for a new passport. He anticipates that he will be able to go home soon. I hope he's right. In the meantime I want to know how long it takes to process a new one so that he'll be ready when the time comes. All the red tape will be out of the way."

"And what about you, are you looking forward to leaving? Because I'm just beginning to get a glimpse of the intimate personal side of you and I like what I see. I'd like to get to know you better."

"I feel the same way about you." Stella reciprocated. "But I have to be honest. I *am* looking forward to leaving. But who knows what can happen between now and then?"

She raised her eyebrows giving him a seductive look, slipped into her shoes, then slung her purse over her shoulder.

"I really must get going. Thanks for the wonderful time," she said as she leaned forward, pecked him on the cheek and left.

CHAPTER 26

Detective Diéz and his partner arrived in Santa Inés without warning. The lab had come up positive for traces of fiber on the weapon. They didn't match   Phil MacAllister's clothing so they wanted to find out if they matched Officer Paredes's clothing. They were prepared for a confrontation.

It was early morning and there were no vehicles parked near the police station. Cortéz tried the door. It was locked. It wasn't necessary to obtain a search warrant for the place, being it was already police property. The judge refused to issue a search warrant for the officers' homes. He said to come back with more concrete evidence. For the time being they were here to question the officers and at the same time they could do some snooping of their own. They came prepared to make an arrest but it would depend on the circumstances.

Detective Cortéz produced several keys on a large key ring and tried several of them before the door swung open. Diéz was the first to enter. He immediately recalled the day he was here to pick up the young prisoner. The place was neater then. He glanced around. Candy wrappers were strewn over the desk. There was a cot set up against the wall, blankets and bedding in disarray. A dog's water dish had spilled over revealing a damp spot on the concrete floor. A stale dinner roll lay beside it, abandoned by the animal for which it was intended. Diéz pointed to the filing cabinet.

"You take the cabinet over there and I'll search the desk."

"What exactly are we looking for?"

"We'll know when we find it."

The bottom desk drawer was deep. When Diéz opened it, it contained a bottle of

Peruvian rum with about three shots remaining. He held it up.

184

"Would you look at this!" he exclaimed.

His partner who was picking through the files looked up.

"Ha!" he laughed, "They left some for us. Did you find anything else?"

" So far, there's nothing here. What about you, did you find anything?"

"These reports are so old. They go back ten years or more. I suppose they keep them here because there isn't enough paperwork to store away in boxes. The tabs on each folder are marked according to the year but they aren't in order. I can't find 2008."

He pulled out a thin unmarked folder.

"What's this?"

Two pieces of paper stapled together fell out to the floor. Detective Diéz was tugging on the top right hand drawer of the desk. It was stuck and refused to budge. Finally it opened exposing the original police report that Officer Paredés had filled out. The officer had intended to destroy it the morning that Diéz arrived to pick up the suspect but the detective had arrived before he did. Then he had planned to do it later but forgot about it. That was a big mistake.

Diéz picked up the report at the same time that his partner was bending over to pick up the contents of the folder. When they discovered that there were two police reports, they placed their findings side by side on the desktop. They wondered why there were two reports. They bent over taking turns reading each one of them. They read them a second time just to be clear about the difference. And there was a huge difference. Detective Diéz pointed to the one he had found in the drawer.

"According to this report, when the officers initially arrived, they spotted the suspects fleeing from the scene. They pursued them on foot but when they realized that the suspects were getting away, Officer Paredés fired a warning shot and ordered them to stop. One of them stopped but the other kept running so Officer Paredés shot him in the thigh in order to stop him. Then the suspect dropped to his knees, produced a gun and fired in his direction. Then Officer Paredés returned fire killing the suspect."

Cortez pointed to the other report.

"This is the report that we received. It says that when the officers initially arrived, the scene was abandoned. Upon searching the area, the suspects were caught backtracking to the plane for cover. Officer Paredés fired a warning shot and ordered the suspects to stop. One of the suspects continued to flee. Paredés shot him in the thigh in order to stop him. When the suspect fell on his knees, he produced a gun and fired at Paredes. That was when Paredés returned fire with the fatal bullet."

Cortéz turned to his partner.

"We have two police reports that are inconsistent with one another."

"And I know why," said Diéz. "The day of the crash, Officer Paredés told me that he had to shoot one of the suspects when he was fleeing because he produced a gun and fired at him. When I questioned Officer Paredés about the position of the body, it had alerted him about the error he had made in his first report, the one that I found in the drawer. And so he had to write up a new one to suit the evidence. The inconsistencies are too great to ignore. Obviously these cops are covering up something."

Cortéz bent over the reports and scrutinized the signatures of Eduardo Paredés.

"Do these two signatures appear to be the same to you?"

Diéz reached into his pocket and pulled out a pair of reading glasses.

" I don't know. They are certainly similar. This one here seems a bit shaky and the capital 'P' is slightly different. Why? What are you thinking?"

"I can't be sure but I believe one of them may be a forgery. Let's take these back for analysis."

Suddenly the two local officers came bursting through the door. They had seen the official police vehicle parked outside and they had every reason to be apprehensive.

"What are you doing here?" blurted Officer Ramirez.

The two detectives were caught off guard and were startled by the rude intrusion. Cortéz scooped up the reports and shoved them into his pocket. He wanted to avoid an immediate confrontation fearing the two would become hostile if they realized what they were up to.

"We have a right to be here. We are conducting an internal investigation into Phil Mac Allister's death."

"Why would you do that?" inquired Officer Paredés shrugging his shoulders and trying to appear innocent although he was gripped in fear.

"As you know it's routine department policy. We just have a few questions for you," responded Diéz.

Officer Ramirez was getting nervous. His eyes kept shifting to the tiny, old, wood stove in the corner. He stared at it as he spoke in defense of his partner.

"Everything is in the police report. The suspect had a gun."

His eyes returned to Detective Cortéz who had been observing him. The detective moved closer to the wood stove trying to look nonchalant but he was suspicious. Immediately Eduardo intercepted him and stood in front of the stove. He tried to distract him which made matters worst for himself. He gestured to the chair.

"Would you like some coffee. Have a seat and I'll put a pot on. We can answer your questions and clarify things over coffee."

Meanwhile, Officer Paredés didn't like the idea of an investigation.

"I shot him in self-defense. There's no doubt about that," he said.

Detective Cortéz ignored his statement and replied to Officer Ramirez.

"No thank you but you can make a fire. It's cold in here."

Eduardo Ramirez gazed at his partner who had no idea what was going on. Unbeknownst to Mauricio, on his own orders to burn the

evidence, Eduardo had thrown it into the stove, added some newspaper and a few sticks and lit a match to it. Now he was in a panic.

'Did I check to see if it was completely burnt? I can't remember.'

"Here, let me help you."

Cortéz reached for the handle of the stove and opened the door.
He bent over and peered inside. Ramirez was praying that all evidence was gone.

"There doesn't appear to have been any wood in here. What have
you been burning?"

He poked around and could see among the scanty ashes, what
looked like a small piece of melted plastic, like the part of a clip of
some kind, the kind they use to clip on money belts or knapsacks.
As he inspected closer, he could see what looked like remnants of a
charred, dark blue passport. He could see the official looking numbers printed on the burnt paper.

"We haven't used that thing in years," Mauricio chuckled, "Sometimes it smokes up so terribly, enough to make one choke. I keep
putting in a request for a new one but the department claims that
the funding isn't available. I've given up on it."

Detective Cortéz motioned to his partner with his arm indicating
that he wanted Diez to approach.

"Detective Diéz, I think you should have a look at this."

Diéz was curious as he bent over and looked inside. He squatted
for a closer study.

Cortéz strolled toward the door anticipating that the two officers
would bolt. Officer Ramirez desperately wanted to do something,
anything, but he froze on the spot. Diéz stood upright and addressed the two now suspects.

"We'd like you to come with us to police headquarters in Lima
for questioning."

"But I thought you said that you came here to ask us a few questions. Why do we have to go to Lima?" retorted Paredés.

"We can't do that on such a short notice. We're not criminals,"
added Ramirez.

Walter Diéz had to make a quick decision. Based on the two different police reports and the remnants among the ashes, he took a risk. He subtly signaled to his partner. The two experienced city slickers were upon the two rural officers in a flash. Before the two officers had a chance to protest they were seized and handcuffed.

"You're both under arrest," said Diéz. "You have a right to remain silent......."

He continued reciting while the struggle was minimal. It happened so fast. The two officers were searched, their weapons removed, and then they were placed into the holding cell. Detective Cortéz locked the door behind them.

"How does it feel to be the prisoners for a change?"

The two prisoners scowled at one another.

"You told me to get rid of the evidence," said Ramirez, " I was just following your orders. I went through the stuff and removed the cash first. I couldn't burn it all."

" Keep your mouth shut stupid! Don't say another word!" threatened Mauricio.

He couldn't believe that his partner could be so naïve. He wanted to literally strangle him.

While Cortéz was being entertained by the two prisoners he put on a pair of latex gloves and carefully confiscated the evidence from the small wood stove. Meanwhile Diéz was on the phone with Lieutenant Amaya arranging for helicopter pick-up transportation back to police headquarters in Lima.

When they arrived and were taken in, everyone on staff stopped what they were doing and stared at the officers who were handcuffed and still in uniform. Eduardo Ramirez hung his head in shame. Much to the contrary, Mauricio held his head high in arrogance although he hid the fact that his pride was hurt and he was embarrassed. The two officers were taken to separate rooms for questioning. Mauricio Paredés attempted to contact his lawyer but he was unavailable. His secretary would relay the message as soon as he became available. Mauricio Paredés was not happy to hear this.

Diéz and Cortéz were discussing their strategy while Eduardo Ramirez was having a lengthy consultation with his attorney. They really wanted to nail Officer Paredés and were pleased to interview his partner first. Diéz had witnessed the excruciating emotional and psychological agony that John Emerson had experienced. It was mostly at the expense of the despicable Officer Paredés but he felt partially responsible.

When they were ready, the two detectives sat across from Officer Ramirez and his attorney.

"We know everything. All the evidence we have supports what John Emerson, the witness, survivor, and the victim in this case, has provided."

Diéz had two envelopes in his hand. He reached in and pulled out the contents opening up the pages for them to see. He could hardly wait to see the reaction.

"We found these in your office," he said. "How do you explain them?"

The officer immediately recognized the original police report that he had signed. His mouth dropped and his eyes bulged. He pointed his finger.

"Where did you get that?"

He looked at his attorney and leaned over with his lips to his ear.

"How can that be? Mauricio told me that he would destroy that report!" he whispered.

The attorney asked if he could examine them. The two detectives watched and remained silent as he read. The lawyer was disappointed and knew right away that the discrepancies were too great to dispute. He leaned over, brought his hand to his mouth and whispered into his client's ear. Before he could respond, Cortéz said to the attorney,

"We found traces of the evidence that your client admitted to burning, the leather travel pouches he took from John Emerson and Phil MacAllister, when they were accosted."

The detectives continued throwing evidence in their faces.

"Did you happen to know that the deceased victim was left-handed and not right- handed? Why would he have a gun beside his right hand when we found him? I'll tell you why, because it was put there beyond a doubt," said Diéz.

Cortéz continued to elaborate. He had found traces of cocaine in the jeep. He didn't have proof that the officers had confiscated any of the cocaine. It could have been from transfer after the officers had searched the plane. But he was willing to bluff.

"We know about the cocaine. We found traces of it in your client's vehicle."

The attorney knew that they were defeated.

"We are prepared to make a deal, plea bargain. My client will tell you everything provided you give him some leniency here. After all, his very life was in danger. He was forced at the hands of a cold-blooded murderer. He believed that if he didn't co-operate with Officer Paredés, he would be killed. He was petrified. He will testify against his partner in exchange for the minimum with parole."

Diéz wasn't convinced.

"Your client had every means at his disposal to stop Officer Paredés from murdering Phil MacAllister."

The attorney drew a scenario for the interrogators.

"What would you have done? Point your gun at Officer Paredés while he had his weapon on Mr. MacAllister and tell him to drop it?"

Eduardo Ramirez elaborated in his own defense.

"Do you really think that my partner would believe that I'd shoot him? He would just laugh at me and tell me to go ahead and shoot, knowing full well that I wouldn't do it. And besides, that would make me the murderer."

Cortéz couldn't refrain from speaking.

"It's your duty to protect the innocent which you've neglected to do. You and your partner are the guilty parties here. Why have you been protecting him? You should have come forward. You are just as guilty of murder as he is? You may as well have pulled the trigger yourself."

Office Ramirez was full of remorse.

"I didn't kill anyone. I couldn't. I'm too much of a coward."

He then bent his head forward and covered his face with his hands because he meant what he had said. His life was ruined. He thought about his wife and little ones. He would miss them. Who would support them? He took a deep breath and glanced at his attorney. His attorney nodded his head in the affirmative indicating that it was okay for his client to go ahead and speak.

"I'll tell you everything but I want some leniency."

"I'll see what I can do. It depends on what I hear."

The detectives smiled inwardly. They were getting the confession they were looking for. Officer Ramirez spilled out the whole story. His account was accurate. It verified John's version of what took place on that fateful day. Diéz remembered his viewing of Phil's corpse at the morgue. He pictured the young student vividly, alive, as Officer Ramirez filled in the morbid details. He imagined Phil's terror and could hardly wait to confront Officer Paredés. He knew that he would have to restrain himself from losing his temper. He was livid. Phil MacAllister didn't deserve to die. He thought about John Emerson and was anxious for him to be to be extricated.

After taking the statement, Officer Ramirez was relieved it was over. He was truly remorseful. Cortéz and Diéz could see some good in the man and felt sorry for him. In a way, he was a victim of his own weakness. He was an enabler. As the prisoner was being lead away, he passed by the interrogation window where his ex-partner in crime was being held. He caught a glimpse of him as he passed. He grimaced and quickly averted his eyes. Then he nodded brusquely as if he were warding off some evil presence. He was sorry he ever met the man.

Officer Paredés was ready to explode just as his attorney walked into the interrogation room. He jumped up from his chair.

"What took you so long? How dare you keep me waiting? You're getting paid good money," he growled.

The irony was that he was being paid '*dirty*' money and the lawyer suspected as much. It wasn't the first time he had come to the rescue of his client. In the past, he had caught his client in a web of lies. No one got hurt because of it, and the attorney was bound not to say anything because of attorney-client confidentiality. This time the lawyer didn't want to be here, given and arrogant disdain displayed by his client. But since he was already here, he would bite his tongue and listen to the charges being brought against Officer Paredés.

He took a seat and kept his cool while he listened to Officer Paredés rant and rave claiming his innocence. Despite each piece of irrefutable evidence Diéz presented, the client would counter. They fabricated the evidence in order to cover up the truth. He didn't have any cocaine in his possession. He was being framed. He admitted that yes, he did shoot Phil MacAllister but it was in self-defense.

He continued on and on until his attorney told him to 'shut up and listen'. When the advice was ignored, the attorney finally gave up and threw his hand in the air.

"Find yourself another lawyer. You're no longer my client," he stated bluntly.

The officer gave him an indignant look and responded with the classic line.

"You can't quit! You're fired."

He made a complete fool of himself. In the end he was taken away and booked for the murder of Phil MacAllister. Diéz was proud of himself for not losing his temper. As far as he was concerned, the man deserved the death penalty for planning and executing such a nefarious deed.

Now that this chapter in the case was closed, he could spend his energy elsewhere. He would concentrate on finding and prosecuting the cocaine traffickers. So far he had one small lead, the identification of José Pares. Since the entire force was concentrating on trying to locate him, hopefully it would only be a matter of time before he was brought in. And he also had a description of the second unknown party.

He planned his next step. The first thing he did was to arrange for John's release. He personally drove to the prison to give him the good news. He signed the release papers and persuaded John to go back to the precinct with him, where his parents, Stella, and Victor would be waiting to welcome him with open arms. It was to be a surprise. Diéz felt that it was the least he could do for John Emerson.

As they left the prison in the police cruiser, John didn't look back. His only regret was that he didn't have a chance to say good-bye to his friend Mike the composer. Mentally, he wished him well.

"I can't believe this ordeal is finally over. I would love to have been there when you arrested those bastards. I would give anything to have seen the looks on their faces. They really thought that they would get away with it and for a while *I* thought they would too. But I guess they met their nemesis when you finally decided to believe me."

He knew that his words were accusingly blunt but he didn't care. He was the one who paid a high price because of this man's mistake. Detective Diéz did not immediately apologize.

"Your defense team was good and you were fortunate enough to have lady luck on your side. If she hadn't picked up that clue in the photo, this case could have dragged on indefinitely."

"And I would still be stuck in that dungeon of a prison indefinitely because you wouldn't believe me," John countered, as he pointed out the would-be consequences.

The detective took a deep breath. He could understand John's attitude but he felt obligated to defend his position.

"Look! I'm sorry you happened to be in the wrong place at the wrong time and you were exploited because of it, but that wasn't my doing. And I'm equally sorry that there was nothing I could do for you after your arrest until we had some hard evidence. Some things in life are not fair and we all make mistakes. But I can assure you, I was doing my job to the best of my ability, and I'm not sorry for that."

For the first time John felt a little sympathy for the detective. He wasn't sure if that was an apology but he was willing to accept it regardless. It wasn't Diéz's fault that the cops in Santa Inéz were murderers, and he couldn't hold the detective responsible for the fact that he had been framed.

"I know what you are saying. I just regret that I invited Phil to come on this trip with me. He would still be alive if I hadn't coaxed him into coming."

Detective Diéz could only imagine the turmoil of emotions his passenger was experiencing, love for his friend, regret, anger, revenge, the quest for justice. He could feel a sense of some of these emotions stir within himself for his own personal reasons.

"I promise the perpetrators will be severely punished. They will be sentenced accordingly if I have anything to say about it, and believe me, I will."

He didn't want to mention the plea bargain. John would be upset. But he had to do what he had to do, whether he liked it or not.

The cruiser pulled into Diéz's parking space and the two proceeded into the precinct, Diéz in the lead. As soon as they entered, his awaiting company spied John, rushed over to him and smothered him with hugs. John reciprocated and raised his eyes. He noticed Detective Diéz watching from a distance. His arms were folded and his stance held a certain kind of dignity as he took pleasure in observing the joyful reunion. Carlos Aguillar was right. He did need John's help. As soon as possible, John would return to do just that, but for now he deserved a couple of days alone with his loved ones.

John, his parents, Stella, and Victor returned to the hotel and spent the rest of the day rejoicing in John's freedom. Keith and Laura would spend the next few days with their son. There would be making long overdue phone calls to their family and friends. They had decided that they would return home, now that John was safe and in good hands. John would have some unfinished business to take care of after they leave. But he would soon follow them back to his homeland.

CHAPTER 27

"His eyes are a little further apart. Yes, like that."

John sat beside the artist who was doing an excellent job putting together a sketch of the escapee. The young man was talented. When he was finished, it was perfect. Detective Diéz had asked for the sketch to be forwarded for comparison and analysis in their database.

When the result turned up negative, needless to say, everyone was most disappointed. Detective Diéz was reluctant to have the sketch publicly posted. The man would be armed and dangerous. Diéz wanted to avoid the possibility of alerting him. He decided to circulate the sketch among the National Police Department and security firms for the time being. He would release it to the media at a later date when John was safely in his own country.

John had signed an affidavit agreeing to return as a witness for the trial if necessary. It would depend on whether or not the criminal was ever apprehended. He was the only witness who could identify the narcotraficante. The drug cartel had at their disposal the ways and means of eliminating any witness who was a threat to them. Diéz was concerned for John's safety. He wanted to make up for his oversight in the way he handled the case. When John was preparing to leave, the detective took him aside.

"We can give you police protection," he said.

"That's not necessary," John insisted.

He had mixed feelings about Diéz. He was very professional and had a gentle disposition but at the same time, he was part of the system that put him behind bars.

"At least let one of our cruisers give you a ride to your hotel."

"No thank you. I'm fine. I'll take a cab."

The last thing John wanted to do was get into another cop car. He was anxious to relish his freedom according to *his* terms. Besides, Stella was there for him. When she had insisted on remaining behind with John, he objected.

"You don't have to do that," he had told her. "I'm old enough. I don't need a babysitter. I really appreciate all you have done for me but you must get on with your life."

But when Stella had explained that she had a developing relationship with Victor and wanted to stay, he smiled.

Before John left, Diéz summoned one of the young rookies.

"I want you to keep an eye on him," he instructed, "I imagine he'll want to leave the country as soon as possible. In the meantime, I don't want to take any chances. Take a minute and change into civilian clothing."

As he was saying this, Detective Blanco, who was standing nearby, overheard him. He slipped out to make a private phone call.

John hailed a cab and gave the driver the name of his hotel. He didn't bother to call Stella. She had planned a visit to the Museo de Arte Virreynal Pedro de Osma. She wanted to see the exquisite collection of colonial art and furniture, as well as metalwork and sculpture from all over Peru. It was a private museum housed in one of the older mansions in Barranco.

He was happy to finally be free. The taxi driver dropped him off, having been given a generous tip. The unmarked car that was following parked a few spaces away from the entrance and waited. John entered the lobby, pranced to the elevator and pressed the third floor button. A mother and her two children entered behind him. The door closed. He smiled at the children and then made a funny face at them when the mother wasn't looking. The children giggled shyly. The elevator stopped at the third floor and he exited leaving his company behind. He walked briskly down the deserted hall and produced his key when he reached his room. He was looking forward to meeting Stella later in the dining room for dinner. He had plenty to tell her. As the door opened, he heard a voice at his back and he froze.

"Hello John!" said the voice as John was shoved into the room and the door was closed. John stumbled as he was being pushed.

" Who are you?"

He turned around to face the man. Then he knew. It was the man in the sketch. He was pointing his weapon at John.

"Raise you're voice and you're a dead man."

"How did you know where to find me?" asked John who was overcome with fear.

"Oh, I have my sources," said the man with the gun. Malcolm Murray smiled.

"What do you want?" John bravely asked.

"Don't play games with me. You know exactly what I'm looking for. Now, where did you hide the cocaine?"

Malcolm was certain that he had taken it and hid it somewhere in the area before the police arrived at the scene of the crash. His informer had access to the confiscated cargo and a lot of it was missing. He wanted it back.

He whacked John across the mouth with the butt of his weapon. John was stunned and stumbled backward falling to the floor. His touched his swollen lip and felt a trickle of blood. He remained there, looking up at the unsightly scar.

"I don't know what you're talking about," he said.

"Oh yes you do! You know exactly what I'm talking about. Nearly half that cargo went missing. Can you tell me what happened to it? Get on your feet right now!"

Malcolm held the gun steady on John as he slowly rose to his feet. John looked around bewildered, as if expecting someone to rescue him.

"You're going to lead the way and I'm going to be right behind you. You'll do as I say. One false move and you'll never see your cousin who is staying here again."

He was bluffing about Stella but it was a vise he had planned to use in order to get John to cooperate. John couldn't believe his ears.

"You have Stella? Where is she? What have you done with her? Please don't hurt her," he begged.

"Just do as you're told and no one will get hurt. Now move! Walk out that door and down the stairs, not the elevator, through the lobby and out the front door. I'll be breathing down your neck so don't try anything funny."

John reluctantly obeyed the orders. Malcolm walked behind covering John with the gun that was hidden under the jacket draped over his arm. As they walked down the hall, they met the same two little kids that were in the elevator on his way up, along with the mother. The children tugged on their mother's skirt and said something to her. She smiled and stopped John wanting to know from which country he came. John's eyes widened with fear. His face became distorted and his mouth twitched when she opened her mouth to say something. She looked puzzled at his expression and quickly changed her mind. She grabbed her young ones by the hand and dragged them down the hall. It was not a good idea to talk to foreigners. Especially when they made weird faces.

As John and his kidnapper continued down the stairs, the rookie stepped out of the elevator and onto the third floor. He noticed a mother and her two small children being greeted at the door of one of the rooms. He walked past John's room and listened for voices. The room was silent.

Stella returned to her hotel in the late afternoon. Although she thoroughly enjoyed her day, she was tired. She stepped off the elevator and noticed a casually dressed gentleman stalling near John's door a little further down the hall. He was looking her way but quickly turned his head when he noticed her. Stella searched her purse, found the key and opened her door. After entering the room, she kicked off her shoes and plunked herself down into the chair.

'I'll take a quick shower and after that see how John's day went.'

As she sat there, a strange feeling of déjà-vu came over her. She was thinking of the man in the hall.

'I've seen that man before. Where was it?'

Then she remembered. She jumped up opened her door and peeked out. The man was still lingering in the hall. She wanted to catch him off guard. Did his presence have anything to do with her or John? What was his business? She watched and waited until the man was looking the other way then she stealthily opened her door and sneaked up on him.

"What are you doing here?" she asked as she caught him red-handed.

The man stepped from side to side showing a little embarrassment. He had only met her once, briefly at the station when she was inquiring for Detective Diéz. He was surprised that she recognized him. He gave her a lame excuse.

"Oh! Um! I was just in the neighborhood and thought I'd stop in and see how you were doing. Then when I saw you coming down the hall in a hurry, I thought you were too busy and I chickened out." He smiled weakly.

Stella had a problem believing him. She was too clever to be fooled and suspected that something was up. His being here was too much of a coincidence as far as she was concerned. Something was wrong and she would find out what it was.

"So you're off duty! You found out where I'm staying and you're hanging out in the hall! If I didn't know any better I'd have reason to believe that you are stalking me! Did Detective Diez send you here? Where's John? Are you following him?"

She suddenly became alarmed and raised her voice.

"Is he all right?"

Since it was difficult to keep a low profile under the circumstances, the man figured he might as well be honest with her. He didn't want her to panic. He tried to be discreet.

"He's fine! Don't worry! Detective Diez wanted me to keep an eye on him. I followed him here and he must be in his room. He arrived about twenty minutes ago. Sorry, but I'm just following orders."

He shrugged his shoulders and tiny beads of sweat were forming on his brow. Stella softened her mood. She could tell that the poor guy wasn't used to this kind of work.

"You can relax! I won't say anything! As a matter of fact, I really appreciate why you are here. But I can assure you that I'll keep John safe and out of trouble. He's a very smart man and quite capable of taking care of himself. I'm supposed to meet him here in the dining room in an hour. If you're off duty then, maybe you can join us."

She smiled at him not meaning to be sarcastic, then walked back to her room. She was looking forward to hopping into the shower and putting her feet up until it was time to meet John for dinner.

CHAPTER 28

A block away the car was waiting, the motor running in case something went wrong and there would have to be a fast getaway. That wasn't the case. Everything was going according to plans. Malcolm opened the back door and instructed John to get into the car. The kidnapper climbed in beside him discretely holding his gun under his jacket. John desperately wanted to know where he was going.

"Where are you taking me?"

"You'll find out soon enough. If you keep your mouth shut and behave yourself nobody will get hurt." Malcolm said firmly.

They continued to their destination. Wherever that was? John remained quiet as he stared out the window. His palms were drenched. He chastised himself for not paying attention earlier that day. When he left the precinct, was someone following him? He didn't think to check. At the time, his focus was elsewhere, on his freedom.

'*Phil was right. They would come looking for us. Only he isn't here right now.*'

He secretly wished that his friend were here with him. The thought made him feel guilty but least Phil would still be alive.

They were now driving slowly through the slums of the city. They passed a skeleton of an old man who was hunched over a garbage bin, rummaging through it hoping to find a morsel of something to eat. Children with dirty faces, some of them orphans, were rolling an old tire balancing it with sticks. A young kid wearing rags for clothing stood in the middle of the dusty side street, haphazardly waving both arms. The driver slowed to a crawl while honking his horn and the kid jumped out of the way laughing hysterically.

Finally they left the slums and eventually ended up in an upper middle-class residential area. John had tried to form a mental map of where he was going, but there had been too many corners turned and too few street signs. By the time they pulled into the short driveway of a gated residence, the sun had set. The driver closed the iron gate then drove up to the house and parked the car. When he got out, he stood against John's door preventing him opening it in case he intended to try. Their eyes met as they read each other's thoughts.

'Let me out!'

'You can't escape. Don't even try.'

Malcolm opened his door and climbed out, the gun still pointing at his captive from underneath his jacket. He motioned for John to get out. John sat there with his arms folded, looking obstinate, not moving, testing his kidnapper.

'I can play this game too. They won't get the best of me. The bastards! What's he going to do? Shoot me here on the spot. They may have command of my physical being but they can't control my mind.'

Malcolm observed that John remained stationary. He wondered if the man in the car was deliberately trying to be stubborn.

'Is he stoic or just plain stupid?'

He bent over at the waist, peered into the back seat and glared at John. He was unaccustomed to complications in his life. He had learned to avoid them over the years, but he had a score to settle with this young man and he was growing impatient.

"Get out of the car!" he ordered.

John reluctantly obeyed taking his time. He stood weak-kneed on the terra cotta interlocking brick pathway leading to the front door. His eyes moved from side to side. He had to maintain a sharp edge if he wanted to stay alive. There was no guard dog or activity on the premises. But he did notice the high stone wall surrounding the property. There were jagged edges of broken glass cemented into the mortar all along the top of it, which is a common sight in Mexico, Central and South America.

The driver guided him into the house through the side door. Malcolm followed closely behind. They immediately entered the living room. From what John could see, it was quite modern. It was furnished with a teal blue sofa and chair, a slate- top coffee table and matching end tables. A multicolored area rug with an intricate Inca design covered a large section of the ceramic tile floor. A forty-two inch flat screen television stood against one wall. He was escorted through a large archway that joined with the open kitchen. Malcolm pointed to one of the straight back chairs and told John to take a seat. It was six feet away from the table. He was surprised to see place mats and utensils set. A delicious aroma filled the air.

John sat there perplexed, not knowing what would happen next. He knew what these guys wanted but he also knew that he couldn't deliver. If they knew the truth, they wouldn't hesitate to kill him. He would have to play along with them for as long as he could. And then what? He had to be observant and stay alert. He had Stella to think about. She was probably being held somewhere else in the house.

The driver disappeared briefly then returned with a menacing look in his eyes. He appeared with a roll of duct tape and a small pair of scissors in his hands. John stiffened as he focused on the tape. His stomach felt queasy. He didn't know if it was fear or hunger gripping it. The driver took a few steps toward him picking at the end of the tape with his dirty fingernail. He was about to stretch it out as he cast a glance in Malcolm's direction. For John, everything happened in slow motion and his mind went fuzzy. He thought he was going to faint. It was as if he were in some sadistic movie, only this was real life.

Suddenly, Malcolm put his hand up and exclaimed,

"Wait!"

The driver backed off. Malcolm looked at John.

"Are you hungry? A man can't concentrate on an empty stomach. You look scrawny," he teased.

The teasing didn't fizz on John. He didn't care if he looked scrawny but his stomach was growling and he knew he was hungry. He didn't eat much while in prison but his appetite was slowly returning.

'It may be a while before I can eat again.'

He hesitated, uncertain how to respond.

"I could eat a little something," he stammered in a low voice.

Malcolm burst out laughing. It was deep and hearty. He crossed his arms and leaned them on the table. He pushed his seat back and dropped his forehead onto his arms. He continued laughing hysterically. When he finally calmed himself, he raised his head and glared at John with an expression of loathing. He then pointed his index finger to his chest tapping it repetitively.

"I'm the one who tells you what you can and cannot do."

He raised his voice for effect. "Do you understand?"

John sat trembling. He shook his head in the affirmative without raising his eyes. He had always thought that he was incapable of hating, but he was beginning to hate this man.

It was time for the tape. The hostage's arms were pulled back behind the chair and his wrists were taped together. The driver then wrapped the duct tape several times around John's upper body securing it to the back of the chair. Then he wrapped it around his lap securing it to the seat. Next, his ankles were pulled together and taped together. John's restraints were so tight that he knew his chances of escaping were slim to nil. He was about to open his mouth and complain, but on second thought, if he kept quiet they might overlook placing the tape across his mouth.

A stout middle age woman wearing a red and yellow checkered apron appeared from out of nowhere. The housekeeper and cook always used the back door off the kitchen. Her thick black hair laced with strands of gray was braided in two, and tied at the end of each braid was a multicolored ribbon. She had a kind face. When she saw the young man in the chair, Malcolm noticed the shocked expression on her face and warned her to keep her mouth shut. He threatened that if she didn't, her family would suffer. He then reached into his pocket and took out a wad of cash. He counted out a substantial sum and passed it to her. The woman thanked him and assured him that she would never betray her generous employer. He knew that she knew how ruthless he could be.

The three spoke cordially to one another in Spanish as dinner was being served. It was diced chicken with mixed vegetables cooked in an herb sauce, rice on the side. John's mouth watered as they continued conversing. His thoughts turned to Stella.

'I wonder where she is? Is she okay? Victor will have missed us by now. I've got to do something. I've got to break free, but how? No I can't! I have to find out where she is first. Otherwise she may never be found. I wish I had a cell phone. I wonder if '911' exists here.'

John dared to steal a quick peek at his kidnappers. They were enjoying their meal and seemed to be oblivious to the fact that he was even there.

'How could he have known that I was just released from prison? And how did they know where to find me? Did someone tip off the kidnappers? But who?'

He felt like he was tangled in a web of conspiracy.

The two men finished their main coarse with gusto. The woman with the apron cleared the plates. She placed them on the counter and returned with a hot dessert fruitcake. Then she placed a beverage in front of each and stirred it with a spoon. As she walked around the table, she gently but discretely kicked John's foot. John thought it was an accident but when he glanced up at her, their eyes met and he experienced a peculiar feeling. It was as if she was trying to convey a secret message. When she quickly averted them, he thought that maybe it was just his imagination. She began washing the dishes and cleaning the kitchen as if nothing happened. After completing her task, she untied her apron, lifted the bib over her head and folded it in two lengthwise. Then she draped it over the back of a chair, as was her habit.

After dinner, it was getting late. Malcolm became agitated. He wanted to interrogate John as soon as possible but unfortunately that would have to wait. He had more pressing matters to take care of. He owed his boss money and tonight was the deadline. Malcolm had procrastinated long enough and he could not afford the extreme risk of not showing up for the meeting. He was dismayed at the fact that he would have to leave John attended by the driver for the time being. He instructed him to stay there and watch John while he went out for a while. He should be back shortly after midnight.

Before he left he tore a small piece of duct tape from the roll and pressed it over John's mouth and warned the guard to be vigilant.

'Not that he will be going anywhere.'

When Malcolm went out, the housekeeper gathered her shawl and exited with her boss. She lived quite a few blocks away in the poorer section of the city but she always walked home. By the time her boss climbed into his car, found his keys, and reached the iron gate, the woman was already there and offered to open and close it for him. Malcolm was in a hurry so he agreed. He didn't know she had a motive. She didn't have a key, so she wasn't able to lock it. As she trotted homeward, she wondered if her employer and his friend had drank any of the beverage she had prepared for them. It was just a coincidence that she had picked up her prescription the day before and had it in her handbag. The side effects were numerous and she had no idea if any of them would take effect.

' I guess that would depend on how much they had consumed.'

She was tempted to make a detour and anonymously notify the police but she changed her mind. She knew better than to double-cross her employer. She had a family to protect. She could only hope and pray that the young man who was taped to the chair would pick up on the subtle message she attempted to leave behind.

CHAPTER 29

Stella was starved. She was looking forward to a big healthy dinner with John. Victor offered to join them but Stella had said no. If he didn't mind, she wanted to spend some 'one on one' time with her cousin. A chance to relax over dinner would be the perfect opportunity. Victor said he didn't mind at all, that he could understand why. He would catch up with some of his friends he hadn't seen in a while, maybe invite them over or go to their place.

As Stella was getting ready, she thought about what she would have for dinner. She smiled as she remembered that many restaurants offered guinea-pig on the menu. Apparently it was quite a common dish in Peruvian homes. At first when she heard this, she was appalled.

'Eating guinea-pig? That's disgusting! Isn't that a rodent?'

She stared in near disbelief as the waiter served the whole roasted guinea-pig on a platter. The animal looked repulsive, lying on its back, limbs sticking straight up in the air, face staring up, smiling, teeth exposed. She would never get used to it.

She checked her watch. It was time to meet John. She entered the corridor. The young rookie was still there. He looked totally bored.

"Is he still in his room?"

"Yes ma'am. It's been quiet."

She hesitated before knocking.

'Maybe I should wait awhile. Perhaps he fell asleep. I wouldn't blame him after all he's been through. On second thought maybe I should wake him up. He won't sleep well tonight.'

She knocked. He didn't answer. She knocked louder. Still, he didn't answer.

"Hey John! It's time to get up. It's dinner time."

She put her ear to the door. The room was silent.

'He must be sleeping really soundly. I'll wait fifteen minutes then try again.'

She returned to her room. Fifteen minutes later the guard was still in the hallway. He spoke to her wanting her to know that he was keeping a close watch.

"He's still in there. He hasn't emerged yet."

Stella knocked as loud as she could without disturbing the other guests.

"Hey John! Are you up?" When there was no response, she became concerned.

"Are you sure he didn't go downstairs? Maybe he left his room when you weren't looking?"

"I'm certain ma'am. I've been here all the time. I was watching. I would have noticed if he had left." He shifted from side to side. He was upset that she didn't seem to believe him but he himself was getting worried about John.

Stella was too impatient to stand around and wait for the elevator. Who knows how long it would take? She quickly took the stairs down to the front foyer. She turned right and entered the dining room. Some of the tables were occupied. She scanned each face. She didn't spy John. He wasn't there. She walked back to the foyer. A man was fast approaching the front desk and she rushed ahead of him hoping to get there first.

"Excuse me!"

"Oh! Hello Stella! What can I do for you?"

"Did you happen to see a tall young blond male in the past hour? He's a new guest here. His name is John Emerson. He's staying in room three-o-four."

The young girl with the long dark hair thought for a moment.

"No, I haven't! Sorry!

"Are you sure?" Stella was getting desperate.

"If I had seen him, I would have remembered. I'm single," she said with a smirk.

"Can you please put a call through to his room? See if he's there?"

The gentleman, who was now beside her, gave Stella a disgruntled look.

"Sorry! But this is an urgent family matter," she tried to explain.

He backed off, picked up a magazine and sat in the armchair to the left.

"Sure I can! What did you say his room number was?"

"Three-o-four." Stella waited estimating the number of times it rang.

'Come on, John! Answer the phone!'

"There's no answer. Maybe he's at the bar or at the pool. Did you check there? Would you like me to have someone check the men's sauna?"

"No! No! That's okay. Thanks." She turned away.

'Where could he be? He wouldn't forget our dinner engagement.'

There was no point wasting her time or anybody else's time searching for him. A touch of panic struck her. *'Okay, relax, think.'* She took a deep breath and counted to ten. It didn't help. The elevator dinged as the door opened. She immediately got on. When she reached her floor, she rushed over to the guard.

"You have to ask the manager to open this door right away. John might be in there. He might be sick or hurt. He was supposed to meet me in the dining room for dinner almost an hour ago and hasn't turned up."

The rookie readily agreed. He was the one who was assigned to guard duty. If anything happened to John, he'd be responsible. He didn't waste any time.

The manager arrived and opened the door to room three-o-four. Stella rushed in calling out.

"John are you here?"

210

She called louder as she checked the bedroom and washroom. "John, are you in here?"

The guard followed closely behind. When he saw that the room was empty he knew what he had to do. He was reluctant to place the call because he knew that somehow he had screwed up. But under the circumstances, he would have to take the heat. He pulled out his cell phone and called the precinct.

Detective Diéz had been working late and was just leaving when his phone rang. He wasn't going to answer it, but picked it up at the last minute. The guard gave him the message.

"Tell her to wait there. I'll be there as soon as I can. I'm on my way."

By the time he arrived, Stella was frantic and felt totally helpless. But she was relieved to see him enter room three-o-four where they were waiting for him. She had called Victor but there was no answer. She left a message for him to meet her at her hotel as soon as possible. She wished he were here.

Diéz questioned the rookie cop who felt terrible. He couldn't understand how he could have been so careless. He shouldn't have let John out of his sight.

" Did you follow him here?"

"Yes I did! I watched him get out of the cab and enter the hotel. I waited about ten minutes more or less so that he wouldn't see me and get upset. Then I came straight up here and stood in the hall outside his room. I assumed he was here because when I asked at the desk, the clerk told me that he took the elevator."

"So you didn't see him at all once you entered the building?"

The young rookie grimaced and inwardly cowered.

" No I didn't, but the clerk said he took the elevator. How was I supposed to know that he wasn't going to his room?"

Diéz became visibly angry and cursed, which was something he seldom did. He really didn't blame the rookie cop for being negligent. It wasn't his fault that he was inexperienced. It would be a lesson for the poor guy. Diéz wasn't going to reprimand him. He was just pissed off at the situation. He was merely taking precautions when he sent someone to keep an eye on John. He didn't expect this to happen. He didn't expect *anything* to happen. But maybe he was over reacting. Maybe John wasn't even missing. It was early. He could have decided to go out and he simply forgot about meeting Stella. It was possible that he left without being seen.

The guard looked tired. It was a long day and he hadn't had a break.

"Why don't you go home, have dinner, and get a good night's sleep," suggested Diéz.

The guard was happy to be relieved of his duty and agreed. He was disappointed with himself as he stared at the floor and walked out. Suddenly he stopped and backtracked in his steps. There was a smear of something on the floor. It was easy to miss because the floor was a blend of mixed earthen colors. He stooped to examine it. He also noticed a speck on the wall about a foot high off the floor.

"Detective Diéz!" he exclaimed." Come over here! I think I see blood on the floor!"

Stella turned as white as a ghost when she heard the words of the guard. She hurried over to inspect it. Diéz held out his arm.

"Stand back!"

He stooped beside the guard then stood up and faced Stella.

"It looks like blood. I'll get someone from the lab over here right away for testing. We need to see the tapes from the security cameras. Maybe they'll tell us something. Can you do that while I get a couple of men to search the premises?"

He gave her a card with his cell phone number on it.

"Here's my cell phone number. Call me if you need me, okay?"

"I'll check the tapes right now."

She was sorry she hadn't though of that while she was waiting for him. She could have saved a lot of precious time.

On Stella's way out, she saw Victor coming down the hall. If there was a time that she needed him, she needed him now. He was walking briskly towards her, a worried look on his face. She rushed to meet him.

"Oh Victor! I'm so glad to see you! Thank God you're here!"

He sensed the urgency in her voice but couldn't imagine what it was.

"I came here straight away, as soon as I got your message. What happened?"

As they headed for the manager's office, she filled him in on what was going on. The manager called the security guard and instructed him to remove the tapes from the cameras. Shortly after, the guard asked Stella and Victor to follow him to his office where they could have a look at them. The office was a small room off to the side of the foyer. They entered and closed the door. The guard was holding two tapes.

"Which one is of the third floor?" she asked. She wanted to see that one first.

The guard looked at her and pursed his lips.

"I'm sorry but the cameras on all the floors are fake. We only have tapes from the camera in the foyer and the camera in the elevator."

Stella and Victor looked at one another in dismay.

"We'll take the one of the elevator first," said Victor as he motioned for Stella to sit in the chair and take charge.

"No thanks! I'd rather stand. You go ahead." She shook her head.

He sat in front of the screen and inserted the tape into the tape recorder and pressed 'play' checking the time frame to make certain that it was correct. Only six minutes into the tape Stella became excited as she bent over Victor's shoulder.

"There's John! He's on the elevator with a woman and two children. It looks like he's making faces at the kids. *'Typical of him!'* Now he's getting off. Back it up! Can you see what floor he pressed?"

Stella was doing all the talking while Victor operated the machine. He backed it up and punched 'pause' at the right moment

"He's getting off at the third floor and everything appears normal. He looks like he's in a good mood. Let's keep playing and see who gets on within the next ten minutes."

Stella raked her fingers through her hair as she stood back and watched the screen. She was getting impatient. This was taking time and John could be in a lot of danger right now, but there was nothing she could do about it. She felt defeated but would never give up. Victor had pressed the 'stop' button and was withdrawing the tape.

"We've seen enough of this one. No suspicious looking characters got into the elevator after John. Whoever it was must have taken the stairs and was waiting inside for him before he arrived. Let's have a look at the other tape."

He inserted the next tape and pressed 'fast forward' stopping at the appropriate time. Upon viewing the tape their hopes faded. John was seen leaving the building with another man escorting him. It didn't look good. It was easy to guess what the man was holding under his jacket. It was difficult to get a good look at him because he walked with his head lowered and the baseball cap hid most of his face. Victor switched off the recorder, pressed the 'eject' button and the tape popped out. He rubbed his chin, turned and looked up at Stella.

"I'm so sorry Stella. We'll find John and we're going to get this guy."

He couldn't say much else because he had no idea where John was taken, who abducted him, or even if he was still alive. And he was afraid there was no way of finding out. Stella sighed as she looked down at Victor with her sad eyes. They both felt the same way, totally dejected. She took the phone in her hand as she felt a single tear drip down her cheek.

"I think I'd better call Detective Diéz right away. I have no idea where he is in the building but he's not going to find John."

She punched in his number and before anyone answered she handed her cell to Victor. He was kind enough to take over for her. She was unable to speak with the unwanted hurt in her throat. She massaged her face with both hands and tuned down her senses while Victor was on the phone. He was such a crutch for her. She could depend on him now. What would she do without him? She was praying for John's safety when Victor handed the phone back to her.

"Detective Diéz is up in John's room. The lab technician is there now, so I told him we would be there shortly. Is that okay with you?"

"That's fine with me. Did he tell you what his next move was going to be?"

"No. When I asked him, he said that he would discuss it with us when we got there."

He gently took her by the arm. "Let's go!" he said.

A technician from the forensics lab tested for blood on the spot. No one was surprised that it tested positive for human blood after seeing the tapes. Stella had regained her strength and determination with Victor at her side to support her. She would play a major role in the attempt to capture John's kidnapper. She would work with the media.

When she told Detective Diéz what she intended to do, he agreed that it was a good idea. Then he called the Channel 7 News Station and informed them that he would be stopping by, to be prepared, that he needed their assistance in solving a kidnapping. It was better for him to appear in person with Stella in order to expedite the airing. Time was of the essence. John's life was in danger and every minute counted. They had to get to him before he was harmed or even worse. Diéz would pick up the sketch at the precinct, Stella would pick up the photo of John that she had in her room and they would meet as soon as possible at the television station.

CHAPTER 30

John's eyes suddenly opened with a start. The house was eerily quiet. He looked around with a jolt when he realized that he was physically restrained. His body ached from being in the same position for such a long time. He had been in a deep sleep. He had been dreaming a pleasant dream. He and Phil were about to run a marathon. Friends and family were there to cheer them on. Excitement filled the air as the athletes assembled. The starter gun pointed to the clear blue sky above. The bang of the gun had coincided with the bang of the book that the driver had dropped onto the floor in the living room. That was when John was rudely awakened.

He looked around to orient himself. He could see the driver through the archway. He was picking up the remote control on top of the television. As he turned around, John closed his eyes pretending he was still dreaming. The man walked over to the couch, plunked himself down and pressed the 'on' button. The volume was loud. He flicked through the channels and settled for a nature program. It was a documentary on whales. He put his feet up and assumed a comfortable reclining position. He fought the desire to close his eyes but he lost the battle. Before long, he was in a deep sleep.

The opportunity presented itself. John wriggled in the chair to see if it he could move it. He pressed his feet against the floor and pushed the chair backwards. Then his eyes slowly scanned over every nook and cranny, every detail of the room, searching for something, anything he could use to cut himself free. He was discouraged until his eyes rested on the kitchen drawers over in the corner. He began to move the chair turning it as he slowly crept along. Then he stopped. There was a barrier. The floor in the cooking area was slightly elevated. He hadn't noticed that before. There was a step that prevented him from getting to the counter. He turned his head looking for something else. There was an apron draped over a chair, the one that the housekeeper wore. There was a large open safety pin attached to it. What good was that? But it was better than nothing. He decided to give it a try. He looked into the living room to check on the status of his captor who hadn't moved. His concentration on finding a means of escaping was so intense, that he had been totally unaware of what was happening on television. He suddenly became alert and his heart skipped a beat when he witnessed the image of Stella on the television. He blinked his eyes. Was he seeing things? No, there she was in full view, holding a microphone to her mouth appealing to the public for the return of her cousin John.

"If anyone knows the whereabouts of John Emerson, please contact the police immediately," repeated the newscaster standing beside her.

His photo appeared on the large screen as she was saying this. Then the sketch of Malcolm Murray covered the whole screen.

"If anyone has seen this man please contact the police immediately. He is wanted for questioning in connection with drug trafficking and kidnapping.

The message was in Spanish but John understood. He couldn't believe his eyes.

'So Stella is safe after all. She was never in danger in the first place. What a ploy! I was coerced into believing they had her.'

Little did he know who else would be watching the Channel 7 news?

CHAPTER 31

José Peres miraculously survived a plane crash, unscathed, and literally escaped from the hands of his potential murderer on the same day. He was a survivor. That day, he made it down to a small cooperative farm in the valley below. The going was rough but he made it. He knew that he was in close proximity of the Rio Apurimac valley where some of Peru's illegal drug growing takes place. He also assumed that the authorities would soon be questioning residents in the area for information that might help them to track down the drug trafficers who escaped. When he arrived, he made inquiries about employment, feigning interest. Actually he wanted a lift out of there, as far away as possible, as soon as possible. But he needed a reason for his being there.

The manager of the co-op explained that employment here was exclusively for the local inhabitants, that he was sorry. He advised José to try elsewhere. Whether or not this was true, José didn't know but it was his excuse to hitch a ride with someone. He ended up in a truck that was piled high with vegetables ready to be taken to the market. It was headed for the coastal city of Pisco.

Once in Pisco, José had no problem making his way north, up the coast to Lima via the Pan American highway. He figured that he would be safer in the big city in which he was familiar. A few of his good longtime friends lived there. Señor Murray also owned a house in Lima. He assumed that it was registered under a different name. He had stayed there several times while working for the man. But he wasn't concerned that that would pose a problem. Lima was a big place. What were the chances of bumping into his ex-boss?

José liked to socialize. Presently he was drinking Inca Cola and playing poker at a friend's house who lived in a poor neighborhood. The stakes were low. The place was small, with a combined kitchen and living room. The men sat, laughing and joking, their voices blending in with those from the television. Suddenly, José became somber. He was ready to raise the ante when he looked up. An image of the young man he had dodged around on the day of his accident appeared on the television screen. Shortly after, a sketch of Malcolm Murray replaced it. In order to avoid arousing suspicion, he faked a broad smile and placed his bet. He was keeping one ear glued to the T.V. and managed to pick up the odd word. When he heard the word 'police', he secretly cringed but when he heard the word 'reward', he perked up. He could use the cash, but how could he tip off the cops and expect a reward? He was a wanted man. It would be like turning himself in. That would be just plain stupid.

It was getting late and the gang was anxious to wrap things up for the night. They played the last hand then headed for home. José stayed behind with his trusted friend. He was stalling. He had a decision to make. His friend noticed that he didn't seem to be himself.

"What is bothering you? You seem deep in thought. Is anything wrong?"

His friend patiently waited for an answer as José contemplated the situation. Should he confide in his friend and tell all?

'If I do, there's a risk he'll betray me. There's a lot of money involved. He could keep the whole reward to himself. How can I guarantee that he'll split it with me? On the other hand, if Señor Murray isn't caught, there's a chance that he might find me. And when he does, he'll kill me.'

For personal reasons he would be delighted to see Señor Murray behind bars.

"When we were playing cards, I watched some of the Channel 7 news," he began. He hoped he wasn't making a big mistake. When he finished telling his story, he added. "I'm not a criminal. Well, maybe just a little one in the eyes of the law. But if Señor Murray somehow finds out that you were the one that made the phone call, his hit man will be after you. Are you willing to take the risk? It's entirely up to you."

His friend weighed the pros and cons.

'Fifteen thousand soles is a lot of money. Thirty thousand soles is even better. But if I keep the thirty thousand soles, José would be more than upset. He'll manage to get word to this so- called 'Señor Murray'. He'll let him know that I'm the one who squealed on them for the reward money. If I turned the two of them in, I may have thirty thousand soles but what good are they to a dead man?'

He liked José and knew that he was just a pawn in the larger scheme of things. "I'll do it! Let's go! There's a phone on the corner just down the street. Are you sure you know where he lives?"

"Sure, I'm sure. I had to memorize the address. Señor Murray was so paranoid. He refused to allow me to write it down on a piece of paper just in case I was caught with it."

The two squealers headed out the door, anxious to place the call. On the way, they speculated how they would spend the reward money. When they reached the phone, José inserted a coin and handed the receiver to his friend who shared the receiver with him.

When the phone rang at the precinct, an officer on duty took the call. He collected the information in a hurry.

"Are you certain this is the address? Are you sure it's him?"

José shook his head in the affirmative as he listened in on the conversation. When the officer hung up, he immediately called his superior.

CHAPTER 32

Now that John knew Stella was safe, his determination to escape mounted. The apron was within reach. He maneuvered his chair closer so that the other chair was back to back with his. As he groped the material with his fingers he could feel something else, the outline of a small pair of scissors, the ones that were used to cut the tape. They were in the bib pocket. The incident with the housekeeper registered. He admired her for her subtlety. He managed to reach into the pocket. After several attempts that seemed to take forever, he finally managed to slip his thumb and finger through the loops of the handle. He gripped the scissors and pointed the short cutting end upward between his wrists and began cutting. He could feel the space between his wrists gradually widening until his hands were finally free. Holding the scissors tightly, he brought his arms around to his side and began cutting the rest of the duct tape.

The news and weather were over. The sports broadcaster stood with a mike in his hand. Peru had won over Ecuador and the crowd went wild as a sudden roar erupted from soccer fans. Just then, John heard a loud moan from the man on the sofa as he changed positions. John froze as he held his breath. He waited, hoping the man would resume his slumber. A few minutes passed and he hadn't moved. John continued to cut himself free. It was awkward and taking too long. He expected the man with the scar to walk in at any time. He was exhausted. He fought the uncomfortable urge to void. Finally, he was free. He was euphoric. He yanked the duct tape from across his mouth determined not to make a sound knowing how much it would hurt. He slowly rose and stood up. His legs were weak and his muscles were aching. He stretched and cautiously headed for the side door. His fingers clutched the doorknob. It wouldn't turn.

'Of course! It's locked.'

He twisted the lock from a vertical position to a horizontal position then tried the knob again. He exited stealthily and turned to silently close the door behind him.

He didn't hear the car door closing when Malcolm arrived. He mind was too preoccupied. Before he had the chance to turn around and escape from the premises, he felt a hand on his shoulder and then heard a familiar voice at his back.

"Where do you think you're going?"

Malcolm was unprepared for what happened next. With one, swift, backward jerk of his arm, John elbowed him in the sternum. It was a sudden impulse, an instinct for survival. Before Malcolm could respond, John had disappeared to the front of the house. Malcolm quickly caught his breath and swore. He remembered he hadn't locked the gate as he quickly spun around and pursued his prey.

John escaped through the gate and raced down the sidewalk. He could feel his heart pumping the adrenaline as his eyes darted from side to side looking for a place to hide. He heard the distinctive clicking of his pursuer's heels on the pavement behind him. He spotted two teenagers walking down the sidewalk ahead of him, a boy and a girl. The boy had one arm around his girlfriend's waist and was pushing a bicycle with the other arm. John caught up with them. He was out of breath and spoke in a whisper.

" I need to borrow your bike. I promise I'll return it to you."

He grabbed it, jerked it away from the owner's hand and ran with it. The owner stood dumbfounded. He didn't understand a word John said. He ran down the sidewalk chasing after the foreigner, protesting in Spanish. John placed his foot on the pedal, swung his leg over the bar and began pumping as fast as he could.

By this time, Malcolm gave up as he watched John take off on the bicycle. He was furious. He would never be able to catch him.

'How could a young punk like that outsmart me? How in hell did he escape? What in hell happened while I was gone?'

He stood on the spot puffing and panting. He realized he was out of shape. He turned and headed back to his house, intent on contending with the driver.

'*That idiot! Wait 'till I get my hands on him!*'

Then after that, he knew he'd have to hurry and get the hell out of there. John was on the loose and he'd be calling the cops any time now. He started running. Just as he was nearing his gate, about a half block away, a police car came squealing around the corner headed his way. Another one followed.

Malcolm's first reaction was shock.

'*How did they get here so fast?*'

He was spied instantly. By the time he pivoted around, police cars were fast approaching from the opposite direction. He glanced around like a trapped animal, head jerking from side to side looking for an escape. All the properties in the neighborhood were enclosed, either by a stone wall or an iron fence. He ran to the nearest gate and violently attempted to open it. It was locked. He frantically tried the next one with the same results. His fingers were wrapped around the wrought iron bars when he heard a loud voice and froze.

"Hold it right there! Put your hands on your head!"

While Malcolm Murray was being arrested, other cops stormed his house looking for John. The driver who was still on the couch, bolted to an upright position. He hadn't been aware of what was going on outside. He hadn't heard a thing. His head felt groggy, as if he had been slipped some kind of drug. He rubbed his eyes. Was he hallucinating or did he see cops with guns standing in front of him? With concentration he was able to focus better. He spied the empty chair with duct tape stuck to it and he vaguely remembered. But there had been someone sitting in it. He had been on the sofa and he was dreaming. As he was being handcuffed he actually thought he was in the midst of a nightmare. He staggered like a drunkard as he was being led out of the house but he sobered up quickly when he saw all the lights of the patrol cars. A pang of fear struck him like a dagger in his chest when he suddenly realized this was reality. Everything was slowly coming back to him.

John heard the sirens in the distance. They were getting louder and louder. Then he saw the flashing red lights approaching. He stopped the bicycle in a hurry and dropped it onto the side of the street as he dismounted. He rushed into the middle of the street. He stood and waved his arms above his head for attention but the police cars zoomed right past him. He watched them until they stopped. He counted a total of six flashing red lights and immediately calculated and concluded where they were parked.

'How did they know where to find me? Did the housekeeper call the police? She must have.'

John picked up the bike and began peddling in the direction of the flashing red lights. As he cautiously drew near, he joined a crowd of curious neighbors. They were gathered around observing the action. The owner of the bike was among the spectators. John saw him before he saw John. John wanted to apologize and return the bicycle to its rightful owner. The teenager was gawking around at the crowd when his eyes rested on John. He walked toward the thief and accosted John. The crowd's attention was drawn to him when he pointed a finger at the thief and accused him of stealing his bicycle.

"Hey! There's the guy who stole my bike. I want my bike back!"

John quickly approached the teen and handed over the bicycle. He apologized but that wasn't good enough. Since the cops were already here, the guy wanted them to arrest him. That was when someone recognized John.

"Hey! Isn't he the one who was on the news tonight? The man who was into drugs or something."

Immediately heads turned and all eyes were on John. A buzz of commotion developed around him. He was relieved to see one of the officers from the scene, walk in his direction. He rushed to meet him.

"I need your help. Is Detective Walter Diéz with you?"

He hoped that the officer would recognize the name Walter Diéz and therefore pay attention to what he was saying. He correctly assumed that the cop didn't understand a word of English. The bystanders parted to make way for the cop who was now just a few feet away from the thief. He immediately recognized John from the photograph he had been given. He said something in Spanish to and indicated to John that he wanted him to follow. Just then, John glanced toward the front entrance of the house where he had been held and witnessed two policemen coming through the door with the driver who was handcuffed. John was tempted to call out to him and give him a piece of his mind but the man who had taped him to the chair hung his head and refused to look up. As they continued walking toward the police cruisers their paths converged and John spoke.

"I hope they put you away for a very long time. Where's your buddy?"

At the recognition of John's voice, the kidnapper's head snapped up. He had a perplexed look on his face as is if he had no idea how John had managed to escape. It was a brief, satisfying moment for John and he couldn't resist giving the kidnapper a knowing smirk.

When he spotted Detective Diéz he made a beeline for him. The back door of one of the cruisers was open and he had his hands on the man in the sketch. Despite being handcuffed, he was reluctant to cooperate and didn't go without a struggle. With the detective's help, Malcolm Murray got into the back seat and the door was closed. Diéz stood on the sidewalk watching as the cruiser pulled away. By this time, he hadn't noticed that John was standing beside him watching as well, observing the whole fiasco. As the car slowly left the scene, Malcolm happened to look up and notice John. As they stared at one another during that terse moment, John had the opportunity to relay his thoughts with one single action. He smiled a big smile at his kidnapper and gave him the finger.

Diéz was startled when he turned and saw John standing there beside him and he breathed a sigh of relief. Since all of the officers reported that they hadn't seen John, he was beginning to fear the worst.

"Where have you been hiding? We've been looking all over for you? Your cousin is very worried. She'll be glad to see you. *I'm* glad to see you."

John's first concern was for his cousin.

"Can you please call Stella and tell her I'm okay. I'll give you her number."

Diéz handed John his phone.

"Here, you can call her and tell her yourself."

John took the phone and called while Diéz took charge of matters at hand. Initially when he first glimpsed the man in handcuffs standing in the doorway, he had assumed it was José Peres. But now, as he was being shoved into the back of a squad car, it was obvious that he was not. He was a stocky man and did not resemble the picture of José Pares in the least. He calmed the spectators answering few questions and gave orders for everyone to return to their homes.

When John was off the phone, the detective told him that he could ride with him in the cruiser on the way back and to hop in the front seat. As they left the curb, John didn't know why, but he looked back at the house where he was held captive. Perhaps it was because it gave him closure to a more than upsetting ordeal. He could finally go home.

"I don't think you have anything more to worry about. We've got the people responsible for your kidnapping and everything ties in with the smuggling. Thank God we got to you! I'm surprised that they hadn't already murdered you. I wonder why they let you live so long? I mean you've been missing for hours and you'd think that they'd be anxious to get rid of you since you're the only one who could identify them."

John had to chuckle, as if things weren't complicated enough!

"The reason why they let me live was to interrogate me. They said that they had their sources and they knew that a portion of the shipment was missing. They thought that Phil and I took it and hid it someplace before the police nabbed us and they wanted to know where it was. I guess I can understand why they came to that conclusion."

Diéz was puzzled. He knew about the amount of cocaine that had been confiscated by the department. He knew that Officers Paredés and Ramirez had taken some after hearing Eduardo Ramirez's confession. But how would the pilot know that some of the cocaine was missing in the first place? Why would he think that a portion of it had been stolen unless he had an inside source. The information released to the public was that a substantial amount was found but the exact amount was not disclosed.

"What did you tell them?

"I told him the truth, that I didn't know what he was talking about but I don't think he believed me. Eventually I suppose, I would have stalled in order to try and save my life. I would have told them that I would take them to where I hid it and hope that I could possibly escape in the process. How did you know where to find me?"

"After releasing your sketch to the media, we received a call from someone who recognized him and gave us an address. He will be receiving a nice fat reward thanks to your cousin Stella."

John had a couple of small pieces of duct tape sticking to his clothing. After seeing the victim's chair covered with the tape Diéz wondered what happened.

"How did you ever manage to cut yourself free?"

The subject brought to mind the woman with the braided hair donned in the red and yellow checkered apron.

"With great difficulty and with the help of an angel sent from heaven."

Diéz had no idea what he was talking about but accepted it at face value. He knew that an apology was due and was willing to accept the blame.

"I'm sorry that you had to go through all this. I should have had more foresightedness and insisted that you stay in protective custody until you got on that flight back to Canada. Maybe none of this would have happened."

"It's not your fault! How did he find out so fast that I was released from prison? How did he know where I was staying? I mean he even knew my room number."

It was truly mind-boggling. Diéz had been wondering the same thing. Although John's whereabouts was supposed to be kept confidential, it was a huge police department. But if there was a leak somewhere, he expected it would have been to the press and that didn't happen.

'There seems to be more to this than meets the eye.'

"Well, we have them in custody now so we should be able to get some answers. In the meantime I'm going to see you to your hotel room and have you watched like a hawk. There's a man out there on the loose, who would probably love to get his hands on you. I doubt very much that he would be stupid enough to come looking for you now, but I'd rather not take any chances."

He was thinking of José Peres. He suspected that he would go into deep hiding, especially if he had seen the news coverage earlier that night of his partner's image being exposed in full view of the public.

As they were nearing the hotel, Diéz called ahead of time and arranged for John to be escorted through the side door and up to his room where Stella and Victor were anxiously awaiting his arrival. He would be safe with them. Diéz respected John's position and wanted to give him some privacy and time to recuperate. He would see John again tomorrow and take his statement then.

He returned to the station in time to witness a scene that would answer many of his questions. As Malcolm Murray was being lead out of the processing room, he happened to turn and get a glimpse of Detective Blanco from the corner of his eye. At the same time, Blanco looked up from his notes and their eyes met. This sudden appearance was totally unexpected for Blanco. He had been on another call and was not on Diéz's team during the arrest. Detective

Blanco immediately spun on his heels hoping that he wouldn't be recognized. But it was too late. Malcolm took a step in his direction before he was caught by the arm and held back. He struggled to get away. Malcolm was ready to kill when his fiery eyes met those of his so-called betrayer. His voice boomed uncontrollably.

"You bastard! You set me up! You told them where I was! Why? Why did you do it? Why'd you set me up? From now on, you had better watch your back! I'll make sure they get you!"

It took two cops to restrain the prisoner when he was saying this and being dragged away. Blanco's mouth dropped in shock as the words reached his ears. It took only seconds to compose himself.

"Who is this man? What's he jabbering about?"

He swept his arm in the direction where the prisoner was being taken. He desperately made an effort to hide his guilt.

"Get him out of here!"

Diéz walked over and confronted Blanco. He made certain everyone heard.

"What was *that* all about? Are you sure you don't know that man because it's obvious to everyone here that he seems to think he knows you?"

The whole room was silent. You could hear a pin drop. All eyes were on Blanco as they waited for a response. Blanco was visibly perspiring.

"Don't look at me! I haven't a clue what he was talking about! I don't know the man! I've never seen him before in my life! I don't know about everyone else but I have work to do."

He turned and stomped to his desk as if he were disgusted with his fellow co-workers. But as far as Diéz was concerned, it wasn't over. He was prepared to go to any length now to complete the puzzle, and he knew exactly what pieces fit where.

News coverage of the entire episode was on every channel, beginning with the crash, how the wrong person was arrested, and how Officers Ramirez and Paredés were ultimately arrested for the murder of Phil MacAllister. They covered the kidnapping of John Emerson and the arrest of Malcolm Murray and his accomplice. Calls from the press kept flooding in, wanting to interview John but he wasn't interested.

Meanwhile, José Peres sat watching everything on his new thirty-six inch flat screen television in his new apartment. Malcolm deserved what was coming to him. He was sorry about what happened to the poor young lad who ended up being the victim in all this and a little guilty because his life had changed for the better because of him.

He had a new wardrobe and makeover, changed his hairstyle, fixed his teeth, and put on some weight. Life was treating him good these days. He even had a beautiful young girlfriend.

CHAPTER 33

John was ready to return home to Canada. Since Officer Paredés ultimately pleaded guilty on the advice of his new attorney, and Officer Ramirez had given a full confession, there was no need for John to stay and appear as a witness at a trial. Malcolm Murray and the driver pleaded guilty to kidnapping and drug trafficking. Detective Blanco was under investigation for conspiracy and aiding and abetting.

Being a guest at the same hotel brought Stella and John closer together than ever. Stella was now like a big sister to him. She had insisted on staying behind for her cousin and he loved her all the more because of it. John had an opportunity to get to know Victor while he waited for his temporary passport to be issued. As soon as it arrived by courier, he and Stella booked a fight to Toronto for the following day. A throng of newspaper reporters would be there to greet them. Phil MacAllister's death and John's imprisonment had been on the news and everyone wanted to hear the story firsthand.

Victor picked them up in front of the hotel and loaded their cases into the trunk. He looked forward to visiting them in two weeks time. He was ready for a little vacation. John sat in the front seat beside the driver.

"I can't thank you both enough for all you've done for me."

"You needn't thank me. It's been a horrible experience for you. I wish we could have met under more pleasant circumstances but it's a consolation that we did meet."

Victor glanced into the back seat and smiled at Stella. She beamed as she inspected and admired the ring on her finger. Victor had bought her a gold friendship ring with a ruby birthstone as a celebration gift. He told her that he wanted to keep seeing her.

During the better part of an hour that it took to drive to the airport, John absorbed the sights and scenes surrounding him, the colorful markets, the hubbub of traffic, the pedestrians and cyclists, the children playing, the slums on the background hillsides. It was the people and their unique culture that gave this city a heartbeat. He would return some day to pay tribute to his friend Phil.

ABOUT THE AUTHOR

Sandra Owen lives in Cornwall, Ontario, Canada, with her husband. She has four children and several grandchildren. She has traveled extensively throughout Mexico, Costa Rica, Colombia and Peru. She enjoys music, nature, trekking and sailing.

While she was travelling through the Central Highlands of Peru in January 2008, a small plane carrying a cargo of cocaine crashed in the Andes and the occupants fled on foot escaping the authorities. This inspired her to write the novel 'Terror in the Andes'.

Printed in the United States
215702BV00001B/5/P

9 781438 961873